BUTTERFLIES

L. A. NETTLES

Paperback: ISBN: 9798408635412
Hardcover: ISBN: 9798408636136

I dedicate this book to Waverly and Lyra.
Waverly, you are my sun.
You burn bright and scorch the world
With your artistry and true self.
Lyra, you are my moon.
Your glow is calming with a light
Bright enough to illuminate
The darkest corners of the earth.

Thank you for all your patience.
My love for both of you is infinite.
And I hope I didn't embarrass you.

And to my dear friend, Happy, I am eternally
Grateful for every second you spent giving
Me feedback and writing edits. Writing a book is a
Challenge in itself, your patience and guidance
Was not only generous, but beyond meaningful
To me. Thank you.

Much to your surprise, I would like to thank you, Keith,
For always encouraging me with positivity and showing
Enthusiasm for a book that you will
Probably never read.

CHAPTER 1

My divorce will be finalized today. I cringe thinking about all the times I ignored my Spidey-sense. My imagination is replaying random instances from my marriage like film clips. I stop myself from recounting every little red flag, like cruel, looping mental memes.

The sun blazes through the uncovered cracks of my window, burning through my eyelids. The sun is bold, sparkling on every object in my room. It illuminates the quiet, dark areas awake, including myself.

The aesthetics outside do not emulate my internal feelings. After forcing myself to leave the comfort of my bed, I enter my bathroom. It was time to assess the damage to another sleepless night. My gaze fixates down to my circular vanity mirror. The unforgiving vibrant light flicks on as it senses me. It has no mercy on my reflection. I mumble, "When did I get old?" I look like someone who just had their mugshot taken after an all-night bender.

My green eyes are bleary from fatigue and stress. The area around my eyes retains hefty, emotional baggage. I examine the lines mapping my face. Each flaw signifies gained wisdom. Am I aging like an expensive bottle of scotch? Or an overripened avocado? When your husband runs off with a younger woman, you analyze imperfections.

I gather my hair up into a bun, then examine my body in the long bathroom mirror. I hold my breath, sucking in my stomach. This is what my thirty-year-old body resembled. I exhale. My stomach returned to its normal girth. This is my forty-three-year-old body. Evaluating my physical mileage, I wonder if I wasted all my pretty years. Leaning in closer to my reflection, I can see a few strands of gray hair. With my natural espresso-colored hair spiraling around my oval face, I see a ghost of a once-vibrant woman.

My self-deprecation ends with the ringing of my cell phone. Startled, I answer quickly to hear, "Mom…are you okay?" The voice of my eighteen-year-old daughter, Harley, is full of concern.

When you have a child, all your best features are infused into one person. They appear to be your "mini me" but with their own personality. She has an emotional fire that I wish I never lost.

"I didn't overdose on antidepressants…but I sure as hell look like I did." I clear my throat to sound more upbeat and positive. "Yes, I am alive. It's nothing concealer and Xanax can't fix." I begin stroking my mascara wand onto the roots of my head to cover my gray.

Harley's voice is soothing. "I just wanted to make sure you were okay." As a way to make me laugh, she turns into a lively caricature of happiness: "Today is the day…my parents will be officially divorced." She pauses, then shouts with glee.

I close my eyes when I hear the word, "divorced." I spent half my life being identified with this man. He was a huge part of my existence. He left so unapologetically. I was disposable after all. I felt like an epic failure with no way of understanding how it even happened.

"Yes…today should be a celebration. Christmas is coming twice this year! Happy Divorce Day to me!"

I let out a nervous laugh. How do women celebrate divorce? I didn't date or have gratuitous sex. My desire to be alone had me holed up watching John Hughes movies. Reliving the innocence of teen love, from the '80s, was addictive. These movies helped me realize that I wasn't unlovable in fact, it was the opposite. I was just in love with the wrong person. Repeatedly watching the movie *Sixteen Candles* made the love story between Samantha and Jake enviable. Love is a series of unfortunate events, layered on top of determination to make it work.

Feeling foolish for thinking of *Sixteen Candles*, I state the obvious, "I never thought your father and I would get back together, but I never thought we would be divorced either. How stupid does that sound?"

Harley is quick to respond. "That's not stupid. You were married to a koala."

I'm puzzled. "Koala?"

She giggles, "You know, super cute and cuddly but probably has chlamydia."

Her silly comment changes my mood with laughter. "Don't forget the sharp claws to stab my heart."

"Dad was actively dating while he was still married, so this isn't hard for him. Your replacement was on hand. Some people are afraid of being alone. Maybe you aren't having a divorce party, but I bet he is." Harley goes from being sarcastic to sounding hurt. "I can't even remember the last time I saw him. At one time, I had this super dad. Now I have no dad."

I process her statement. "One day, you will have to forgive him, because he's your dad. Forgiveness from me is something that isn't owed to him. It will be a process… of the utmost longevity."

She quickly corrects me. "Just because I have his DNA doesn't mean he's entitled to my love."

I look at the clock and panic at the time. "Harley, we will talk more after court. I have to officially make myself single again." My name will now be known as Miss Emerson Vaughn, and not Mrs. Emerson Vaugh.

After hanging up, I digest our conversation. He probably would celebrate today. And we would still be married if he didn't have someone waiting in the wings. He was probably miserable for years and stayed out of commitment to his daughter. I always thought the adultery was about me, but it wasn't. It was about him. It's funny how the person who retains the most pain thinks they brought it on themselves.

******

Time can dismantle what we hold ideal. My body trembles walking into the courthouse. It's that roller-coaster-induced nervousness that sparks adrenaline. Your stomach clenches in preparation for the drop-off. You scream to release the sensation of free-falling. My anxiety isn't from the divorce hearing but the fear of seeing my soon-to-be ex-husband, Dylan Vaughn. I cringe knowing he may be lurking around the halls. Dylan now has the ability to make me feel full-blown PMS, just from the sight of him. I consider this his X-Men superpower: cramps.

My divorce attorney, Olivia Henry, waves at me to come over. Olivia is a spunky, young mocha-skinned beauty, with a weave that can rival Beyoncé's at

Coachella. Her pristine, fabulously styled whip-smart confidence quiets my fears. She is pumped about getting "what is owed to the wife." This means my husband is about to get fucked by another woman who charges $500/hour. Divorce becomes a game of who has the biggest dick, and Olivia makes me feel like Ron Jeremy.

Every divorce is unique like a snowflake. It isn't just the variations in design but also how it lands before dissolving. My brain recounts the past year in a split second. Olivia puts her hand on my arm. I instantly snap back to reality. She guides me into the courtroom and explains the procedure. I look around the courtroom as she speaks. She says, "Don't worry. It's just us. Dylan's presence is not required. Only one of you needs to appear in court."

I say, "Well, that sums up the last two years of my marriage. His presence wasn't required."

My clenched jaws absorb an internal wildfire, raging, swirling with emotions. I'm relieved not to see him with his smiling younger girlfriend. But I'm angry at how he couldn't show up to his own divorce. After twenty years together, there is some expectation to see it to the end.

When the judge enters the courtroom, we stand up. Olivia introduces my petition for divorce. After reviewing the case out loud for ten minutes, the judge directs a question to me. "Is this marriage irrevocably broken and unable to be fixed?"

My reaction to such a preposterous question is to burst into laughter. Olivia and the judge are not amused waiting for my response. I must appear deranged. Pulling myself together, I answer, "Yes, this marriage is beyond repair."

At the crack of the gavel, I become single. I am no longer married. I wasn't a Missus, but now a Miss.

Olivia pats my hand and cheers, "Well, that's it. Let's go downstairs and get a certified copy of your divorce papers...and then you can celebrate!" It's only 11 a.m., and I've heard the words *divorce* and *celebrate* twice. I never associated those words together until today.

Before leaving the courthouse parking garage, I sit idle in my car. I look down at the notarized copies of my divorce papers. I can now call myself "certifiable." I have a certificate of divorce. Crying would be expected, but there's nothing left but emptiness. My situation isn't unique, but I feel alone. I turn on the car, and the song "Everything Is Everything" by Lauryn Hill is playing. It is a moment of clarity.

CHAPTER 2

Day 1

Ashley and I plan to meet for lunch at the Ty Bar inside the Four Seasons Hotel. I am the first to arrive. Walking up to the host, I reevaluate my appearance. It's been a while since I wore a dress, heels, and makeup. My closet full of trendy clothes and shoes had been abandoned for anything with Lycra or a drawstring.

I patiently sit at my table with a Bootlegger Vodka martini and a plate of Marcona-stuffed olives. I nestle myself into a big, cozy red chair and inspect my surroundings with wonder. The beauty of the red walls adorned with black-and-white photos of New York City displays simple elegance. The martini warms me like a calm blanket.

When Ashley enters the room, everyone's eyes focus on her. She resembles a *Playboy* centerfold yet unassumingly armed with a doctorate degree. She's a magnet of energy that has to be recognized. Her "girls" are peeking out of her cobalt-blue skintight wrap dress. The Tiffany diamond pendant dangling from her neck enhances her bust line. I stand up to greet her with open arms. She reciprocates with a colossal hug.

After all these years of being a New Yorker, Ashley still holds on to her Texas twang. "Hello, sweetheart! I'm so happy to see you."

She orders her poison of choice, bourbon, and we eagerly catch up on weeks of occurrences and family gossip. We've been close friends for over twenty years, so reconnecting has always been easy. Being here with Ashley feels like absorbing vitamin D from sunlight. The social interaction nourishes my mind and heart.

I ask about her life and husband. "How are you and Edmond doing?"

Ashley responds in her charmingly southern voice, "Edmond is a hedge fund manager, not a snake wrangler. He lives a non perilous existence in his office." With an arched eyebrow, she adds, "After ten years of marriage, he still surprises me. His wily and adventurous side keep things fresh. He may be much older in age, but very young at heart."

The waitress places our drinks in front of us, and Ashley takes a sip of bourbon, then she continues, "My practice is booming. Just about everyone in New York City is in need of a psychiatrist. Other than work and the typical bullshit life doles out, Edmond and I are great."

Warm with authenticity, she asks, "How are you doing, Emme?"

My face softens, and my eyes shift down to play with my martini glass. "I was a hot mess during the divorce. I had to dig in deep and figure my shit out. I realized I needed to leave my old life behind and sell the house." I pause long enough to taste the sweetness of my martini. "Packing makes you sentimental…to see all these material things. They mattered once, but not anymore.

Memories are perfect because they already happened. I'm looking to the future now."

Leaning in with an inquiring look, she says, "What does your future hold?"

In fortune-teller fashion, I motion my hands in a circular pattern over the top of my martini glass. Smiling until my wrinkles crease around my eyes, I say, "It's been six months since my divorce. Moving out of the safe suburban confines of Chappaqua, New York, will motivate me to leave the past and move forward. My second act in life will be entirely for me. I want to travel, return to professional writing, and figure out how to be single as a middle-aged woman."

Ashley's bold red lips flash an enticing smile of approval. In quintessential Texas fashion, she declares, "Look at you strutting while you sit down. Where will you move?"

Confident in my resolve, I reply, "I want to move back to New York City. I have loved the eclectic energy ever since we went to NYU. But before I move, I want to travel. Moving can wait until I see the world." Removing my typical stoic expression and mirroring Ashley's smile, I add, "With Harley gone, I am free to do whatever the hell I want."

Looking at me for signs of distress, Ashley's psychiatrist side seeps out. "First divorce, and then your baby chick has flown away. How's empty-nest syndrome?"

"I experienced random emotional moments leading up to Harley leaving for college. Growing up and leaving home was an eventuality. I didn't feel like a mom anymore." Before Ashley could interject, I clarified, "Yes, I know I'm still her mom. I'm not doing routine daily mom things. I'm not needed anymore. It feels like another divorce but without anger and resentment."

Crossing my arms in front of me, leaning forward for transparency, my smile relaxes as I reconcile my thoughts. "Believe it or not, I'm fine. We both require independence to figure out our new lives. I'm excited for both of us."

My eyes were glossy with emotion, not from sadness but with gratitude. "Thank you for this opulent divorce gift. Seven days at the Four Seasons in Midtown East would even make Robert DeNiro smile."

Ashley's centerfold appearance of large envious breasts, fair skin, and voluminous, long blonde hair was no match for her heartfelt and boisterous laugh. She accepts my appreciation with adoration. "You are my soulmate, a sister, and there isn't anything I wouldn't do for you." Winking at me, she throws in, "I'd even hide a body with you."

Forming my hands and fingers in the shape of a heart and holding it up to my chest, I satirically respond, "You complete me."

Our typical silly banter shifts gears when Ashley asks, "I want you to try something during your stay." She slides a business card over to me.

Puzzled, I pick up the black linen card. Etched in white calligraphy is the name "Dr. Alexander Jameson," with the title "Sex Therapist" underneath. A look of horror creeps over my face.

Not one to hold things in, I blurt out, "Why do I need to see a sex therapist?" I point out the obvious: "Don't you need to be having sex to have sex problems?"

She anticipates my reaction and begins laughing. "You don't need a sex therapist, per se. I'm not asking you to sit there and discuss your sexual depravity. He won't be playing 'Puppetry of the Penis' with you. I think you need to discuss your issues with intimacy with someone…other than me."

Alcohol makes her adamant. "Please hear me out. He is a very well-respected therapist. His specialty just happens to be sex. He has an elite clientele just based on word of mouth." She briefly pauses before adding, "Since he is so highly recommended, I sought him out for myself."

She slings back the rest of her bourbon. "Even though I'm a behavioral therapist, I needed therapy." She snickers, "And yes, I feel the irony."

She relaxes her shoulders and crosses her arms. Leaning forward, she rests her elbows on the table. "There's a point in every woman's life when she has doubts about her husband. Is he happy in our marriage? Is he still attracted to me?"

I stare at her in disbelief. I decipher what she is truly saying. "Is Edmond fucking someone else?"

With deep admiration, she says, "I love my husband, and he loves me. There have been times I've questioned his fidelity. I needed reassurance that my doubts were just paranoia."

Ashley plays with her glass. Her fingers slowly rub around the crystal rim to process her thoughts. "I am much younger than Edmond. I can never assume I meet all his needs. My younger age might leave me lacking in some areas."

I'm surprised by this revelation. I look her up and down before asking, "Exactly what areas are you lacking in?"

Her beautiful red lips curve into a sneaky grin. "I was basically flying off the handle over nothing. She bats her curled lashes flirtatiously. "Honey, I'm not lacking in anything. The problem was Edmond. He was dealing with erectile dysfunction. Instead of talking to me about it, he avoided me intimately."

She assures me we'll discuss the complexities of her issues at a later time but reminds me that this vacation is about me, not her. "Rest assured, my marriage is strong and intact." She winks.

"For Christ's sake, you scared me. I thought Edmond was cheating…or gay." I sit still, digesting our conversation. "Your personal reasons for needing sex therapy are understandable. There's no sexual drama in my life. Is that the issue?"

"Honey…for the past two years, you've become a social hermit. There's so much apprehension in moving forward. Life isn't going to knock on your door and ask you to participate. This is the time to try new things."

"New things? Like vaginal steaming? Vampire facials?"

Ashley rolls her eyes. "Have you had sex yet?"

"Yes, I actually have proof I've had sex. Harley is my sex trophy." I giggle at my analogy.

"Have you had sex after Dylan?"

My eyes shift down. "No. I haven't. The thought of sex scares me. You were my emotional crutch throughout my divorce."

I look up to meet her twinkling eyes, with a grin, I add, "You've saved me thousands of dollars in therapy bills. You are the gift that keeps giving."

"This is why you need to see a sex therapist. You told me your sex life with Dylan was routine and lacking in everything from romance to fantasy fulfillment. Dylan was not only cheating, but it was with a younger woman, and you told me how undesirable this made you feel. You couldn't see yourself as sexy at this age or even sexual.

"Sex with someone new, especially after divorce, is scary. Then again, it might be 'Jesus, Take the Wheel' amazing," she counters.

Placing her hand on mine, she puts her explanation in the simplest form. "As Justin Timberlake says, you need to get your sexy back."

I stare at the card to hide my thoughts. Post-divorce sex terrifies me. It's like eating grilled chicken every night, and then switching it up with Thai. Spice can be an explosion to your senses. It might give you heartburn.

I accept her challenge. "You're right. I'm ready for Jesus to take the wheel."

"That just dills my pickle." She pats my hand to reassure me. "Seeing a sex therapist is definitely something new, but don't sweat it. He was nothing but professional with me. I found his technique unusual, but beneficial. I'm sure his session will be a doozy."

I question her choice of words. "A doozy?"

She replies, "There's nothing traditional in his methodology of treatment. He will catch you off guard, piss you off, and cross boundaries, but he gets to the core of the problem. It will be memorable."

"How can sex therapy be memorable?" I scrunch my face in disbelief.

Ashley continues with her description, "Just be forewarned; he is a tall drink of iced tea on the hottest day. The good Lord spent extra time on his type of pretty." She smiles thinking about him. "His family is considered the bee's knees. You'd think he'd be some stuck-up asshole. He's very proper, educated, and charming. I've met his mom and sister at a lot of charity events. They are good people, not the least bit hoity-toity."

"Wow. You just described the perfect man. Beautiful, rich, and he listens to you. He has to be gay." I raise my hands up to the heavens. "Let my sexual healing begin."

"Whatever is causing you anxiety, tell Dr. Jameson. Sometimes it's just good to talk to someone who is neutral. Perception and wisdom are occasionally better with a stranger, especially if they're from the opposite sex."

I understand what she is saying. Telling your story to the same social circles makes the feedback monotonous. It might be beneficial to share my fears of intimacy with a total stranger.

"You know what I miss more than sex? Those quiet moments of intimacy through touch we take for granted. I miss cuddling on the couch. He would place his hand under my shirt to feel my stomach or to hold me closer. Or when we were driving, he'd reach over to place his hand on my thigh."

I subdue my smile in recollecting better days. "I could make lists of these types of moments, but I can't say that about sex. Intense sexual moments are isolated incidents. Passion is brief. True intimacy is what my body misses."

Ashley coyly winks at me. "Who knows? Maybe you'll meet someone while you're here. He might throw in a good spooning after some fine French dining, with *la petite mort* as dessert."

"What the hell is that?"

"It's that moment before climax when your mind is free of bullshit and you feel heaven for a few seconds."

While explaining this to me, Ashley comically reenacts Meg Ryan's deli scene from *When Harry Met Sally*.

I satirically reply, "Is that when I let Jesus take the wheel? When I'm unconscious in my euphoric state?" In response to Ashley's sexual pantomime, I decide to sing the chorus to Britney Spears's "Baby One More Time." "My loneliness is killing me…"

Ashley chimes in with me, "Give me a sign…. Hit me, baby, one more time!" The waitstaff, along with the bar patrons, just stare at us. They are horrified either by our singing or that we found enlightenment in Britney Spears. She wastes no time in giving me another surprise. "What are your plans for tonight?"

I laugh. "I'm a sexless domestic shut-in staying at a five-star hotel centered in this great metropolis. I am totally free."

"I figured you might be." She begins chuckling at her proposal. "Don't be pissed. I set you up on a blind date."

I feel ill. "You what?! What if I *did* have plans tonight?"

She says, "You can't fool me. You need to get out there and grab the bull by its horns. You just need a swift kick in the ass. The point of my gift isn't to hang out with me every day. I lured you out here to jump-start your libido mentally and physically."

I have this mixed expression of fear and excitement on my face. "It's funny. Divorce made me scared of being alone. Now that I'm alone, I'm scared of being with someone. It's a mindfuck."

"Tonight is about just having dinner and nothing more. You need to build up your confidence."

I asked, "Do you think dating is the solution to my confidence?"

"No. You are confident in all areas in life except love. It's time to put yourself out there, and if you hate it, then give it time. " She sneaks in, "And until you meet Mr. Right, casual sex is a viable option."

Her point is valid. Besides the absence of male companionship, I do miss sex. I know it's not medically possible, but I feel like my vagina is sealing itself. I think about the urban colloquialisms about vaginas growing cobwebs and eventually shriveling up from being unused. My vagina is turning into a haunted house that needs an exorcism to rid it of my ex. I reluctantly ask for the details.

CHAPTER 3

Ashley's wealth means her gifts are Texas-sized in grandeur. Reserving the Ty Warner Penthouse at the Four Seasons was meant to make me to feel special. It is like living out a movie montage makeover scene. The plot would be about a divorcée staying in an opulent penthouse in a quest to get laid.

I call Harley to check in. "I just wanted to let you know that I arrived safely, and Aunt Ashley set me up on a blind date."

Harley immediately squeals, "Aunt Ashley is my hero. I can't wait to hear about this date."

"I want to go into this with positivity, but I can't," I confess. "Dating has drastically changed since I met your dad. Life was slower and simpler. Everything is fast and complicated now."

"You're overthinking this," she counters. "Dating hasn't changed, you have."

She advises, "Yes, technology has made dating more or less complicated, but if you don't try, then you won't experience anything. Get back out there to test the waters." She chuckles profusely before advising, "Just steer clear of 'booty calls'…just go on 'foodie calls.' Go for the free meal."

"You're right. I'm missing out on all these free meals. The world is an all-you-can-eat buffet." I grin at her college freshman dating advice. She was clearly thinking with her stomach, not her heart.

I needed to get ready for my date. Harley's fresh enthusiastic worldview was infectious. Unfortunately, I lacked that enthusiasm, but her reassurance encouraged me. I knew the odds of my blind date working out were null.

After showering, I evaluate myself in the long bathroom mirror. I have to be more attentive about my grooming habits, by removing all the excess hair from my face to my ass. I have no intention of having sex on a first date. But just in case, I shear myself into bald perfection, like a wolf shedding her winter coat.

I walk over to the closet to examine my options for undergarments. Thankfully, I packed my Spanx. The purpose of Spanx is to replicate human bondage. Wearing this ensures I won't have sex. This is the epitome of a condom made for the female body, a necessary evil to give myself a mannequin-looking physique. Once I wiggle the Spanx up, I squat. Situating my torso and ass into a sausage casing is like a weird predate workout.

Choosing an outfit makes me panic. Staring into the mirror, I hold different dresses up to my chest. I didn't pack any date-type clothes, like jeans and a cute top. I focus on the mantra "Serenity now!" and my deliberation ends with a navy sheath dress. The dress makes me look classy and slim. My greatest accessory are my shoes. I slip into my nude Fifi Louboutins and smile. These shoes always make me look Halloween-caliber sexy.

I preview myself in the mirror with uncertainty.

I was with the same man for over twenty years. I'm about to meet someone new. When people say, "Just be yourself," they aren't referencing your personality on the first date. What they mean is, be the best possible version of yourself, or he won't ask you out again.

I pull out my phone to text Ashley.

Me: Okay. I feel like I'm seventeen going on my first date.

Ashley: Consider this a test.

Me: I'm assuming I can't CLEP this test? What does he look like?

Ashley: His name is Quinton Porter. He is a banker, sixty years old, and bald. Meet him at TAO at 8:00 p.m.

Me: WTF! Bald hotness like The Rock?

Ashley: You will just have to wait and see.

Me: What a waste of pubic grooming!

Ashley: You might like it. This is about putting yourself out there, not actually putting out.

Me: Bald head. Bald vagina. One is more preferable than the other.

Ashley: Bald head in the bald vagina is the most preferable. He's sweet.

Me: Personality pandering means he is hairless-cat-wrinkly-type bald. Gross.

CHAPTER 4

The drive to TAO Uptown is only thirty minutes. It is enough time to soothe my nerves. I scan the forefront of the restaurant before walking inside. TAO looks unassuming, considering its famous reputation. I drop Quinton Porter's name to the hostess, and she escorts me toward my table.

Walking through TAO is a visual baptism. TAO's internal personality doesn't resemble the exterior, prismatic with a scenic blend of lucky-red paint, brick walls, eclectic hanging lanterns, and Chinese scripture infused with art. A giant Buddha at the base of the restaurant is the eye-catching focal point. The Chinese decor placed inside this old movie house gives an "East meets West" visage.

My heart vigorously palpitates. The blend of commotion created by music, moving dishes, and the voices of people mingling set off all my senses. The restaurant patrons remind me of a J.Crew catalog. The men are groomed and smartly assembled. The women look Juno-esque in proportion, from their perfectly painted faces to their physicality. I feel out of place trying to integrate into single social norms.

Before reaching our table, I notice open spots at the bar. "I'd rather wait at the bar than at my table," I inform the hostess.

She cheerfully obliges and assures me she will let Quinton know my whereabouts. Giving her my fake Mentos smile of enthusiasm, as if to say, "Thanks!" I redirect my attention toward the drink menu. The bartender's generous pours are the perfect medication for my predate jitters.

The bartender places two lychee martinis in front of me. I don't hesitate slamming the first one. The sweet nectar of the lychee fruit blended with vodka treats my nerves. My second martini is being saved for the awkward first encounter with Quinton. Relaxed but cognizant of the people at the bar, I can smell the rampant pheromones. Everyone's body language signals availability.

Glancing across the bar, I notice hypnotic midnight-blue eyes fixated on me. The way his eyes bore into me make my ovaries explode. I don't turn away. The attention is too gratifying. His square, chiseled jawline is a distinctive distraction from the surrounding faces. He stands over six feet tall with thick, wavy dark-chocolate-colored, well-styled hair. Dressed in a polished gray tailored suit, navy tie, and a crisp clean white shirt, he looks divine. His clothes are cut to fit his lean body. He is sexual napalm.

Like a child full of amazement, I feel excited and warm. He is Christmas morning. Our exchanged looks enable me to bask in the color of his eyes. Where have I seen that shade of blue? I reminisce about photographs in *Travel + Leisure* magazine. The destination was Lahaina Beach, Maui. The beautiful dark ocean meeting up with the sky is captured in the color of his eyes. Watching me as I admire him, he backs away from his crowded section and moves toward me.

Placing his drink down next to my second martini, he faces me with self-assurance. My deprived inner voice screams, *Holy shit! He's here.* There is no formal introduction but a galvanizing smile. A million colors amplify the ambiance of this room, but all I see is Lahaina Beach. I fumble with my empty martini glass as I push it aside. Suddenly, I want to chug my second martini with infinite purpose. Instead, I try to come off as uninterested and bored. The ignorance of being newly single is having a resting bitch face.

My self-assured Apollonian fantasy initiates conversation: "Do you mind if I wait here? It's pretty crowded over there." He motions to where he was, and then continues, "Unless you're not alone. Are you waiting for someone?"

He is British. I listen to his accent as if he is singing a song. I am just watching his full-bodied mouth form those questions. His lips look soft. I wonder if they taste like the glass of red wine he is holding. My body craves his sex. I visualize this moment ending like an episode of *Red Shoe Diaries.* Trying to refrain from being a gawking whore, I put my inner pervert back in her cage. I have to wonder, *with all these beautiful women, why is he with me?*

His simple questions seem important enough to demand my immediate attention. My inner teen emerges by stumbling with words. "Yes, and yes…I mean, yes, you can stand anywhere you want. Yes, I am meeting someone."

His eyebrow arches. He playfully asks, "Boyfriend? Husband?" His tone shifts to intrigue. "Girlfriend?"

I almost choke on his words. I quickly reply, "No…no husband, and definitely no boyfriend. And I've never had a girlfriend. Maybe, I should consider it. Women haven't fucked me over yet." Feeling defeated, I say, "I am meeting a blind date."

His smile ignites my insides until my cheeks blush. It feels wonderful to be seen and approached by such an exquisite-looking man. I am at a loss for my typical cleverness. All this visual stimulation mutes my ability to conjure basic conversation. My small talk is less than brilliant.

A double tap on my shoulder provides an unwanted reality check. A carbon copy of Yul Brynner introduces himself, "Are you Emerson? I'm Ashley's friend Quinton."

I contemplate an escape, but there is no rock to crawl under. There are exit signs by the bar. Knowing I can't run fast in these heels, I surrender myself to the predicament. Quinton is the reason I am here. It is important to follow through with Ashley's challenge of a blind date. I agreed to do this.

Forcing a smile, I say, "Yes, I'm Emerson."

My warm insides are now turning frigid. I feel no attraction to Quinton's perfectly round head and smiling emoji face. He is the antithesis of the eye candy next to me. With his deep brown doe eyes, Quinton looks like one of my dad's friends. He is older, with a short and husky build.

My mystery man's deep indigo eyes shift from Quinton to me. He grins. Gently placing his hand on my arm, he quips, "Have fun."

Speechless, my face pleads for help. A voice inside cries, *Take me with you!*

Our moment was brief, but impressionable. I wish for another serendipitous encounter as he walks away.

Quinton's positive demeanor makes it impossible to resent him. After being seated at our table, my eyes scan the room for the mysterious gentleman at the bar. He isn't hard to find. Attraction is an epic paradox. My focus is on him, not the date in front of me. It doesn't matter if Quinton is relationship material. It is the nameless stranger who has this magnetic power over me.

Quinton genuinely seems interested in getting to know me. I oblige his curiosities by answering his questions. I look up to observe the sexy Brit engaging with two young ladies, a blonde and a brunette, in their late twenties. Flirtatious body language is easy to decipher. The blonde one puts her hands on his shoulders and tilts her head, giggling. She has game and works his ego. She places her hand into his to lead him out of the restaurant. As they leave together, he looks up to catch me spying on him. Red faced and warm, I quickly face Quinton.

I am an older woman succumbing to the millennial disillusionment of dating. If dating is like riding a bicycle, then it's the Tour de France set in hell.

******

The buzzing sound of my phone vibrating startles me awake. Eager to hear all the details about my date, Ashley calls to interrogate. I compare my date to a Disney movie, rated PG and family friendly. I told her about the Brit with the cobalt eyes. A date with him would have been comparable to porn. She asks if I want to see Quinton again.

"No, thanks. The chemical reaction of Pop Rocks in soda is more exciting than Quinton and I were. I'm not interested…at all."

Ashley chuckles. "I'm proud of you for having the cojones to go on a blind date. The first date is the hardest.

Do you feel ready to start dating again, or no interest whatsoever?"

I smart off, "As G. I. Joe says, 'Knowing is half the battle.'" Surprisingly, I admit, "Yes, I want to date, but I'm not looking for anything serious."

"Speaking of knowing…Dr. Jameson is meeting you at the penthouse at 10:00 a.m."

Before ending the call, Ashley lovingly encourages, "Dating is not easy. I'm proud of you for trying. Let's hope the next date is with someone you have chemistry with."

I wonder if this will be fun. My entitled nervous breakdown from divorce has remained dormant. Maybe all this pent-up angst needs to be unleashed on a therapist. Discussing my libido with a stranger is not how I wanted to spend my week. I get out of bed, muttering two words, and saluting the day with my middle finger.

CHAPTER 5

Day 2

Session 1

At promptly 10:00 a.m., there is a call from the front desk announcing Dr. Jameson. He is allowed entrance to my penthouse via a private elevator. Waiting for him feels like being in a paper dress on an examining table before a pap. He is going to see all of me, yet I want to be presentable. I hear the elevator door chime open. My feet feel sweaty as I hear footsteps in the hallway.

I announce, "I'm in the library."

As he walks around the corner, and my skin tingles to my core. His face sends my heart pumping fire through my veins. I freeze when I see him. In a familiar British tone, he simply states, "Good morning, Emerson."

It was the gentleman from the bar. "You…you were at TAO last night?"

He graciously responds, "Let me formally introduce myself. My name is Dr. Alexander Jameson. I will be your therapist for the next few days."

My wish for another serendipitous encounter has been fulfilled. A fusion of emotions ranging from shock, curiosity, but more importantly excitement, had come over me. We both stand silently staring at each other like opponents ready to battle. Breaking the tension, I motion my hand as an invitation to the leather seat, with a quiet, "Please."

Sitting idle across from him, I wait for him to speak. Deeply examining my discomfort, he begins, "My being at TAO last night was no coincidence. Ashley told me you would be there on a date. I wanted to observe you. Ashley described you as having social anxieties. She worried you might suffer from dating paralysis." With an apologetic grin, he continues, "I assured her you were totally fine."

I'm not sure how to process this discovery. Is this some psychological experiment? I've been a recluse but nothing in the realm of Howard Hughes. I stopped wanting to go out because people would only identify me with being divorced. Everyone wanted to be my personal Oprah. I became lactose intolerant to their vanilla-milk-flavored advice. My personal prison was the time needed to discover myself.

He startles me out of my thoughts by asking, "What are you thinking?"

Stumped by this simple question, my thoughts run rampant. I take a long meditative breath before responding, "I admit to being socially unhinged, but it's normal to grieve the loss of a marriage." I pause long enough to rationalize. "I know Ashley worries about me. I tell her everything. Her knowledge of me runs the gamut of favorite hangover food to all my marital woes."

My pale game face flushes into a rosy peach hue. "I want to feel confident as a single woman, physically and sexually. I need to find Emerson 2.0. Ashley thinks you can help unlock this side of me."

"Everything you're feeling is pretty normal." Dr. Jameson leans back in the leather chair, settling himself. "Ashley has given me brief details about your life. I would like to hear who you are…from you."

Hunkering down into my seat for a long sorted tale, "I can tell you who I used to be."

Wiggling around for comfort, I reference the details of my past. "After graduating from NYU with my journalism degree, I wrote for magazines covering the local music scene. Determined to be a music journalist, with dreams of being the editor of *Rolling Stone*, I was focused."

Looking angelic with a curious need to know, he asks, "What made you lose that focus?"

My heart tries to tame the rampant adrenaline by remaining still, "Dylan."

Compressing my folded hands until they felt warm and sticky, I breathe out. "I was twenty-years old, with no relationship experience. Being goal-oriented had made him an unwanted distraction. Kids and marriage were not for me."

Needing a few seconds to keep my feelings in check, I continue. "He was completely charming, intelligent, and hard to resist. He totally captivated my heart by doing little unusual things, like separating my M&M's by color, because I liked the red ones. Or he would leave me love notes in the most obscure places."

I sounded naïve. "I'd never experienced true love. With graduation approaching, I had to make a choice between committing myself to Dylan or fulfilling my dreams. We married right out of college."

Shifting my eyes around the room to avoid eye contact, I admit, "I put Dylan before my career goals. The first couple of years of marriage were bliss. I was a contributing entertainment writer to *New York Magazine.* I had everything, great job and marriage, and there was balance. The dynamics of our marriage changed when Harley was born. Everything seemed to fall to shit. Dylan's growing business had him working longer hours, then I quit my job to be a stay-at-home mom. Life shuffled into disarray pulling us in different directions."

Feeling the lines in my brow crinkle, I cross my arms and legs creating an imaginary barrier. "We became strangers in our marriage. We both had different needs that weren't being met. We were like perfect roommates. He paid the bills, and I did everything else.

"I fell in love with being a mother rather than a wife. The love Harley gave me was unconditional. It didn't feel that way from Dylan. In the end, it was easier for Dylan to cheat and leave. I was willing to do anything to save our family, but he didn't. All this happened because we couldn't talk to each other."

I tap my finger on my lips to help me think. "Divorce is the mother of reinvention. I'm a work in progress."

In an effort to equalize the thickness in the air, I joke, "I used to be 'the Walrus.' You know? Silly but serious, strong but insecure, like the disorienting lyrics of The Beatles song, 'I Am the Walrus.' Now, I am more like Lizzo's, 'Good as Hell.' I practice self-love…even when I don't want to."

Smiling at my analogy, his face lights up. Dr. Jameson leans to the edge of his seat, before cross-examining. "Self-care is never easy, but we need it for growth. You are divorced, and Harley has left home. What's next?"

A brief moment of silence helps me regain my composure. Not wanting to come off as condescending, but straightforward, I respond, "I want to return to writing. Not only did I love it, but I was good at it. All this grief has given me ideas for a novel."

Mentally racing through a multitude of scenarios, I blurt out, "But for now, I want to travel. I don't want to travel with friends, but alone."

Intuitively, he interrupts, "Socrates said we should know thyself. But why travel alone?"

My deadpan response slumps me down further into my chair. "I've never been completely alone until now. Traveling alone scares me. It's not about safety. It's about being selfish, no itinerary, and for once, not catering to others. For once, it's what I want to see and do."

I innocently ask, "Do you travel alone?"

His eyes widen, devoid of emotion. His magnetic confidence diffuses. "Once upon a time, I had an amazing travel companion. I miss sharing those experiences with someone. That side of myself is gone."

Without hesitation, he steers the conversation back to me. "What kind of relationship are you looking for?"

I prepare for a clinical judgmental stare down. My knuckles turn white from gripping the arm rest. "I have no desire to marry again."

Dr. Jameson searches for a reason. "Why?"

Balling my hands into a fist, I feel morose and washed out confessing. "I lost myself in a man. I will never do that again. Love isn't supposed to shit on you. Divorce is an amped-up breakup, especially when children are involved."

His elegant stature absorb my words. "I'm the last person to chastise your thoughts about marriage." His hypnotic blue eyes squint slightly, curving his mouth into a million-dollar smile. "You took a huge leap of faith going on a blind date. Maybe you should try online dating?"

"The modern aspects of dating seem so complicated and fast. People tend to be in a hurry for everything, and that it seems unnatural to me. I don't want technology to be the middleman in meeting someone." I sigh. "But I guess this is how people date."

Dr. Jameson states the obvious, "Dating is a personal preference. A lot of people use technology as a tool to help them choose someone they might be interested in. It's a good way to meet people."

Restraining my laughter, I ask, "Why not use the Sorting Hat at Hogwarts? I could use it to get a clear glimpse of every guy's intention without the bullshit. Let's face it; most of those men would be in Slytherin."

Focusing on my last statement, Dr. Jameson responds, "Even if you had the Sorting Hat, you would have to find a guy to put it on. Meeting people is the first step in figuring out what you want in a partner."

"You're right. Dating seemed so much simpler when I was young." Giving him a wink, I say, "I'll have to submit at some point."

Showing consideration for my uneasiness, he compassionately asks, "I know you didn't ask for therapy. I'm a stranger asking you personal questions. In all fairness, would you like to ask me anything?"

I said the first thing that popped in my head. "Is being a sex therapist some code word for being a gigolo to the elite? Are you a real doctor or a pervert with a PhD?"

His voice remains dry and tempered, as he responds, "I've spent a lot of time studying and writing papers. I lack the street smarts or business sense to be a gigolo."

Cautionary in approach, he discloses, "As we begin, you may feel my methods are unconventional and, possibly, obscene. I can assure you that I am not a prostitute in a suit."

Sitting up tall, he commands. "Ashley asked me to treat you on a trial basis, due to your short visit. Don't let time constraints hold you back. If this type of therapy works for you, we can schedule regular visits later. I will try to help alleviate whatever mental blocks you are having pertaining to sex or relationships."

For a brief second, I feel relieved knowing he is an actual therapist and not a man whore. I try to digest his words as he further explains. "A lot of my patients are married. I tend to deal with their sexual issues verbally. Psychotherapy lasts an extended period of time, not a few days."

He adds this disclaimer: "There are couples who prefer a more 'hands-on' approach, which requires a sex coach. They need help by touching each other. I don't do that."

Smiling wryly, I ask, "I haven't been touched in almost two years. Can I get the 'hands-on' approach? I was under the impression this was the platinum package, which entails talking and touching."

I play down the lewdness of my comment by snickering. Sensing my playfulness, he asks with false concern, "Do you feel you need help?"

I chuckle. "You mentioned your therapy might be obscene. What makes it obscene? Are we watching porn together while eating large quantities of Häagen-Dazs?"

"Let's just determine what you want emotionally, before we discuss physical pleasure."

Being a complete jackass, I blurt out, "Physical pleasure? Doesn't that fall under touching? I think that requires an extra set of hands…or will I be touching myself?"

He acknowledges the seriousness of my question. "Why do you want to do this?"

Without hesitation, I say, "I want to experience love again." I pause to collect my thoughts. "The kind that gives me butterflies."

He asks, "When was the last time you felt butterflies?"

I want to tell him it was the moment he spoke to me at the bar. In fact, I am feeling them now. Childlike in expression, I throw up my hands, kicking my feet forward. "I don't know. Maybe my internal butterflies have migrated to Canada."

Delving deeper, he asks, "Did your husband give you butterflies?"

Rolling my eyes, I respond, "In the beginning, we fall in love with the best of intentions. We are all meant to be loved with a fierce passion. Our romance was replaced by comfort. There is a point where you have to decide to evolve for the better or adapt to the worse."

I had bound myself to the idea that being in a lonely marriage was better than being alone. For a lot of women, the perception of having a perfect family defines you. You strive harder to hold on to an image than the actual marriage.

"I know I have trust issues, but can you blame me? My husband was dating while he was married to me."

Dr. Jameson explains the basics of human nature in a textbook manner. "Monogamy is not considered natural. Since we are humans with cognitive capabilities, we choose to be faithful to our partners. It is a choice that is done out of loyalty or love. Humans are designed to be promiscuous. Couples lack intimacy when they stop communicating with each other. It gives them purpose to bond sexually with someone else."

I feel ashamed. "Dylan mentioned that we didn't have enough sex. But he was so distracted with work."

Dr. Jameson confirms, "When he told you that he wasn't getting enough sex, he was indicating that he was hurt by your lack of desire for him." He proceeds, "I'm not justifying what he did. Men connect through sex. Abstinence made him feel disconnected from you."

I squirm with uneasiness. "Feeling disconnected can go both ways. It's hard to desire someone who makes you feel invisible."

He analyzes my mannerisms while I speak. "Are you ready to open yourself up again?"

I rest my head back and look up at the beautiful chandelier. "Even if opening myself up to love again means experiencing pain, I want to try."

Suddenly snapping to attention, I add, "Oh, by the way, my date last night was a total disaster. I wanted to look past the physical aspect, but I couldn't."

In a revealing moment, I recognize, "I feel like I've lost that spontaneous spark that made me interesting. Divorce doesn't just take away material assets, but also a part of who you are."

He watches me for a moment. "What is something spontaneous you want to do?"

Without any hesitation, I respond, "Go to Paris. I've always wanted to see Paris."

I impotently slouch further into my seat. "I've always thought once Harley left for college, I would see the world with my husband. All I ever talked about was going to Paris to enjoy the architecture, food, and art. There were so many things we were supposed to do. But for whatever reasons, we never did them. They were considered missed opportunities to be made up at some indefinite time. Your child's needs always come before your own. When your needs become relevant again, it doesn't seem to matter anymore."

Controlling the sudden surge of adrenaline, I rub my sweaty palms together. "For once, I want to do something for myself. Going to Paris would be a monumental symbol of independence to me." I surprise myself with that statement. Seeing Paris represents something I truly want.

I lower my eyes to my hands. "It appears Dylan found the Fountain of Youth in female form. She's like Botox and Viagra all rolled into one big pill. He takes her like a daily vitamin because she makes him feel good."

Leaning forward with interest, he engages, "Aging makes you interesting, not unattractive. Women in their forties radiate beauty due to life experiences. In my opinion, they are more appealing than women in their twenties."

Trying not to fidget by crossing and uncrossing my legs, I force myself into stillness. "Men don't age like women. Men are like the cans of Spam you keep in your cabinet for emergencies. You can pull it out ten years from now, and it'll look the same, but with added jelly on top. Women are like sponges. We start out bouncy but end up dried-up and worn-out. Men can toss out the old sponge and get a new one."

Smiling at my analogy, he jests, "I would never compare you to a dried-up sponge. You've just lost focus on what makes you feel beautiful."

Amused by his response, I ask, "How old are you?"

"I'm thirty-five."

"Of course you are," I say, putting my hands to my mouth to hide my razzed, pouting lips. "Your confidence in me is based on an external viewpoint. You are young, single, and perfect. You've probably never felt rejection."

"It's presumptuous to think I am single...or perfect." He is forthcoming in his sincerity. "And I do know what rejection feels like. You don't know anything about me."

I shrug. "You're right. Some serial killers fit your pretty-faced professional stereotype. I don't know you. You just seem so self-assured."

Amused by my derisive comment, he responds, "I promise. I've never killed anyone. I can't be timid if I'm giving guidance." He pauses before he asks, "Would you like to be the assertive one?"

"Sure, I'll be assertive." I arch my eyebrow and request, "Let's begin today's session by analyzing *The Complete Illustrated Kama Sutra* positions. Which position gave Sting the seven-hour-long orgasm? I need to make up for lost time."

Suppressing laughter with a half grin, he comments, "Yes, I will introduce Tantra to you...just not today." Deepening his voice to command my attention, he continues, "I am going to ask you to do things that will make you feel uncomfortable, and they might seem unethical."

He assures me, "You don't have to participate if you choose not to, but I ask you to at least consider it. Due to our short amount of time, I don't want to just talk. Sometimes you need to do something scary to remove normal self-reactions. It might make you feel less stifled to be impulsive."

My body tenses into a paralysis of worry, before asking, "What exactly do you want me to do?"

Without flinching, he directly states, "I would like for you to stand up and take off your dress."

CHAPTER 6

"Excuse me? Did you just ask me to take off my dress?"

"Yes. I want to see what you're wearing underneath."

Offended by his audacity, I release my acidic tongue. "Why don't you just go fuck yourself? I'll judge your technique and give you an assessment of your personality."

He remains unusually calm with his request. With a devil-may-care presence, he leaves my remark unchecked. He speaks as if this request is ordinary. "You can tell a lot about a woman from her underwear and bra choice. It's an expressive part of your personality. Do you prefer the comfort of cotton Calvin Klein boy shorts? Are you a repressed teenager with cartoon character designs? A flirtatious Victoria's Secret Angel in silk bikinis? Or are you seductively confident in wearing La Perla lace to the grocery store?"

My stomach feels heavy with nerves. "What I'm wearing underneath has no bearing on what's rattling in my head." With exasperation, I acknowledge, "I don't even think my ex-husband saw my panties until our third date."

My inner Nicolas Cage from *Honeymoon in Vegas* is about to lash out. I have that neurotic slow build to crazy in my voice. "Remind me to put this on your Yelp review…clothing optional!"

He calculates my reaction and proceeds to clarify, "You were forewarned that I am impractical. I generally spend months with a patient, not a few days. This will help me get the basics out of the way." In an effort to console me, as well as bait me, his charisma proves motivational. "I normally wouldn't even take on a patient for such a short amount of time. Ashley's love for you persuaded me to do this."

I snapped rhetorically, "Ashley's love for me…persuaded you to ask me to take off my dress?"

"It is rare to find a friendship like your bond with Ashley. Her love for you was very apparent. It's like I said earlier, I'm trying to be creative with our short amount of time."

Part of me feels pissed off by such a humiliating request. My curious half wants to hear his analysis of my underwear. His logic seems inane, but it provides insight to the male mind. He is right. When you try something scary, it's better to be impulsive instead of rational. This is not the time for me to puss out.

"What if I told you what I was wearing? Does that count?" I sound like a sullen teenage girl trying to be understood.

He has this triumphant look of arrogance. "No, it's not the same if you describe your undergarments. I need you to trust me."

I glance down at myself. My hands gesture to my body. "I can assure you, there's nothing sexy going on under here."

I feel punchy defending my virtue and prolonging my inevitable embarrassment. "How many women have you asked?"

"You are my first. I'm not trying to be insensitive or demeaning. This helps me understand how you see yourself sexually. How we proceed is entirely up to you."

I cringe knowing what is underneath this dress. I look like a mom, not a seductress.

Stalling for time, I argue, "You must realize the dichotomy of analyzing comfort versus how I feel. I tend to choose my underwear based on my activities. I would never let a thong ride up my ass in the vegetable aisle of the grocery store. Sexy is a state of mind."

He's quick. "But I want to see how you see yourself on a daily basis. Every day you put these knickers on, and no one sees them. Who are you underneath?"

I stand there, eyes closed, contemplating this question. I convince myself this is like modeling a swimsuit. Cajoling myself with the positives. I groomed, therefore, I won't resemble Chewbacca's sister. And I won't look like a female hog casing, since I'm not wearing Spanx. My bra and panties match. They don't appear worn-out or stretched.

I open my eyes to see him fixated on me. There is a quietness to his decorum. It's as if he doesn't want to spook me with any sudden movements or sounds. Proceeding with caution, he says, "We can just sit and talk if you prefer practicality."

My thoughts escape my mind. I ask, "What is the point of this?"

"I am just trying to read you." Tenderness creeps across his face. Dr. Jameson measures each word down to this ideal. "It is amazing how the simplest things are interpreted into something complicated. Sometimes these simple things can bring the most pleasure physically and visually. Ultimately, you control the situation."

Calmly, I slip off my Louboutins. They will have to take a back seat to my uncouth, virginal striptease. My underwear will be on display, not the shoes. As I step out of each shoe, I slide them to the side with my foot. Facing Dr. Alexander in a hushed determination, I slowly open the first three buttons of my olive-green shirt dress. My hands proceed to slip each button free. I abruptly stop. Gripping the knotted belt, I hesitate before its release.

We both concentrate on each other for different reasons. He studies my actions as if my body is a tarot card in a psychic reading. Feeling naked regardless of still being dressed, I ask, "What do you think I'm wearing?" The softness in my voice makes it sound like I'm flirting.

He quickly answers, "I see you in beige, because you don't realize your beauty. You want everything to be hidden."

I delve into the situation by wriggling my knotted belt open. I undo it and pull the ties back until they spill down. The front of my wrap dress is slightly open, revealing a peek of what is underneath.

My self-esteem takes charge saying, "Fuck it." Pulling the dress open to rest on my shoulders, I release my grip, allowing myself to be exposed. I slowly slide the dress down my arms, until it drops to the floor.

CHAPTER 7

"I guess you called it. I'm beige."

He examines me. "My guessing beige was easy. There is more to this than color."

His eyes are staring at my chest. "Your choice of Victoria's Secret means you are specific about the feel and fit of your undergarments. You didn't just pick up some random set at any department store. Your breasts are emphasized by a demi-cup lace bra. The cut of the bra elevates your size-C cup. You feel this gives you an attractiveness to your figure."

Holy shit, he has a sixth sense for boobs. Tension creeps over me as I listen to every description. The fact that my underwear reveals a deep subconscious revelation astounds me. He smiles and winks at me.

His words catch me off guard. It reverberates throughout my body, relaxing my stance and warming me with curiosity.

Delving deeper into his visuals, he says, "You groom yourself, maybe out of habit, but you want to be prepared for anything." His lips slowly form a devilish grin as he finishes the statement.

He sits up, then taps his bottom lip with his index finger. His eyes scan every inch of me. "You physically care for yourself, evidenced by your toned physique. Wearing bikini panties in lace means confidence in the appearance of your bottom. Choosing lace makes you feel innocent, romantic, and sexy at the same time. But the color beige makes you feel practical and safe."

Needing to puncture the stress bubble around me, I parody the situation by being an ass. "Does your skill set list a proficiency in tits and ass? It should. Maybe you can judge the swimsuit competition at the Miss Universe pageant."

Not the slightest put off by my mouth, he absorbs it with a smile. "If you changed the color or style of your undergarments, it would have an entirely different meaning. Even though it is hidden underneath, the simplicity of change is in your attitude. Being bold is a state of mind."

He stands up and begins walking toward me, then stops. With just a few inches between us, I forget I am half naked. He whispers, "Thank you for trusting me. I wish you could see how beautiful you are."

His words have bite. It's like venom streaming in my veins, which turns my cheeks a rose-colored hue—the perfect shade of sun-kissed humility. My hands instinctively creep from my sides to cover my pubic area. I feel the urge to shield my vagina. Even though he ogled my body in order to deconstruct my sexual type, I allowed it. I liked it.

I watch him kneel in front of me. He reaches down by my ankles to collect my dress. The movement seems slow and calculated. He drapes my dress around my waist, gliding it upward against my spine. It is a soft feathery tickle on my skin. The dress moves upward as he stands up straight. He walks behind me to hold my sleeves open. Easing my arms back into the dress, I feel his fingers on my shoulders. This intense closeness makes it hard to dress myself. My hands reach to the ends of my sleeves, and he steps back. He folds the front of the dress shut like a kimono. He never takes his eyes off mine. I take over from there. Distracting myself by lining up the buttons to be closed.

Taking a few more steps backward, he explores my mindset. "Why did you agree to let me see you undressed?"

As I tie the belt back into a knot, my hands smooth down the dress. After I ensure I'm presentable, my eyes move from my hemline to meet his gaze. "Maybe I did it for shits and giggles."

"Hmm…shits and giggles? I must annotate that in my notes." He seems to enjoy the absurdity of my answers. "We've killed two birds with one stone. I was able to get a general assessment of your personality, and now you know what it feels like to have someone other than your ex-husband see your underwear."

He surprises me by asking, "Do you want to change your style of undergarments? Or are you content with what you have?"

I think about all the times I go out to eat. I always mull over the menu to try new things. I put more thought into ordering food than my underwear.

Ready for change, I apply logic, "Will I feel different?"

In his patronizing, yet exquisitely proper British accent, he says, "Let's find out…for shits and giggles."

"You want me to try on lingerie in front of you? What does your girlfriend think of your methods?"

Wryly amused, he says, "Who says I have a girlfriend?"

According to my mental calculations, Dr. Jameson implied he wasn't single. His unscrupulous and cunning play on words drove me to assumptions. He's gay.

He explains how some women use sexy lingerie as a tool to boost their confidence. Looking at myself in different lingerie might change my perspective on my own sexuality. Maybe these small changes might not feel drastic, but they're a start. This all seems so comical to me. It's more interesting than traditional therapy.

CHAPTER 8

Exiting the hotel, he holds out his arm as an invitation to join him for a stroll. I intertwine my arm in his as we walk, a platonic gesture that felt personal. Being close to him felt nice. We look like a couple.

Casually strolling down the street, I am thrown for a loop when we pass a Victoria's Secret, assuming we were going to shop there. Pointing my finger at the passing store window, I'm puzzled, "Aren't we going to stop in there?"

"No. That is where you would normally shop. I have something else in mind." He says this with a smug look on his face.

"Are you taking me to some kinky sex toy shop?" I look up at him. "Is this part of my induction into your sexual healing?"

His British smart mouth plays along. "I was hoping we could do the toy store later in the week. I thought you might like something more high-end for your sexual awakening."

I jest, "Why would you assume I would like high-end lingerie? Maybe I want to be a freaky bitch. Today, I'm in the mood for a patent leather strap-on harness and a dog collar."

"We can pick those items up after you're done shopping for something less fetish." Feverishly sarcastic, he emphasizes, "But only if you promise to model it for me at the store."

I look up at him and give him my own compromise. "Only if you bring in your sex coach. Please show me the joys of deep penetration and how to stuff a ball in my mouth without gagging."

Walking toward Madison Avenue, I can feel the cool breeze blowing across the chaos of traffic and pedestrians. Chaos can be distracting in a good way. Glancing around, I see women looking at us. I know they are admiring his physical beauty. They are probably wondering why he is with me.

I start to snicker, "I look like a cougar strolling down the street with you."

He shakes his head. "Do you feel that it's impossible for a younger man to be attracted to you?"

"I just can't imagine a guy your age looking at me…the way older women look at you. Younger men generally don't appreciate an older woman for what we represent. I'm not saying it doesn't happen, but it's rare. Women my age carry themselves differently. We are already established in our views and life experiences."

Dr. Jameson asks, "Have you ever heard of the Half Your Age Plus Seven rule?"

I crinkle my eyebrows and shake my head in disbelief. "There's a dating age rule?"

Dr. Jameson explains, "Theoretically, there is a socially acceptable formula that determines your dating age range."

He jokes, "Now this is hypothetical, but a formula was developed to calculate what is socially acceptable. You take your own age, divide it in half, and then add seven. This would be the youngest age you could socially get away with dating. The equation for the maximum age limit is your age, subtract seven, and then double that answer. This would be the oldest socially acceptable age to date."

Doing the math in my head, I respond, "I'm no Steven Hawking, but this formula is batshit crazy!"

I break down my age group. "I'm forty-three. According to this logic, I could date a guy as young as twenty-eight years old. I can't imagine showing up to my daughter's dorm room with a guy she could date! Harley would be mortified." I follow the second formula to calculate the age of what is too old. "According to the second equation, I could date a seventy-two-year-old man! That's like dating one of my dad's friends. Gross!"

Dr. Jameson smiles as he explains, "This all in theoretical fun. Men seem to adhere to the formula more than women do, especially in figuring out how young a partner can be. Most women tend to go for a man closer to their age, one that has been born at least in their decade."

He offers another viewpoint. "Generally speaking, women in their forties aren't really looking for men younger than thirty-five years old. It appears I'm at the perfect age. Women both younger and older than me would be satisfied."

"That is a bold conclusion, Dr. Jameson. Who would be more sexually gratified in that scenario?"

His smirks. "This is about you, not me. Maybe you will experience this newfound sexual fulfillment with your new panties."

I can't see a younger man asking me out, yet stranger things have happened since I've arrived to the city. I wonder what type of woman he would date. "You said you don't have a girlfriend. Why is that? Being so proficient in relationships, aren't you like the Dalai Lama of ass?"

Insinuating a sexual preference, he remarks, "Who says I like girls?"

CHAPTER 9

My insides feel compressed, like a crushed Coke can. I joked he might be gay but never imagined it. Then again, there are no stereotypes in sexual taste nowadays. Maybe that's why he's so unfazed by women. At least now, I won't be self-conscious when I pick out lingerie. It's like going shopping with my hot girlfriend.

We suddenly stop walking. He announces, "We are here."

I look up and notice the name Agent Provocateur. I stare at the window dressing. The mannequins pose seductively while wearing see-through lingerie. The display demands your attention. The bras and panties selected to showcase the store are a roadside distraction. It is like rubbernecking at the female body. It makes you wonder if just a few pieces of fabric could make you look that desirable.

Stepping inside the store unleashes a self-esteem check of epic proportions. I notice the lingerie is decadent, hypersexual artistry. The store's decorum is muted with neutral grays, blacks, golds, pinks, and browns, but the lingerie and shoes dilate your eyes with color. The assortment of color and styles appear delicate, yet sex-provoking. This underwear would definitely alter my confidence.

A beautiful ivory-skinned ginger named Dusty greets us. She looks voluptuous in her curve-hugging pink Agent Provocateur uniform. Her flaming-red hair matches her pouty lips, and black stilettos emphasize her long lean legs. She resembles a high-class naughty nurse. Admiring her uniformed "Healthcare Harlot" outfit, I don't hear her offer us assistance, but I do hear her offer champagne.

Dr. Jameson interrupts my thoughts. "What are you looking for, Emerson?"

Dusty's personality bubbles like the champagne in my glass. Sparkling with enthusiasm and full of assurance, she examines my body and inquires, "Can I find you anything in particular?"

"Can you help me find my dignity?" I respond.

My eyes study the room in unadulterated fascination. I imagine supermodels skimping around with their wealthy lovers in exotic cities. Minimalistic in coverage turning into pure seduction. Composed with expensive silk and lace, these clothes make feeling sexy obtainable.

I blurt out, "Black. I want to try on black lace. What do you think?" I look at Dusty, as if she is the fortune-telling Zoltar of lingerie.

She smiles. "Of course! First, let's get you into a fitting room. I'll select some items for you to try on."

Dr. Jameson takes a seat outside the room enjoying his champagne, content, like a lion finishing a meal. Dusty guides me into a steel-colored room with large cream-and-gray-colored drapes. The drapes cover the doorway to each dressing room. They are pulled open by large black tasseled ropes. Looking up, I notice the rose-colored lighting from the pink bulbs. At least the light will be flattering. I won't look like a corpse in a morgue.

I remove my dress and bra to be fitted properly. Dusty begins measuring my chest for an accurate size. She is spot on just from her visual assessment. She writes it down for my "profile." I chuckle. I realize it is only early afternoon and already two people have seen my chest today.

Dusty is my personal assistant in picking things out. She seems knowledgeable and eager to help. She leaves for a few minutes, then returns with a selection of black lace bras and panties. The notable black lingerie has my imagination in full gear.

She says, "You look like you usually have a sophisticated taste. Let's try something different. I'm sensing burlesque and risqué. Your boyfriend will love it."

I am about to explain that he is my therapist, not my boyfriend, when I start chuckling. Who brings their therapist lingerie shopping? My laughter makes Dusty question her selections. She assures me the black Sally bra and brief set are to die for. She leaves the dressing room for a split second, then returns with more items. Dusty's nonchalant behavior in opening and shutting the curtains without warning is startling. She isn't trying to be intrusive, just helpful.

Dusty storms back inside holding a black Mercy corset. She is giddy with excitement to have me try it on. This ravishing Victorian era lace corset is intricately embroidered with an unusual design. I slip into it carefully and hold it against my chest. Dusty ties the laces by weaving it up my spine. She pulls the laces tight. It feels like suffocation through constriction. Looking in the mirror, I am flabbergasted by my bombshell appearance. The corset forms my figure into an hourglass shape.

"Do men like corsets?" Smiling back at my reflection, I add, "I do feel sexy."

Dusty explains her logic about men. "Some men enjoy the beauty of what a woman wears before sex. Look at the form of your body in this corset. Undoing the tie in the back is pleasurable because it requires them to take their time. You are a gift needing to be unwrapped."

My sexual awareness is diminishing with age. I've lost myself in being a wife and mother. I am first and foremost a woman. I drink in my reflection. Lingerie has changed my attitude and posture. I had no idea I was capable of looking like this.

"I can't believe this is me. Wow."

Dusty asks, "Would your boyfriend like to come and see how amazing you look?"

"I think he's seen enough today."

My statement makes Dusty assume Dr. Jameson and I were intimate earlier. I am not going to explain anything. I just need the corset undone to resuscitate my lungs.

Dusty hands me a ravishing deep crimson ensemble, the Denver set. It comes with a bra, brief-style panties, and a top cover. A sheer French lace design with embroidered leaves, it is an abstract visual of passionate love. A mandarin-collared jacket accompanied by a diamond-shaped front enclosure makes the top look regal. This ensemble would make any woman feel unmistakably sensual.

I tell Dusty I want to try this on without assistance. Agreeing with a nod, she leaves the room. I slide into each piece carefully, beaming with admiration while looking in a mirror. I had trivialized this lingerie expedition. It wasn't just the color, but the style. It changes my perception of my body. I'm not frumpy.

The ever-flowing champagne on an empty stomach empowers me to show it off. I poke my head outside the heavy cloth dividers and request for Dr. Jameson to come inside. He appears skeptical while approaching the drapes. I ask him to shut his eyes. Ensuring his eyes are closed, I take his hand and guide him inside the drapes. I situate him into a prime viewing spot. I remind him, "No peeking."

I fluff out my hair, creating bedhead around my face, and cascade it around my shoulders. Placing my arms above my head, like a centerfold, then crossing my legs to elongate them, I pose. My platform Louboutins and sexy lingerie make me comparable to a high-priced prostitute.

Provocatively, I pose against the mirror behind me.

In a soft bedroom voice, I ask, "What color do you think I'm wearing?"

He responds, "Black."

"I'm sorry, Dr. Jameson. You are incorrect."

His eyes pop open to my suggestive pose. He approaches me with a smoldering stare. The electric pull between us makes me feel hot and nervous. He's quietly examining my body. Breaking his silence, he explains, "In each culture, the color red has a different meaning. It represents love and luck. The embodiment of energy, passion, and action. Some men think the color red is an aphrodisiac. It signals an awakened sexual energy. Personally, I find red lingerie to be very erotic."

His eyes map every angle of my body. "What does it look like without the lace jacket?"

I feel self-conscious. My fingers fumble at the small hook-and-eye fastenings on the mandarin collar. I portray more klutz than sex goddess. My frustrations lead to nervous giggles. "I can't seem to undo the collar."

He asks, "May I assist you?"

I give permission with a nod. He positions himself within inches of me. Gazing into my eyes, he blindly searches for the latch by touch. I relax my head back against the mirror, exposing my neck, my breasts perched out, enjoying his slight touch. My body is responsive to his flirtatious exploration of my collar. A gentle tugging with his fingers releases each latch. This simple act give me pleasure without sex.

"Now, what about the tie on the back?" he asks.

Puzzled, I replied, "What about it?"

A tulle strap is tied behind my back. I begin to reach my arms backward to undo the bow. Dr. Jameson stops me. Deviously grinning, he says, "It would be easier for me to do it."

I'm not sure where this is going. My body is responding on its own. His sliding hands pace slowly down to my waist. He reaches behind me. My natural physical response is to touch him. I maintain restraint. He pulls me in closer with a firm grip against my back. Our faces tease close enough to scorch my skin. Breathing in his masculine smell is deeply arousing, warm, and delicious.

Perplexed at what is happening, I'm not sure if this is part of his therapy or something platonic. "What are you doing?"

He whispers, "I'm loosening you up."

His hands softly travel to the lower part of my back. He undoes the tie, smoothing the straps down to my sides. Ever so slightly, he places his hands on my curves as a starting point. His fingertips move upward, exploring me, stopping at my shoulders. He navigates his hands inside the jacket with precision. He peels away the lace off my shoulders, and the jacket tumbles to the floor. I let myself feel desire for a fleeting moment.

Examining my exposed chest spilling out of my bra, he shifts his eyes back to meet mine, and inquires, "Do you need help with anything else?"

I clear my throat. "No. I think I'm good."

He takes a step back to admire me. In a sweet tone, he says, "You are better than good."

The combination of alcohol and a sudden urge to pounce on Dr. Jameson swelters me like a storm. I'm compelled to confess my thoughts. "For a second, I felt like you wanted to fuck me. Are gay men turned on by lingerie?"

Astonished by my accusation, he asks, "What makes you think I'm gay?"

I remind him, "You clearly stated that you don't like girls."

Laughing at how I read too much into his comment, "Well…I don't like girls, but I am very heterosexual. I love women."

He responds to my assumption with a hearty laugh. "You felt confident with me…when you thought I was gay."

Seeing the look of embarrassment on my face, he extinguishes my uneasiness. "Red was a great choice. I am surprised by the color, but not by how stunning you look." Suddenly, he becomes very controlled in his demeanor, and he takes another step back.

I feel flushed. "Your version of therapy can be confused with being a pervert. Unlike this morning, this went beyond analyzing into a physical examination."

He addresses my frustration. "I never made you do anything you didn't want to do. It's the power of suggestion and a person's desire to know someone's opinion." He prided himself. "Yes, I suggested a way to speed up my analysis of you, but you took your dress off on your own."

Cowering to the truth, I hunch back against the mirror. He goes further in his evaluation. "You took charge of this situation by calling me in here, having me close my eyes, and then shutting the curtains for privacy. Maybe I come off as perverse, but my technique seems to be working out for you. You probably haven't been this assertive in quite some time."

Recognizing my discomfort, his voice softens, "Thank you for trusting me enough to bring me in here."

I stand there half naked wearing heels. Being daring is something I am not accustomed to. I want to do it again. It's been a while since I tapped into this side of me. Wearing this red lace ensemble combined with the champagne instigated my carefree behavior. The change in the undergarments seems so subtle and simple. I want to show it off.

"Are you upset with me for seeing you stripped down?" He pauses before continuing, "Or not pursuing something more?"

"I'm not upset with you at all. I'm more perturbed by my own actions. You are trifling in your innuendos."

I gesture my hands all over my body. "Look at me! I thought it would be fun to be a vixen for a gay man. I just assumed the female anatomy was like vanilla ice cream to you."

He puts his hands in his pockets and stares me down. "I'm sorry I confused you. I'll try to be more forthcoming, but it's in my nature to be aloof with patients. Then again…you aren't really a patient, are you?"

He lightheartedly jests, "And I love vanilla ice cream."

Dr. Jameson tries to contain his laughter. I know my reaction was over-the-top dramatic. I hate his sexy smirk, because it disarms me.

He affirms my thoughts. "You are absolutely correct. This seems mental. I will let you get dressed. Or would you like to continue exploring more options?"

"Actually, I want to try on these other items." I hold them up for him to see, then add, "I can manage these alone."

He walks out with a pleased look on his face. I stand behind the curtain, feeling flustered. I distract myself by examining the other items Dusty brought in for me, then I take my time trying them all on. The way the lingerie makes me look and feel invigorates my nonexistent libido. I need this variety in my boudoir. At some point, I want to have lingerie-worthy moments. Until then, I'll store it in my arsenal for change.

When I exit the dressing room, I see Dr. Jameson seated on the sofa. I wonder how many women he's taken here. I walk up to the register to check out. He watches me from afar and gives me a nod. He seems proud of my newfound boldness. I buy four new sets. Dusty packages everything up into a beautiful pink box with a black bow. She puts the box in a big pink bag with "Agent Provocateur" written in cursive on it. I'll walk out of here with a perfectly packaged box of sex.

Outside the store, Dr. Jameson holds out his arm. His gesture represents a peace offering. I accept it by intertwining my arm into his. Strolling arm and arm, I am captivated by the beauty of fall in New York City. Fall truly is the time for renewal. I share my good news. "By the way, my sizes are now on file with the store. Dusty thought my boyfriend might want to surprise me later." With a side-eye glance, he responds only by smiling at my comment.

Out of the blue, I feel the urge to eat. "I'm starving. Could we stop off and eat somewhere? Maybe get another drink?"

He glances around to get his bearings. "We can grab a cab and head over to The Roof on top of the PUBLIC Hotel. The view of the city is spectacular."

"Perfect." Peering out at the city's landscape at night is the ideal way to end this day.

CHAPTER 10

The panoramic view of New York City from The Roof bar is worth the overpriced food and drinks. The interior is dark and sophisticated and sleek with sexiness. The city resembles a postcard silhouette showcasing its vibrant glow. We glide past the long bar of glimmering bottles of high-end liquor to find our way onto the terrace. It looks like a tranquil botanical garden set against artificial night lights and skyscrapers. The cozy seating area is separated by an arrangement of plants to allow each group privacy. It is open and exposed, but we search out privacy. Sitting at a corner table against the clear balcony rail, I consume the city view. I walk over to the railing and gaze down at the bustling city. The sun is going down, and it is going to be a clear, cool night. I close my eyes and just listen to everything and absorb it. I turn toward the table to see Dr. Jameson staring at me with a grin.

Returning the smile, I disclose, "It's funny. I don't live far away from here, but I never fully appreciate how close I am to the city. Everything is changing so quickly."

"Where do you live?" he inquires.

"I live about an hour and a half away from New York City, in Chappaqua. I am surrounded by grass and trees and nothing concrete, but who can resist this view?"

I glance down at the menu to see what my champagne-filled hunger pains crave. The waitress comes to our table, and I order a Moscow mule and something heavy to absorb the previous drinks. My body wants a plate of nachos, but junk appetizers aren't on the menu.

Trying to appease my growling stomach, I order, "Okay. I would like the Long Island sea scallops with honey butter."

Dr. Jameson orders an IPA beer from the Montauk Brewery. I am surprised that he is a beer guy. He seems like someone who would drink scotch in an old-fashioned glass. We sit in silence for a few moments, just looking around the enclosed terrace. The rooftop is cozy with the intimate landscape and thriving with the sound of young couples socializing and listening to music.

In an effort to figure him out, I ask, "Other than lingerie shopping, do you normally dine with your patients?"

"Actually, I don't take any of my patients lingerie shopping. I do not dine with them either. You are my first. We've established you aren't a real patient." With a wink, he continues, "I have an office, but most people like house calls for convenience and privacy."

Rejecting his statement, I snap back sarcastically, "You said you didn't have a girlfriend. Why is that? It seems odd to me that you are an expert on relationships, but you aren't in one."

Mocking my response, he says, "I normally don't discuss my personal life with my patients."

My you're-full-of-shit look shuts him down. "I'm technically not a patient…right? There was no money exchanged or paperwork filled out."

His stance relaxes with his quick response. "Oh yes, that's right, or I would have been arrested by now."

I stare directly into his eyes with a slightly crooked grin. "Why can't you just answer the question honestly? As we both agreed, I was kind of thrown into this, so nothing about this situation is normal."

He is silently contemplating whether to answer me. He fumbles with his beer by swirling it around. His thoughts seem to be lost in the swirling foam. He shifts his gaze up to me and softens his voice. He rests his arms on the table and leans in to confess, "Yes, I have loved deeply, but the loss felt deeper. I am not intimately close with anyone at the moment. Is that a better answer?"

He raises his brow at me to seek a verdict. "I'm not in a relationship because I choose not to be. I am complicated in how I approach my own relationships versus helping people with theirs."

I glance around the room. "There are women here tonight who can't take their eyes off of you. That must be strange…to know you are desired, and you choose to be alone."

He jokes, "Does changing your underwear make you the therapist now?"

I wonder, "What do you want in a woman?"

"I usually know it when I experience it, not see it. Finding a beautiful woman is easy, but finding one who holds my interest beyond sex is something else."

I look around the room again. I notice young women together on a night out. I can see them laughing and telling each other stories while they drink. A woman in her late twenties is conspicuously staring at us. She looks like a Mediterranean beauty with long wavy dark hair and light brown eyes. I start to bite my lip to control my giggles.

I confide to Dr. Jameson, "Look—I think you have an admirer. She has balls to be checking you out while you're sitting with me. She doesn't know if I'm your girl-friend, wife, or sister. There's definitely an interest in you, with those 'talk to me stares.' Why don't you talk to her?"

He is astounded by my observation. He quickly glances over at her. She gives him a shy smile while tuck-ing her hair behind her ears. She coyly looks away, then back again.

He flatly responds, "No."

I let out a puzzled, "Why the hell not?"

"First, I'm here with you, and I'm giving you my fullest attention. Second, she looks too young and imma-ture for me. And finally, she is by no means a munter."

I interject, "What the hell is a munter?"

He laughs at my curiosity. "A munter is an Irish term for 'ugly woman'. She is attractive. I wouldn't have noticed her if you didn't point her out."

I feel flattered by his undivided attention. "I went out with a portly, old bald guy last night. He was unat-tractive to me, but sweet. I'm amazed at how it's okay for me to surrender to these situations, but you can't do it yourself."

"Maybe that's the best analysis of me. I can't seem to surrender myself to anyone."

Gazing at him in disbelief, I reveal my observation. "You and I are very similar in a weird way. We both want to appear open-minded and laid-back. In truth, though, we are both pretty uptight. By coming here, I've succumbed to what was asked of me. I'm amazed at what I've done these past two days." I shake my head as I look around the room.

"I suddenly feel sad for you. You live in this huge city full of alluring, successful women, and no one has captivated you. And *I'm* the one who needs therapy?"

Dr. Jameson's eyes light up with an infectious smile. I am about to open myself up for his "Therapy for Dummies" analogy. "You have no reason to feel sad for me at all. I was deeply in love once. Maybe one day, when I'm ready, I'll fall in love again." He goes on to explain, "Love doesn't make anyone complete, but it does make you connect with people. It is in our nature to love and be loved. Love is what brought you to me. Ashley loves you and wants you to be okay."

In a surprisingly revealing moment, he adds, "And who says I'm not captivated by anyone?"

"Well, I know you're not captivated by me. Men might find me attractive. I'm not being insecure or self-deprecating, but I'll never be the hottest girl in the room. It's just a factual observation."

We sound like some weird couple comparing our attractiveness. "Ashley exudes sex and has a great personality. She will always be the hottest girl in the room. I will always be the cute sidekick with a dirty mouth."

Dr. Jameson finds my analogy amusing, but he is in the same league as Ashley. People will always notice them when they walk into a room. Maybe it's their self-assurance or confidence giving them physical divinity.

Dylan was the first guy who made me feel beautiful. He had this ability to make me feel remarkable without makeup and wearing ripped jeans. Our personalities were so opposite, but our quirks made us complement each other. Reflecting on Dylan makes me wonder what happened to us. The innocence of so many beginnings have the most tragic endings.

Dr. Jameson has the luxury of choosing anyone in this room. Beauty creates a strong first impression, and it can be overwhelming to some people. It's like having a special power. Attractive people can use their beauty to their advantage, but it can also be their kryptonite. In Ashley's case, she has doubts in her marriage. She had never questioned her physicality until her husband didn't seem interested. Dr. Jameson seems to use his beauty like a priceless vase at a museum. You can enjoy looking at it, but don't try to touch it or an alarm might go off.

I scoff, "A great personality is spectacular, but let's be real. If I had a choice between you and Quinton last night, I would have chosen you in a nanosecond."

Dr. Jameson takes a dig at me. "But both of us did approach you. You walked away with him."

I let out a sinister laugh of serial killer proportions. "That's not fair. I was obligated to walk away with him. Believe me. I knew where all the fire exits were located."

Feeling like a schoolgirl, I twirl strands of my hair around my finger while scanning the room. I notice a hot, bosomy blonde. She has sparkling sapphire eyes. "Take a look at the corner table. If you had to choose between that buxom blonde and me, you would walk out with her in a heartbeat."

He is perplexed. He seemed to be puffed out in stature by sitting upright in response. "Unbeknownst to you, men are not that simple. You shouldn't assume that men prefer big jubblies over natural beauty. I've spent all day with you. I doubt I would pick her over you."

I am genuinely surprised by his answer. I feel frustrated. "Why are you even here with me? You said you don't dine or lingerie shop with patients. With me, you are a huge contradiction."

"I don't know why I've strayed from my normal process. Maybe I like talking to you. I would be a walking contradiction if you were an actual patient."

As the waitress gives us our dinner and drinks, Dr. Jameson seems amused by my appetite. I can tell this casual setting is an unusual experience for him. I take a sip from my Moscow mule. "This feels like a date, but without all the typical stressful bullshit."

I've caught him off guard. He responds, "Are you always this unfiltered? Did your ex-husband enjoy this about you?"

I start laughing. "My ex-husband left me for someone born in another generation. He apparently needed less conversation and more sex. You would have to be a strong man to handle my mouth. I'm destined to be with cats." I direct my glance outward toward the twinkling city lights. "Perhaps I'm a walking contradiction too. I have no problem speaking my mind, but I couldn't communicate my needs to my husband."

I grin at Dr. Jameson. "I guess we're both fucked."

His body stance leans into me with interest. "I'm curious. You seem so blunt. How did you react when your husband asked you for a divorce?"

I sit up straight in my chair, preparing to control my emotions. "He emailed me."

"He emailed you?"

"He was gone on a business trip overseas. I checked my email before I went to bed. I read this simple email. 'Our marriage is dead. I want a divorce.' Try going to sleep after reading those two sentences."

"You had no idea this was coming?"

"Marriages come to a complacent plateau at some point. It becomes normal. He found something new and exciting on his trip." I take a sip of my drink, then add, "He denied he was having an affair for the longest time. I was batshit crazy wondering what I did wrong. He just left me and my daughter. He doesn't speak to either of us, and we can't figure out why."

Dr. Jameson's facial expression reflects compassion when I tell my story. I try to diffuse this from becoming some bitter rant. I confess, "I don't want to be a hateful or disgruntled woman, and really I don't want this to consume me. All these emotions have held me prisoner. Coming to New York City has made me see myself differently. I am feeling relaxed and hopeful for new possibilities."

"I've just met you, and I would never say you were someone who swallowed a bitter pill. In fact, I think you have quite a unique perception of things. Your blunt humor makes me laugh. Even in my line of work, I've heard everything from couples with peculiar fetishes to depraved sexual fantasies, but the cruelty some people can inflict on others is still shocking to me."

Dr. Jameson takes a drink of his beer before asking, "What do you physically miss?"

My fingers tap the sides of my copper mule mug. I am relaxed enough to indulge his question in full disclosure. I place my hands to my mouth as if to savor something delicious. "I genuinely love kissing. Kissing is so sensual to me. I love the anticipation of brushing our lips together but not fully committing. Letting my mouth tease his neck and earlobes, before meeting up with his mouth. I just love the way it evolves from something so soft and innocent into full-on passion. Your mouth sets the pace for sensual examination. It's the intimate starting point that creates the eagerness to pursue other parts of the body."

Looking at him dead in the eyes, I illustrated. "Deep kissing can lead to amazing foreplay. Sex is the ultimate reward. Most people would argue an orgasm is the reward. To me, the sexual performance can be the most enjoyable part. Allowing ourselves to freely give each other pleasure orally or by touch is heavenly."

Engrossed by my detailed description, Dr. Jameson asks, "Why did you and Dylan stop foreplay or oral sex… if you enjoyed it?"

I reply, "I can't articulate a logical explanation. I don't know why we stopped being adventurous. Maybe it all started after I had Harley. He was preoccupied with building his business. My focus shifted to creating a wonderful family life, and away from being a good lover. I wonder if I gave all my love to my daughter instead of equally loving them both. Since our needs weren't being expressed, we drifted apart."

Feeling ashamed, I shifted my eyes downward before I spoke, "As a family, we were together in stature, but as a couple, we were pretty distant. For some reason, I couldn't talk to Dylan anymore. It was easier for Dylan to just be with other women. It became too much work for both of us at some point. We both knew there was a problem, but we didn't fix it."

Dr. Jameson's eyes are sympathetic. In a moment of realness, he explains, "I know you feel your husband left you suddenly. Marriages never just abruptly end out of the blue. It is a slow process of warning signs that lead to betrayal. I'm impressed that you can look back and see things from a different perspective and understand that there was a timeline of events. It's important to look into yourself and not just constantly be pointing the finger at your ex. The only way to heal is to figure out what you did wrong as well. You will find love again."

I feel comforted by his analysis. Maybe I did need therapy. I start thinking about Dr. Jameson's profession. He just sat there with no reaction to my description of kissing or oral sex. It must be strange to ingest all this personal information and stay contained. He must masturbate after his therapy sessions. He watched me passionately explain what arouses me. Then he hit me with an emotional revelation about divorce.

He circles back to the topic of my physical needs. "Did you enjoy giving oral as much as receiving it?"

My face turns brick red from this question. "I can't remember the last time I performed oral on my ex."

"Did you not like performing oral on him?"

I reply, "Once the passion was gone, there was a lack of desire just to go down on him. He never conveyed any need for oral sex."

Dr. Jameson clarifies, "Most men genuinely won't ask for oral sex, but they always want it. It's more of a turn-on if their partners do it willingly."

Dr. Jameson's thoughts on oral sex appear to be more of a personal opinion than medical fact. He seems more animated with his expertise. He seemed jovial explaining how men love their penis. "There are so many layers to what you feel physically during sex. The one main thing a man consistently loves, above anything else, is his penis. He wants his lover to enjoy his penis by putting it in their mouth and show physical excitement. It's like he's trusting you with his most important body part. He wants to watch you enjoy his penis. Men find this submissive act to be deeply intimate. The amount of pleasure you give him and the amount of pleasure you feel doing it helps him sexually connect with you. The dynamics of how a woman performs on a man orally can be more exciting than regular intercourse. There is an explosion of sensations a penis feels in a woman's mouth. A penis can feel gratified vaginally or anally, but there are so many specific maneuvers a tongue can do to a man's shaft, from the tip to the scrotum."

Dr. Jameson clarifies, "When you stopped performing oral sex or foreplay, he probably felt physically rejected by you. He couldn't sexually connect with you because you couldn't fully enjoy him or his penis."

I chuckle, "Believe me, his penis was being enjoyed…just not by me."

I giggle at the abstract image that pops into my head. I simplify my views of marital sexuality through the wisdom of Martha Stewart. "When I bake a cake, I can't just stick it in a cold oven and expect it to become moist and fulfilling. I have to preheat the oven for at least fifteen minutes before the temperature is right. It helps make the cake bake evenly. My vagina is like that oven. It needs to be preheated before placing anything inside, so it can come out satisfying and enjoyed by all."

He almost chokes on his beer and starts coughing from laughter. He is boyishly charming when he laughs. "I thought I'd heard everything, but that one literally takes the cake. Brilliant."

Removing his professional self out of the equation, he engages in the discussion with swagger. "I'm not disagreeing or placing any blame on you. I am just speaking from a sexual therapist's perspective. Men don't want to ask for it. Men want you to do it as a way of giving them the deepest physical pleasure. But more importantly, they want you to enjoy it as much as they do."

I gave him a quizzical look, "Is that what you enjoy?"

Knowing his analogy will disclose personal preference, he hesitates. "Fellatio feels unbelievable for any man. The pleasure we feel is indescribable. It's like this strong physical sensation of feeling phenomenally happy. A man's penis being pleasured in a woman's mouth with her tongue and lips is extremely erotic and exceptional. Oral sex is affectionately special for both sexes."

Hearing Dr. Jameson explain oral sex with such enthusiasm, I feel fellatio illiterate. "You went into such great detail about emotions and physical response. You make women giving head sound like some sort of religious experience."

His seemingly altruistic suggestion sounds arrogant. "To a lot of men, it *is* a religious experience. If she's good at oral, then it feels like heaven."

Instantaneously, I let out a nefarious laugh. "I doubt you reveal your personal take on oral sex with your typical patients. You probably speak in clinical or theoretical terms with them. I'm getting the deluxe package with the 'sucky sucky conversation' on penis needs. What about what I want after a long day?"

He asks, "What did you want?"

I school him on the dynamics of suburban motherhood. "In a perfect world, when you and your spouse are not bothered by kids, and nothing has to be done or made, you can achieve sexual nirvana. When you have a normal family, it can be hard to carve out sexy time. It isn't impossible, but on occasion, you have to plan it out. Being a homemaker doesn't entail watching TV all day. From the house itself to the people, I took care of every single thing, but my own needs. I was the quintessential people pleaser. At the end of a typical day, I was exhausted."

I look at Dr. Jameson dead-on and drop this revelation: "I never thought 'a nice warm dick in my mouth' would be the perfect ending to my hectic day. If my husband had shown me a little appreciation, I might have put a blow job on my to-do list."

Dr. Jameson bursts out laughing at my logic. He looks at me with a warm glowing smile. His attention was completely on me. "I'm sorry for sounding insensitive on the topic of oral sex. I was just expressing my personal views as a man and a doctor. I'm enlightened from your comical perspective. I appreciate this about you."

I start to fidget with the paper straw in my drink. Leaning toward him, childlike with curiosity, I evaluate his mindset. "When you talk about sex like this all day, does it desensitize you? Is that why you aren't in a relationship?"

He clarifies, "I have no problems talking about sex with patients, but you technically aren't a patient, so my conversations with them are nothing like this. I never put personal input into my guidance."

He takes another drink of his beer and continues, "I'm not desensitized from talking about sex at all and having a relationship has absolutely nothing to do with sex. I am not in a relationship because no one interests me."

I point out his errors in my befuddled state of candor. "It's incomprehensible for you to tell me to put myself out there. You literally don't practice what you preach."

"I never said I was perfect." He leaves it alone and radiates curiosity in changing the topic. "What type of guy are you interested in?"

I twiddle my fingers on the table. My eyes shift up toward the left. I lean back and fold my arms on top of the table as if I were praying. "I know it sounds funny, but with billions of people on this planet, there's no way that I lost my only chance at love. There has to be someone else, because there's enough people on this planet to create more than one great love."

Dr. Jameson finds this revelation logical. He grins at me and listens as I describe my perfect avatar. I continue, "I'm not going to settle for any warm body. We all want someone attractive. I want someone who has their shit together in every way. More importantly, he not only talks to me but wants to hear what I have to say."

Sentimentally revealing something fantastically cheesy, I close my eyes long enough to put my thoughts together. His piercing gaze makes me feel like the only person in the room. I explain, "In movies, when couples are lying close together in bed before or after sex, the woman looks up to see her handsome guy looking down at her. He gently touches her face and tells her how beautiful she is. I would love to know what that feels like. It's a beautiful, stripped-down moment of truth. That type of reassurance is out of pure love."

He has a gaze of nostalgia. "You seem to know what you want. It isn't easy for me to describe what I want. It would be something about that person that sets me off internally."

I reply, "How will you ever find this person if you never date anyone?"

He leans back to finish his beer. He shrugs. "I meet people all the time. Dating means finding someone interesting enough to pursue something more."

My blood alcohol level has made my smart mouth feel liberated. "Spending time with you sounds like some freakish job interview. You haven't hired anyone for the job yet because they are unqualified. You are probably some asshole type A boss with high expectations. How will you ever know someone can do that job if you never give anyone a chance?"

He doesn't seem offended by my comment. Smiling ear to ear, he responds to my sense of humor, "Maybe you're on to something."

He slyly changes the subject to refocus our conversation back to me. "You said you wanted to write a novel. Any idea on what you'll write about?"

I sound defeated. "I haven't written in a long time. I lack inspiration. Why do you ask?"

Looking at me wholeheartedly, he hints at my aspirations. "You just seem to have an unusual outlook on things. People might find your insight enjoyable. You should start writing again. Self-expression might build your confidence. Even though you have no problems expressing anything with me."

I place my elbows on the table and rest my head on my propped-up fists. "I think I'll write my novel about a middle-aged divorcée having sexual adventures in New York City. Maybe, I'll have her attending sex therapy with a rigid British dude who doesn't believe in love."

Dr. Jameson's response is hypothetical. "Maybe, the rigid British dude has a broken heart, with no rush to find a replacement. He would rather focus on growing his practice, writing his own book, and possibly doing seminars at universities. He doesn't have time for dating. Relationships are a lot of work."

I roll my eyes at him. "Perchance, this British dude is you. You're a sex therapist for Christ's sake! You probably know more about connecting with women than any man here does. Not only are you good-looking, but a doctor. You should be swimming in ass."

Prodding him on, I say, "Just so you know, today has been more like a weird date, not a session. Plus, you got to see my panties. You are capable of dating a woman."

My comments set off a grandiose smugness in his voice. He hits back. "I'm very particular in how I spend my time. Pursuing a relationship isn't a priority for me at the moment. And being alone doesn't necessarily mean I'm unhappy." He tosses out some scholarly advice. "Tolstoy had a quote on being happy. 'If you want to be happy, be.'"

His entrancing eyes soak in my silent reaction. Sweet in tone and demeanor, he offers, "You're right, this seems more like a date than a session. I actually enjoyed myself, which is unusual."

"Why is that, Dr. Jameson?"

"I love my work, but some days are emotionally taxing. Today was not a typical workday." He suddenly stands up, lays down cash for our bill, then looks at me with a revelatory wink. "You summed it up when you said we're both fucked." I am thrown off by him using the word 'fucked.' My impropriety is rubbing off on him.

As we stand up to leave, we admire each other with a newfound understanding. He contemplates saying something but catches himself. Instead, he holds out his arm and leads me out of the terrace. We proceed to walk back to the Four Seasons.

******

The night is clear and cool. I keep my arm tightly looped with his for warmth. Even though it is platonic, there is emotional comfort. I feel safe.

Out of the blue, I surprise him. "If being alone doesn't mean you're unhappy, why do you think I'm unhappy? Don't you enjoy feeling secure in being single?"

Glancing at me sideways before he speaks. "I never said you were unhappy. Fear keeps you from doing new things. Today was probably the first time you displayed audaciousness in a long time. Why is that?"

"Maybe you just had a profound effect on me." Breaking from the lighthearted moment, I ask, "Who's this woman who broke your heart? What happened?"

His body tenses up with silence. I start to wonder if I crossed a line, but I'm sure that line was crossed once my dress dropped. Noticing the hotel up ahead, I realize our time is up.

Smiling through anguish, he softly answers in a hesitant voice, "Sometimes when things are broken, they can be repaired with precision, but on occasion they are beyond damaged." Cryptically, he adds, "I lost her a long time ago. She is never coming back."

Mystified, I ask, "Lost who? Where did she go?"

His smile draws downward pulling his eyebrows closer, no response. We reach the entrance of the hotel in uncomfortable silence. Deciding not to push for a response, I untangle my arm from his. Once I let go, I take a few steps backward. The smiling doorman automatically opens the polished glass door.

I disrupt the unintentional tension by expressing compassion, "You don't have to answer. This seems extremely painful to you, and it's none of my business. I don't want to ruin an enjoyable day from prying."

Pretending the last five minutes didn't happen, I ooze Disney princess charm, "Thank you for getting me out of my clothes, twice. Your keen observation in undergarments let me tap into my inner vixen at Agent Provocateur. I can't imagine how tomorrow's session will top this."

He reaches out to grab my arm in an effort to prevent me from going inside. "Spending this entire day with you has made me feel less guarded." A seriousness creeps over him making him vulnerable. "I want to answer your question. I needed a moment. I never talk about Victoria."

Before substantiating his statement, the silence mollifies every sound around us. He brings to light his past. "She didn't go anywhere. In fact, she was my wife. She died."

CHAPTER 11

Day 3

Session 2

The hotel lobby calls to announce Dr. Jameson's arrival. I wait for him in the library hell-bent on keeping my inquisitive mouth shut. Standing patiently by the Bösendorfer grand piano, I'm lost in thought. My eyes fixate on the stupendous view of the city, until I see his reflection behind me. Constraining myself to maintain a friendly greeting like nothing happened.

The skyscrapers' mirrored windows reflect the sun, and the city is blinding.

The moving cars and busybodies make everything look tiny and animated. Breaking away from the panorama, I observe his profile. I clear my throat, before addressing the elephant in the room. "Yesterday began and ended in two different directions."

His posture rigid, he acknowledges my words with a forced smile, but his eyes betray his English stoicism. He faces forward. Something about his demeanor compels me to apologize, "I'm sorry for inquiring about your personal life. I shouldn't have pried."

His mirror-like blue eyes reflect comforting warmth, while he speaks. "You did nothing wrong. I thoroughly enjoyed our first session. You didn't pry." He softly whispers, "I surprised myself wanting to answer you."

I am a captive audience when he unexpectedly opens up. "I met my wife, Victoria, while studying at Cambridge."

Searching his thoughts to recount the past, he says, "I was enamored by her. She was this statuesque English beauty, ivory skin, long wavy mahogany hair, bright royal-blue eyes, and an extremely talented artist."

His description of Victoria painted one thing plain and simple: "She was the love of his life."

His voice shakes with discomfort as he recollects, "She suffered from manic depression. There was something inside her that no amount of love or expertise could fix. Tired of feeling despondent…she ended her life by taking a bunch of prescription pills with a bottle of gin.

"Victoria was an art history major when I met her. Because of her interpretations of life, she helped me become a better therapist. I began to figure out unique solutions to mainstream issues."

He expounds, "She tried to discourage our relationship. She knew that being with her meant I would experience her would be a roller coaster. I would experience her manic episodes caused by severe depression. Victoria wanted to protect me and to be sure this was the life I wanted."

He sighs. "Even with her incandescent glow, she could cast a dark shadow. There was a definite coldness during these brief moments." His mirrored image revealed his pain, "Once I fell for her, all the red flags become invisible."

He sees my reaction echo in the glass. I was befuddled, mournful of his loss.

He explains his intentions. "Maybe it's the age-old tale of finding someone beautiful and damaged, and then trying to fix them with love. I've coped with so much loss in my life. Maybe I was drawn to it."

Not wanting to interrupt, but needing clarification, I ask, "Why did you move here when she was so fragile? Wasn't your life established in England?"

Proudly, he affirms, "It's true. My family is established with wealth and prestige, but I wanted to make my own way. I walked away from running my father's company to pursue my own interests. I chose to further my doctorate at Harvard, because I've always dreamt of living in America and opening my own practice."

The calmness in his voice cracks. "My extra years of schooling triggered Victoria's episodes of mania. Victoria didn't want to leave England for Boston. She did it for me, which made her more vulnerable to stress and anxiety. The transition was difficult on her, as well as our marriage. All this sudden change made her unhinged. She could be totally normal for a month, then without warning, the symptoms would hit full-on, and last for weeks."

The word *unhinged* made me think of a mental patient from a horror movie. I wondered how Victoria spent her time. "What do you mean by unhinged?"

He closes his eyes in remembrance. "Victoria stayed busy by painting and teaching art classes to children. Some days her mind couldn't shut down, constantly needing to stay busy. She became an insomniac, painting day and night. She barely ate with this constant stream of energy. Some days she had extremely high energy, then without warning, she would crash hard into a depressive sleep state. Once the episode passed, she would be her old self…somewhat like Jekyll and Hyde."

I ask, "What was she painting so feverishly?"

He describes one of her episodes to give perspective. "Victoria found old pictures of my family. She wanted to paint these images on canvas. She was driven to turn these photos into masterpieces. Even if you found her rendition phenomenal, she would destroy it and start again. She coped by becoming overwhelmingly negative and increasingly hard to talk to."

I wondered aloud, "What set her further into a downward spiral?"

"She stopped taking the medicine that regulated her moods. She felt the medication was making her into a zombie. Oddly enough, Victoria concluded that having a child would enliven her. She convinced herself that having a child would somehow bring her normalcy."

Dr. Jameson looks at me and tries to rationalize Victoria's mindset. "One of the main side effects of stopping medication is a relapse into a deeper depression. She became agitated by daily life and felt stifled by marriage. Victoria's ability to show or feel love subsided the longer she stayed off medication. When she wasn't able to conceive a child, she felt cemented down."

He continues, "Victoria told me it felt like being at the bottom of a jar. She could look up to see light but couldn't quite seem to get out of that emotional rut."

I sense defeat in his voice. He explained, "I tried treating her with the best doctors. I endured these manic episodes with compassion and patience. Sometimes love can't fix everything."

"I needed time away. My mother lives in New York City. Knowing I needed a brief escape, she invited me to stay with her, encouraging me to take a step back from everything, just for a couple of weeks."

Any lightness he had dimmed as he admitted, "Being here in the city was phenomenal, I fell in love with New York City. I figured it was a great place to start my practice and create a new life with Victoria. Surprisingly, she wanted a fresh start, too, and agreed to move here."

I cringe. "How could you sustain a long-distance marriage?"

He shoots me a sideways glance. "It's always easy to look back with regret, but you can't change anything."

He continues, "Victoria agreed to resume taking her medication. She seemed enthusiastic about the move, as well as the art museum job prospects."

The rest of his narrative was based on his own assumptions. "The night before she was supposed to fly out to New York, Victoria must have hit rock-bottom. She never resumed taking her medication. I guess she only said that to appease me. The imbalance in chemicals gave her suicidal thoughts. She felt barren."

His brooding eyes cast down as he recalls her last moments. "I was in the middle of seeing a patient. Victoria deliberately called during this time, knowing I wouldn't pick up. She left me a simple message. She calmly told me that her love for me was infinite…and she would make things right."

He pauses to take a breath. "That was all she said. Right then, I knew she had done something to herself. She took a bottle of her unused antidepressants and consumed it in its entirety with measured patience. There was a half-emptied bottle of gin on the nightstand. My phone number was her last call."

My eyes swell with tears, hearing his voice.

"Her death nearly destroyed me. I wanted to die myself. But I made myself keep living. I knew I would never heal from this grief. But in time, it would be more manageable, and it has been."

His voice declines into a gentle murmur. "It's hard to determine which scenario would have been best. Finding her lifeless or dealing with it from a far. Either way renders you helpless."

His trauma becomes his truth. "You have to let the pain go to rebuild the relationship with yourself. Acceptance doesn't mean forgetting; it means forgiveness."

We were both transfixed on each other. Changing his tone to reboot the mood, color returned to his cheeks, and his posture eased. "I know it is ironic. I'm trying to open you to new experiences, as I shy away from it myself. We always know what's best for others. Sometimes it's easier to believe in an ideology rather than live by one."

Instinctively I reach out for his hand. He squeezes it with appreciation. His eyes cast a storm of torment hovering over a cerulean sea. My commiseration mutes any sort of response. I take a deep breath, before letting out. "I am truly sorry."

I empathize with his grief and wonder how trivial my problems appear in comparison. I am a divorcée, and he is a widower. The dichotomy of loss is vastly different. I feel so stupid complaining about my cheating husband, while he has coped with suicide. "I suddenly feel so little. My problems must seem preposterous compared to what you've been through."

"That's not true. Everyone's pain is compartmentalized into different forms of grief. I truly enjoy helping people." He reiterates, "No matter how you lose someone, you want to figure out why. Or what you could have done differently. Those questions need a resolution, even if you never find one."

His eyes shift down toward the bustling street. He tries to disguise his broken heart by saying, "Everyone has some dark cloud over them. Yes, that encompasses me too. I am far from perfect, no matter how manicured I appear."

A random thought hits me. "During my divorce, I didn't want to think about the 'could have' or 'should have' scenarios. It's an endless hole of sorrow I didn't want to go down. I had to pull my shit together and start moving forward."

He is focused on the concrete skyline where sunlight radiates off the windows. The frantic city pace exudes tranquility from this height. Grief orbits around us at warp speed, and I try to pacify the situation. "No one can be responsible for another person's happiness. Everyone is on their own in that department. We're all alone in this world. You can't carry around that baggage forever. Dragging it around just lets it control you. Victoria's decisions were her own. Just remember…you experienced a wonderful love while it lasted."

He sighs. "I've already surrendered a substantial amount of regret. It did take time, but I am in a good place in my life."

"I'm not a therapist, so this is my undignified opinion." I turn to him to profess my mantra on life. "Horrible things happen to good people every day. Life tends to serve up an occasional shit sandwich. All you can do is eat it, slowly digest it, and understand why it left an awful taste in your mouth."

He purses his slow grin to prevent laughter. "Should I diagnose some of my patients with emotional indigestion? Should I call it Shit Sandwich Syndrome?"

Needing to diffuse the heightened sense of empathy with levity, I advise, "Sure, Dr. Jameson. My advice isn't polished, but it's effective. I won't charge you for today's session."

Our hands are still intertwined. He didn't let go but held on tighter. Feeling uncomfortable with this romantic vulnerable moment, I resort to snarky humor. "Are you taking me to seedy fetish stores today?"

I playfully offer, "Imagine us buying 'Kochi the Anime Doll'. She has three holes and a blurred demonic face. Nothing says super fun like a sex doll derived from our darkest nightmares. You can demonstrate all my pleasure points on a sex doll. It will be educational."

My freehand mimicked the gesture along to me singing the television commercial for "The More You Know."

He showcases a charming Colgate smile, then suggests, "We can sit in your $50,000-a-night penthouse, or we can venture out. Let's tour the Met on Fifth Ave. Art is the best form of escape."

He doesn't release my hand but pulls it up to his chest, firmly pressing it to his heart. Everything falls silent. His heart is pounding, but all I can hear is my own. My cheeks smolder into a scarlet blush, and my body tingles from warmth.

He plays against my instincts by not letting my statement go unchecked. "As for later, why would we need a doll? Wouldn't it be better to demonstrate pleasure points…on you?"

CHAPTER 12

Dr. Jameson and I settle into the back seat of a Rolls-Royce Phantom. Astonished by the lavishness of my car, he asks, "A driver and car come with your room?"

I shrug without braggadocio and confirm, "I guess it does. Ashley wanted me to get the full experience."

"Brilliant. I wish I had a friend like Ashley. Have you spent much time with her since you've been staying here?"

Giddy with excitement, I reveal, "Her husband, Edmond, is out of town. I will be accompanying her to some society function tonight. I guess it will be a glammed-up girls' night out."

"My calendar is peppered with the proverbial society function. My mum drags me to these events as her date. I participate out of obligation and respect for my mum, but I loathe these things."

My interest piques hearing him speak of his mom. "You have a date night with your mom? That's sweet. What's she like?"

Not wanting to discuss his mom, he redirects the questions back to me, catching me off guard. "How is Harley?"

With all our conversations focused on sex and relationships, Dr. Jameson asking about Harley felt remarkably personal. "She is hilariously rambunctious, is loving college life, dating for free meals, and giving me daily dating advice."

I pridefully look at him with a huge grin. "She's great. Thank you for asking."

He marvels at my response. "Why wouldn't I ask about her? She's your heart." He then asks, "What is she studying?"

"I guess…I thought you were only interested in my divorce, sex life, and undies, not me being a mother." Laughing out of discomfort, I add, "She's at Georgetown University in Washington DC. She's studying to be a child psychologist. She has an affinity for teen girls trying to figure out their shit, especially ones from broken homes."

"Being a woman first, then a mother is what defines you, not divorce, sex, or even beige panties." The blueness in his eyes glow in merriment. He asks, "You are surrounded by a lot of psychologists. Does that make you self-conscious?"

Biting back swiftly, I ask, "What if I was surrounded by proctologists? Would that make me a walking asshole?" Shrugging off his analogy with my own, I respond, "I'm actually glad I have all this free mental health care. I need all the help I can get."

His laughter is subdued by the clearing of his throat. He reminds me of a Rubik's Cube, a three-dimensional puzzle with each side revealing a different color. I have to keep twisting and turning in order to get one side to align, while simultaneously trying to solve the other sides. Normally these sorts of things make me surrender in frustration, but with him, I don't want to stop trying.

We arrive at the Metropolitan Museum of Art, and I realize I've forgotten how majestic it is inside. It's been years since I enjoyed this museum. We look like a couple wandering around the museum together. Dr. Jameson reminisces about the National Gallery in London. He fondly recalls time spent with Victoria looking at art and people watching.

Even though Dr. Jameson is a therapist, he is well versed in art history. He details each artist's work in a fascinating manner and makes each piece come alive with his descriptions. He asks my opinion about various sculptures and paintings, as a way to open me up. Unlike him, I can't articulate a scholarly opinion. Even though I am out of my element, today seems more about his healing than mine.

We casually stroll around, until we end up on the second floor. We look for a place to sit in the twentieth-century European early paintings and sculptures section, where works of art by Pierre Auguste Cot are displayed. *The Storm* rests on the wall before us as we situate ourselves on the bench. The painting is whimsically romantic. A young man and woman, half naked, run carefree in the rain.

Dr. Jameson glances at me and asks what I see in the painting. "Is this my Rorschach test?" I ask.

"What if it is? What do you see?"

I know more about pop culture than I do brush strokes. My thought process spills out through song lyrics or movie scenes, not specific images. "This painting seems innocent, because the perversion is camouflaged. The couple live in an era when openly displaying affection was inappropriate. They were restricted to what was deemed morally right. It's kind of how we all felt as teenagers. Parents dissuaded our sexual curiosity, but teen hormones prevailed."

Dr. Jameson questions me, "How very textbook. What do you really think?"

Trying not to laugh my ass off, I remain composed. He knows I'm not being authentic.

I truthfully respond, "The star-crossed young lovers are looking for a safe place to fuck, not make love. She's paranoid but willing to fool around in the bushes. The guy longingly gazes at her with desire. This forbidden behavior, which excites them, will intensify the sex."

Dr. Jameson agrees. "Your description is pretty astute for someone who doesn't feel confident in defining art."

My description feels like our flirtatious game of cat-and-mouse. I blurt out, "I don't understand why you distance yourself from relationships. Do you feel like you need some sort of permission to fall in love again?"

He eloquently answers, "I just require time to reconcile the past. We all grieve at our own pace."

He waits a second before adding, "And I agree with what you said last night. There are too many people on this planet to limit myself to one great love. I should open myself up to dating again."

I smugly state the obvious, "Sometimes when you aren't looking, love will find you."

Dr. Jameson whispers under his breath, "As of late, I'm realizing this."

The young lovers in the painting compel me to share, "I miss the pleasure love brings. Do you miss that pleasure?"

Startled by my question, he asks, "Who says I don't feel pleasure? There is a difference between pleasure and love. You don't have to be in love or a relationship to have pleasure."

Not expecting such a blunt answer, I look away from him. In an effort to hide my embarrassment, I focus on another painting. I must be a closeted misogynist. I've always put love and pleasure in the same category. Theoretically, they are incomparable. I lacked a lot of pleasure during my marriage; therefore, he is correct. I amaze myself in having my Oprah "a-ha" moment at such an obscure time.

"I guess you can have one without the other. I always thought my lack of love caused me to not have pleasure, and vice versa."

He begins his inquisition. "You don't even need a partner to feel pleasure. Do you pleasure yourself?"

I shamefully look down at my hands, before confiding, "For me, fingering or touching myself isn't the same as having a man do it. And before you ask, yes, I own a vibrator. But the real thing is so much better."

He replies, "You must have some mental block about pleasuring yourself." He pauses long enough to ask, "Haven't you heard of flicking the bean?"

"I'll remain lazy with my big purple vibrator."

He counters, "As a form of foreplay, did your husband ever ask you to masturbate in front of him? Some men are aroused by watching women masturbate."

"No, he was a lights-off kind of guy. I'm sure he has a closet full of sex toys and a new bag of sex tricks for his youngling." I threw off his questioning with a retort, "Why don't you show me what to do."

His eyes widen considering my request. "Let's figure out the basics. What arouses you physically?"

Letting my guard down enough to feel humble, I softly speak, "When I tried on lingerie yesterday, I looked like someone out of the Moulin Rouge—sexy, empowered, and in charge. I want to be that way in the bedroom, as well as outside a dressing room, without lingerie."

Uncertain about what to disclose, I share the basics. "Physical stimulation can be generated by the slightest gestures: soft kisses on my neck, tasting my earlobes, sucking and teasing my breasts, and enthusiastically tasting me orally." I quickly add, "And he's not there for a small taste but enough to get me off."

I redirect the question to him. "What gets you sexually excited?"

Dr. Jameson should be a spokesman for Penis Anatomy for Dummies. Delving into further detail, he continues, "To get the blood flowing, stimulating the area above the pubic zone is really arousing, and of course, the scrotum is the equivalent to the vagina in nerve endings. There is an area called the perineum that occasionally gets neglected. This is the area between the anus and the scrotum. When a woman applies pressure in this area, it feels astounding."

Rambunctiously laughing at his tutorial, I say, "Did you leave any part of the penis out? You seem to know more about penis exploration than Magellan knew about the Spice Islands."

"It's a shame the $150,000 spotty banana duct-taped to the wall 'artwork' isn't here. We could discuss that for hours. It resembles a penis being restrained."

Whipping his head to pivot in my direction, he questions my intentions, "I'm trying to be clinical, but you aren't really asking about men per se, but more about me, right?"

At first, I was sexually drawn to his looks, but it's becoming something more. After spending hours disclosing intimate information about ourselves, there is something magnetic between us. I hope this isn't some sort of psychological illusion created by him to unlock a disconnected side of me.

I sense his eyes searing into me for a response. Trying to find a distraction to change the topic, I rampantly search the room. Homing in on another painting by Pierre Auguste Cot, named *Springtime*, I nonchalantly examine the picture. "This young man and woman are at the beginning stages of infatuation. Her slight smile is longing; there is a look of adoration. Her arms are wrapped tightly around his neck, like a lifeline. She can't let go. Her desire for him is deep. He tempts her with seductive touches. Her virginal armor is worn down. He longingly feasts his eyes on her for some sort of physical permission. He cleverly positions himself by wrapping his legs around her. She allows his charm to envelop her. You can visually smell the pheromones between them."

Interpreting my observation, he boils it down. "When was the last time you had sex?"

I cut back sharply, "Truthfully, I can't remember. Dylan and I quit having sex at some point. I haven't pinpointed a date and time. It's easier to use a menstrual cycle app to track my period." Improvising, I pull out my phone. "Maybe…I should ask Siri."

"Siri, when was the last time I had sex?"

Siri's robotic voice responds, "I do not understand your question."

Ignoring my shenanigans, he asks, "Why haven't you had sex?"

I throw my hands up trying to find a plausible excuse. "I've been with the same guy since college. I'm now in my forties, and I don't go out to get laid. Imagining myself randomly picking up men in a bar is hilarious."

Not wanting to justify my abstinence out of embarrassment, I explain, "Even though my body desires pleasure, my heart needs an emotional connection."

Trying not to sound stagnant in growth, I continue, "Since I don't want to be a spinster, I need to take risks. Casual, no-strings sex may seem lonely, but it might be a necessary evil."

Probing for a more substantial answer, he asks, "How was your sex life with Dylan?"

I look over at the previous painting *The Storm* to prove a point. "Our love life was like that painting. In the beginning, everything was exciting because we wanted each other badly. We had sex everywhere, from the kitchen counter to a baseball dugout."

I close my eyes. "As time went on, sex became more mechanical and inhibited. Maybe becoming parents took away our spontaneity. Sex became habitual, not fun. Having any sex was better than no sex, though, right?"

"Do you miss sex?" he challenges.

My inner teen mouths off. "Well, duh! Of course, I miss sex. Don't you?"

He quips, "Who says I don't have sex?"

Unknowingly sounding naïve, I ask, "I thought you weren't looking for a relationship. Are you dating someone?"

Dr. Jameson is getting a kick out of our quid pro quo type of therapy. "Just because I'm not in a relationship doesn't mean I quit sex…it feels too good. Some days it just feels comforting to have someone intimately against you. The power of an orgasm is like dopamine."

I feel more stripped down by revealing my sexless life while his is expansive. "This is the textbook scenario for why I shouldn't make assumptions. I feel like an ass."

Wanting to know more about his personal life, I ask. "When was the last time you had sex?"

He isn't bashful in acknowledging the time and place. "The night I met you at the TAO bar. I left with someone."

I recall my blind date. My TAO tryst was composed of awkward conversation, a plate of olive fried rice, and a fortune cookie. He shows up and gets laid.

Dying to understand his seduction technique, I ask, "Do you wake up one day and decide 'I'm in the mood for some pad Thai and a side of oral sex. This woman will do.'"

Trying to unlock his secret vault of sex tricks, I plead, "How is sex so easy for you?"

Dr. Jameson displays his amusement with a half grin. "Women can be just as sexual as men. With every sexually charged male, there is always a female counterpart. Nature has engineered its version of yin and yang. Some women are assertive in getting my attention."

"How do women get your attention?"

Getting pointers from him is invaluable information. He begins to illustrate pick-up scenarios. "You can tell when a woman is interested in you sexually when she's physical. She's constantly touching your arm or rubbing your back or leg. She will make sexual comments, but more importantly, she draws attention to her mouth. She makes her mouth a focal point with bold lipstick, or putting things against her lips, like a straw or her fingers, implying very sexual things. Regardless of the physical sexual innuendos, she might be forward enough to ask me to take her home."

Sounding like a stalker, I scrutinize, "How do you choose these women? Is that why you picked the blonde over the brunette at TAO?"

"She projected a sexy, fun confidence, unlike her friend. She's not the type I would bring home to my mum…or even date. She's a one-night stand."

He allows me to hear what transpired that night. "We left TAO to go to another bar, and then back to her apartment. She was forthcoming in expressing what she wanted sexually. We didn't necessarily talk about our hopes and dreams."

I can see his mind racing. He wants to answer the question without sounding like a douchebag. "I guess I'm drawn to the crazy one."

I flinch before letting out a weak laugh. Dr. Jameson continues, "It's not a very professional answer, but it's the truth. There is this wildness that makes them sexually provocative. Being a therapist, it's in my nature to rescue her, even if it's just for a one-night stand."

He runs his fingers through his hair to ward off my judgmental glances. He finds my perception of him troubling. "You're thinking I'm being a perv around New York City…romping with loose women. We live in a world where two people can randomly meet, feel a strong attraction, and have no-strings-attached sex. There's no drama or emotional attachment. When the situation is favorable, I enjoy myself free of guilt."

"Really? You don't feel…anything?"

Dr. Jameson doesn't sugarcoat his response. "Feeling enjoyment doesn't require love or a need to pursue anything more. It serves a purpose for that moment."

Deflecting the interrogation back to me, he asks, "Hold on…let's back things up a minute. Were you watching me at the bar with those two women? Why weren't you focusing on your date?"

I've gone down this rabbit hole, and now I have to climb out. There is no magic potion to evade this question. "When you approached me at TAO, I was completely confounded by you. You don't know what it's like to have someone notice you. Women probably throw themselves at you. You're gorgeous. Our brief encounter was an EpiPen to my heart…a rush. I couldn't take my eyes off you during my date. You were this huge distraction…until you left with bachelorette number two."

Burning red with humiliation, wishing I had a rock to crawl under, I want to be invisible. Sensing his stormy eyes staring at me, I feel compelled to sit up. He places his hand under my chin, softly guiding my face in his direction. With a slight tilt of his head, we both lean in to close the space between us. Licking, then biting my bottom lip, warm with impatience, I swallow hard anticipating his taste. His thumb delicately strokes my bottom lip in a sweet-tempered teasing motion, reading me. My blunt mouth is silent craving his kiss.

Without warning, he freezes up, ceasing to move forward. He doesn't pull away but suspends his stance. Longingly looking at my lips, his self-control extinguishes any physical response. He is the female equivalent of a cocktease.

He apologizes, "I'm sorry. I shouldn't have done that. I don't think we should be crossing any lines." Holding me at his attention with our eyes locked, he confesses, "If it makes any difference, you have been a distraction for me as well."

I quietly sit disarmed and highly aroused, contemplating what the hell just happened. Facing forward to concentrate on the wall to make heads-or-tails of what is happening between us. For what felt like eternal purgatory, we remain in dead silence. In an effort to break the dead air, I seamlessly begin deciphering the painting titled *The Birth of Venus* by Alexandre Cabanel.

I act like nothing just happened by proceeding with a critique and offering up an amplified description purposely including an underlying meaning. "I see an ethereal woman. She is the embodiment of beauty. She emerges from the sea as if she is contemplating a devious act. Her purity is protected by four cherub angels hovering over her. She lies still in a sleepy manner with her arm draped over her forehead. Distraught from loneliness, she can't feel true passion with the constraints of angels and being trapped surrounded by the sea."

He questions my interpretation, "Are you contemplating casual sex due to personal constraints?"

Challenging his question with defiance, I ask, "Why not? You're the Yoda of vagina. You've detailed the perfect play-by-play for getting ass. Apparently, crazy girls don't go home alone, but I do. I don't want to inhibit myself sexually anymore."

"Casual sex is pretty much a mindset you either have or don't. I built a wall around myself. I'm the stereotypical emotionally unavailable man, so it's easy for me. After my wife died, I didn't miss being in a relationship, but I missed affection. Sex can mean instant gratification when you refrain from getting personal."

His eyes narrow, voicing concern, "I don't recommend that you meet some guy tonight and shag. Earlier you said sex is emotional for you. Casual sex might be an experimental quick fix, but the aftermath it may make you feel more alone. The emotions you'll establish from your encounter might not be reciprocated, leaving you rejected, questioning yourself. Don't seek out sex, but let it happen organically."

The contemptible look of bitchiness masks my face. "I'm not asking for your permission. I would never put myself in a sexual situation I can't handle. Maybe I have a wall around my heart too—"

He cuts me off, "Professionally, I am here for guidance. You will always make your own decisions."

I face him out of consideration of what he said. I want to point out something bothering me. "If life were to happen organically, you should admit there is some sort of attraction between us. Or is this my imagination?" I flick my hand back and forth between us, with over-the-top enthusiasm. "You know what? I'm not crazy…this is crazy."

Dr. Jameson feels repentant. "Sharing intimate parts of yourself with someone can make you vulnerable. Our feelings are transcending beyond what's normal. It's inappropriate for me to talk about my personal life, but it seems to help you trust me. I feel unusually comfortable with you, which is out of character for me."

His flirtatiousness is cooled with professionalism. "This new method of therapy has expedited my evaluation of you. I still need to remain platonic and neutral."

Frustrated by his self-induced emotional boundaries, I identify the problem for him. "You have developed feelings for me." Taking a deep breath, I continue, "I know I have feelings for you."

He tries to snuff out any suggestion our time together means something more. "It would be wrong of me to have a sexual relationship with you." I realize he is pondering about me sexually as well.

I roll my eyes at him. "I only mentioned that you might have feelings for me. I never mentioned sex. You just had a Freudian slip. Human nature will occasionally supersede your uptight British ethics."

Guarded, he sits composed with a Mona Lisa smile, mysterious and unreadable. He calmly clarifies, "You are something totally new and brilliant to me. I have never been this way with any woman…since Victoria."

Hearing this made me growl in annoyance. "For a therapist, you are thick in the head. Let's analyze what you just admitted." Excitedly looking around, I joke, "Where's the Robert Mapplethorpe exhibit? Mapplethorpe's 'Self Portrait' showcasing a whip up his ass would be fitting to look at, but in your case, it wouldn't be a whip. You'd be putting your head up your ass."

Putting Pandora back in the box, he suddenly ends our session, stands up, and faces me. Extending his hand out like a gentleman to help me up, he pulls me toward him, until we are face-to-face. "I fancy our sessions. We need to remain proper regardless of my unusual tactics. Please understand, I don't want to lose sight of my purpose with you."

Feeling bold and unapologetic, I spit venom. "Your emotional constipation has made you full of shit."

Immediately turning away from him, I move with purpose searching for the closest elevator. My insurmountable frustration rivals drinking a Red Bull before meditation. I need to get away from him. He casually strolls down the hallway knowing we will end up at the same point. Waiting with uneasiness for an elevator outside the Greek and Roman art section, I wish the elevator doors would open. Feeling his presence behind me, I refuse to turn around.

Once inside the elevator, I ooze contempt, while tensely leaning up against the wall. He stands in the center of the elevator unabashedly staring at me. Resting both his hands in his trouser pockets, his eyes feasting on me becomes hypnotic. We stand there sizing each other up.

My antics seem to entertain him. "For someone full of verbal rapid fire, you are suddenly speechless. What's on your mind?"

Shaking my head in dismay, I feel discombobulated. "You are provoking me with innuendos and flirtations. Stop acting like you're interested in me. Just be a stereotypical therapist by listening and giving advice. No more middle-school level of emotional footsies."

He removes his hands from his pockets and moves toward me, stopping inches from my face. An electric current surges between us. The enticing smell of his neck is an intoxicating mix of pheromones and bergamot. A paper-thin margin of air separates our lips. He stops to retreat. Pulling away before committing to the intensity of a long-awaited kiss, he suppresses his actions.

With one hand on the wall for balance, and his other hand slightly touching my neck, he moves his mouth up to my ear. "You are making things difficult for me."

His breath tickling my ear releases my inner butterflies. My hands remain motionless like a broken clock. The ticking in my heart can't be heard but felt. I confine my hands behind my back to restrain my urge to touch him. He creates these minuscule sensual moments with false implications. I try to play along by not being reactive.

I brutally bait him with honesty. "Is this part of your treatment too?"

Before he can comment, the elevator doors chime open. People shuffle inside filling the surrounding space. He retreats back to the center like a child caught making a mess.

Deliberately caustic, I patronize his behavior. "As a licensed physician, maybe you should examine my balls. Divorce didn't give me a ballsectomy. In fact, I think they've gotten bigger since we've met." I snap, "Maybe you should grow a pair."

The elevator patrons acknowledge my comments by briefly looking back, before returning to face the gold reflective doors. The tension in the enclosed box is thick with discomfort. He ingests my salty words with a cocky grin. I am now his Rubik's Cube to figure out. With all the twisting and turning he's put me through today, he's almost solved the red side, my personality.

We exit the Met in silence. He offers me his arm as we walk down the concrete steps. I graciously decline. He waves to my driver, indicating to pull the car toward the entrance. His eyes burrow into me, but I won't acknowledge him, not even for random chitchat. As the car pulls up in front of us, Dr. Jameson helps me inside the car, but I push him away and step in myself. He ensures that I'm safely inside before shutting the door. He taps on the window to tell me something.

I look up at him with confidence before rolling down my window. Oozing with graciousness, I tell him, "I guess I'll see you tomorrow. Thank you for taking me on a tour of the Met. The lewdness you've extracted from me, in front of priceless works of art, will always be memorable. I'm sure while you're out tonight, a woman wearing bold red lipstick, rubbing your thigh, and exuding sexual perkiness will unemotionally ejaculate your ego. Enjoy hunting vaginas."

He leans inside the car ensuring that I hear him clearly. He responds to my comments by serving up his own sarcasm-laced politeness. "Yes, Emerson, today was lovely. You may perceive my behavior as being randy; give me credit for being open and honest. The lewdness seen in the art was your own pent-up sex dying to be released, not mine. Despite your opinion of me, I doubt I'll be having it off with anyone tonight. I dare say, there is no amount of red lipstick that could distract me from your smart mouth."

Before he shuts the door, he mockingly adds, "And my engagement tonight is with my mum. Don't assume everything about me is sexual." He gives me a wink and shuts the door.

CHAPTER 13

Upon returning to my penthouse, I was notified that Ashely left a gift for me. I notice a jaw-dropping deep green Burberry silk dress hanging on a hook in the foyer. Suddenly excited about attending the gala, playing dress-up, and schmoozing with NYC's finest, I rush to the bathroom to get ready.

The knocking on the bathroom door startles me. Ashley's voice booms, "I'm sorry for being late. Since the world has gone to shit, I'm booked up with patients."

Opening the bathroom door in my bra and panties, I resemble Alex from *A Clockwork Orange* with one false eyelash glued on. Expecting to find her disheveled from rushing over from work, Ashley is a striking doppelgänger for Jayne Mansfield. Wearing a fitted black mermaid gown, her beauty outshines the wattage from her mega-carat diamond drop earrings. Even the brightest star, Sirius, dimmed in comparison to her glow.

"Busy my ass! How on earth can you pull this look off on a whim?" Blowing her a kiss, I say, "You're gorgeous."

She flicks her hands out shooing me into the direction of the dress.

Wiggling into the dress in front of a mirror, I examine myself before smoothing out any creases. Twirling around to see Ashley's reaction, she immediately grabs my hands. Holding my arms out open to proudly inspect me, her approving smile lights up the world. This is a distorted version of a mother hoping her daughter loses her virginity on prom night.

Ashley hands me a box with "Harry Winston" written on it. "I want to loan you some jewelry tonight." She glances at me with spirited approval, then adds, "Tonight, we'll paint the town…and the front porch."

"I feel like Julia Roberts in *Pretty Woman*."

Ashley cradles my perfectly painted face with her hands. "Honey, you are not even close to a street hooker. You are beaming."

"It's the jewels." I wink at her while tapping the necklace.

Examining the weary look on her face, there is something deeper. I inquire, "You seem exhausted lately. Is everything okay?"

She sighs. "I haven't had much of a life outside the office. I've always wanted a successful psychiatry practice, a self-assured man, and to enjoy sipping Tears of Llorona Tequila at the end of the day. Lately, I've been as busy as a hound in flea season."

Stopping herself to let out a toothy pearly white grin, she adds, "I haven't had the time to enjoy anything…until now."

"Why aren't you enjoying this life you created?" I ask.

Our eyes meet long enough for her expression to mirror my frowning face. "Have you ever just wanted to say, 'Fuck it!' …and run off to breathe?"

My internal voice shouts, *Hell yes!*

"My life is blessed with more than just material stuff. Lately, I just feel tired of everything, but I love so much. I love my job, but on occasion, I want to slap the shit out of someone. And I love Edmond more than myself, which can be suffocating timewise. Let's not forget how I love my tequila, but it's hard to find a quiet corner and savor it."

"How can I help you?" I jest, "Want to do shots of tequila?"

"Having you here is a vacation for me. It's selfish escapism. You're my excuse to check out of the daily grind." Delicately placing her hands on my shoulders, her half grin opens fully to rival Miss America. "My emotional cup is just empty right now. When life is hectic, I miss living. Right now, I'm taking the time to fill my soul. It's a 'me' problem…a funk. Hell…it could just be menstrual."

"Well, if you're menstruating, I sure as hell hope it's an emotional cup and not a Diva Cup. That needs to stay empty. Remind me not to drink a Bloody Mary tonight." Our hysterical laughter is only held in check by our need for oxygen.

She turns the conversation back to me. "Don't worry, darlin', we'll kick that funk in the ass tonight. I plan on filling my cup with that well-to-do booze while hobnobbing. All I ask is that you keep up."

I think about what she has said. Her cup is empty, but she should have free refills—a Big Gulp of constant sugary sweetness.

Ashley spins me back around toward the mirror. We both stare at our reflection. She props her cheek next to mine to reminisce. "Back in college, we talked about what we wanted out of life. We built the life we want, and now we occasionally want to hide from it. Our needs change on a daily basis. Sometimes we need a mental vacation to appreciate our beautiful messy lives."

Her logic provokes my mind into a eureka moment. I speak feverishly, "I know we need to leave now, but I want to take a moment to do something barking mad."

Humored by my request, she asks, "I'm all for going crazy. What are you doing?"

"I'm buying a ticket for Paris…right now…before I change my mind. For the first time, I in my life, I can do whatever the hell I want. When my time in NYC ends, I plan on seeing Paris indefinitely." In a state of excitement, I yell, "This is me saying, 'Fuck it!'"

"A one-way ticket?" she asks.

"For now, it's one way. I have an abundance of free time. I know what's here—you and Harley—but what's there?"

The apples of her nude blushed cheeks are perched up by her perfect smile. She applauds my audacity. "This is the spontaneous chick I roomed with in college. Go fill that emotional cup in Paris, with tons of wine."

******

It's been a while since Ashley and I have had a fun ladies' night out. She didn't question my desire to see Paris. She was proud of me for doing something rash and spontaneous. Sipping my champagne in the Rolls-Royce, I discuss my therapy in great detail for Ashley to dissect. She absorbs every nook and cranny spoken. A sense of elation pulls the corners of her lips into a wicked grin. She articulates her thoughts with brassiness. "When I did my sessions with Dr. Jameson, it wasn't remotely romantic. It was real therapy."

Thrown off guard by her opinion, I question, "Romantic? How did you come to that conclusion?" I ask, "Why the hell were you in therapy, anyway?"

She chuckles at my response but answers in kind, "Edmond and I found ourselves in a stagnated marriage." She looks at me with seriousness before continuing, "I thought Edmond was cheating on me from his disinterest in sex. I assumed he was getting it elsewhere. Edmond is suffering from erectile dysfunction. The mental stigma curbed his desire for sex. Dr. Jameson prescribed one of the greatest scientific discoveries, Viagra."

I am having a pity party, while Ashley tells me she thought Edmond was cheating on her. I feel like a shitty friend. "Why didn't you tell me any of this before? I can't write a prescription for Viagra, but I would have crawled out of my '80s movie cave to be here for you."

"As much as I love you, I needed a marriage counselor, not my best friend. We did counseling with Dr. Jameson for a year, not a few days."

I ask, "Is everything functioning properly now?"

Saucy with wisdom, she responds, "Honey, he's like the Energizer Bunny on cocaine. He can pound the hell out of me for an hour, we'll finish together, and surprisingly, he's up and raring to do it again. We both have multiple orgasms. I'm at my sexual peak—I love this."

Squeezing my hand, she continues, "Every marriage is tested in some way. It was a period of figuring out our insecurities as a couple." Wrinkling her dimples with a huge smile, she says, "We are great."

My eyes look at her hand squeezing mine. "I'm an asshole. I'm sorry for not being there for you, like you were for me…even now."

"Don't be ridiculous! Your world was shattering. Divorce trumps a limp dick on any anxiety list. I just needed to fix Edmond's plumbing problem. The shower head is running at full pressure now and not a drip is wasted."

Her laughter flashes into a sparkling grin. "We just need to work on your current plumbing situation. And it seems you found the right guy to unclog everything you have pent up."

Tilting my head, thinking about what she implied, I say, "Is there something between me and Dr. Jameson?"

"There seems to be an extraordinary connection. You are getting to know him personally. Therapists never reveal personal details to their patients. He said you are the exception, in how he treats all his patients…or even the women he bangs. There must be feelings."

I look out the window wondering why am I the exception. I ponder, "It's not just his looks but the way he thinks and see things. His intelligence is infectious. We can literally talk about anything. Nothing is off-limits. This is entirely new to me."

"Why wouldn't he be interested? You are a stunning intelligent woman."

I try to reconcile with my previous explanation. "I'm not implying that I have a butter face. I'm just saying that if Dr. Jameson were on *The Bachelor*, I wouldn't get a rose. In the grand scheme of things, I have too many miles on me."

Regardless of her New York City lifestyle, Ashley has never forgotten her roots. She grew up riding horses, driving a pick-up truck, and drinking cold beer with her Tex-Mex. "Honey, it's not the miles, it's the model. You're a Bentley. We will find a driver to check your oil and get that engine started."

"What if my driver turns the key and the ignition stalls?"

"Well, any experienced driver would make sure the connection isn't loose or corroded." She assures me, "Tonight, there will be all kinds of makes, models, and years to choose from. Be sure to check his tires to make sure he's balanced."

She holds up her glass to toast and announces, "Let's go car shopping."

"With my luck, I'm going to find a lemon complete with duct-taped seats."

CHAPTER 14

The charity event is held at Cipriani Wall Street. The outside resembles the architecture of the Parthenon in Athens, Greece. The large pristine granite columns look historical in design, which make the building appear monumental. It's aged with elegance by enduring New York City history. The entrance to Cipriani is roped off and lit up with a spotlight. A grand red carpet is rolled out from the entrance door all the way down the steps to the street. We wait in a long line of luxury cars.

Our Rolls-Royce is directed to pull up to the red carpet. Ashley and I give ourselves a once-over to ensure our lips look injected and our skin airbrushed. We want to look like the best fabricated versions of ourselves. When our car door opens, I overcome nerves as a stranger to this world. The driver holds out his hand to help Ashley out of the car. Once outside, she holds out her hand for me to grab. Seeing the distressed look on my face, she comforts me by weaving her hand into mine.

Gripping her hand as if my life depended on it, I whisper, "Let's do this." We proudly walk down the carpet like lipstick lesbians.

The event is held in the Cipriani Ballroom. We enter from the balcony level and walk to the rail to look down. The room looks like a birchwood forest, with bunched white Ranunculus resting on its wooden stems. Little white lights wrap around the tree's limbs, giving them a magical aura. The sparkling birchwood forest outlines the stage and the dance floor, giving it a fairy-like quality. The whole room is moving with voices of people getting acquainted. We grab some martinis and mingle in this huge room of wealthy people.

The event is hosted by Millie Pritchard, a statuesque British beauty in her mid-sixties. She has aged with grace instead of looking pulled or injected. She must have been a natural beauty in her prime, like the British model Twiggy or a muse for a '70s rock band. Her smiling rosy cheekbones are accentuated by her spectacular sapphire-blue eyes. She looks glamorous and refined as she greets her guests with ease. She makes small talk look easy. She is gifted in the art of being hospitable and interested in what you have to say. Everyone walks away from her, smiling from her acknowledgment.

While we sip our drinks, Ashley gives me a brief backstory on Millie's life. Millie is married to an American businessman named Carlisle Pritchard. They lived at her estate in England until Carlisle was diagnosed with leukemia. They relocated to New York City to try out experimental treatments. During this time, she established herself as a New York City socialite. Planning events and hosting charities seemed to be her coping mechanism until her husband eventually passed.

I ask, "Did they have any kids?"

Ashley smirks. "Yes, she has a son and a daughter with her first husband, but he tragically died in a car accident."

Looking around the room, she giggles, before coyly remarking, "Her kids are most likely here. I'm sure you'll meet them soon. Her son is pretty hot."

Calculating Millie's family dynamics, I point out, "She loved her first husband, but Carlisle was the love of her life.

"There is hope for me, then…." I laughed and referenced my conversation with Dr. Jameson. "With the billions of people on this planet, we can't be destined for just one great love. Some people are blessed enough to find love more than once. Life can be blatantly ironic. You have to endure the worst pain to understand real happiness."

We begin to descend the majestic marble staircase to introduce ourselves to Millie. The orchestra plays Vivaldi's "Autumn" from *The Four Seasons* concerti. We make our way through the crowds of vanity-driven friendships, high-end couture, and glasses brimming with alcohol. Millie's assistant gives us a proper introduction once we reach the front of the line.

Millie's personable radiance makes her startlingly beautiful. She genuinely seems interested in knowing who you are and what you are doing in New York City. Ashley reaches out to give her a Texas-sized hug and kisses Millie's cheek. Their affinity for each other is apparent in Ashley's Southern affection. Surprisingly, she pauses all propriety by reciprocating.

Millie and Ashley converse about people I don't know. I shyly glance around as they speak. I feel flustered when their conversation transitions over to me. Buzzing with pride, Ashley introduced us. "Edmond couldn't make it tonight, so I brought my next great love. This is my best friend, Emerson Vaughn. She's enjoying a much-needed vacation at the Ty Warner Penthouse."

Millie shakes my hand, then inquires about my vacation. Even though I hear her question, I just stare at her. Millie's eyes are a familiar mesmerizing blue.

Snapping back to reality, I stammer out something random like an imbecile, "My vacation has been educational."

Millie is intrigued. "How so? Are you enjoying the museums and restaurants?"

My martini helps facilitate a satirical answer. "Ashley felt my vacation needed some panache. She hired a sex therapist to come out to my penthouse. Apparently, I have social anxieties about sex and dating. Touring the city's restaurants and museums with my sex therapist has been kick-ass."

Ashley's hearty laughter erupts, as Mille looks flummoxed by my unfiltered answer. Immediately regaining her composure, she inquires, "Did you say sexual therapist?"

Millie isn't offended, but rather delighted. "If you require a good sex therapist, you should meet my son. He's a psychiatrist who specializes in that field."

Millie turns around and waves her hand at a gentleman socializing with a group. Distracted by women in beautiful gowns walking by, I didn't notice his approach. Millie grabs his hand to introduce us. To my amazement, Millie's son is Dr. Jameson. He looks at me like a deer in headlights.

She politely introduces us, "This is Ashley's best friend, Miss Emerson Vaughn. She is visiting New York City. Furthermore, she's apparently having a kick-ass time with her sex therapist. Maybe you know her doctor."

Dr. Jameson reaches out to greet me. Placing my hand into his, he gently squeezes it as an unspoken "hello." Releasing my hand with a peculiar glowing grin on his face, he says, "My name is Alexander. My mother likes to act as my publicist. She's always trying to advertise my services to people."

He kisses her on the cheek and then directs his attention back to me. Dashingly handsome in a tuxedo, he greets me with a seductive grin. "I am deeply honored to meet Ashley's best friend." His searing words bloom the apples of my cheeks a shade darker than my blush.

Out of pure mischief, I pretend this is our first meeting. "Thank you for the compliment, Dr. Jameson. It is a pleasure to meet you too."

He surprisingly asks, "Emerson, do you like the therapist you're seeing now?"

My alcohol-induced boldness won't let this opportunity pass. With a spirited sense of humor, I decide to play dirty. "You know, Dr. Jameson, my therapist is very unusual. Tell me if this is typical of a psychologist of your stature."

"What makes him unusual?"

I boldly detail my situation. "During my first session, my therapist asked to see me in my underwear. He was like some lingerie soothsayer. He could determine who I was from two pieces of fabric. After my striptease, he took me lingerie shopping at Agent Provocateur." I turned to Millie to explain, "My panties apparently needed a sexy makeover. After I showed him most of my body, he bought me dinner, and then explained how women love his penis. He gave me the full-body experience. Are your sessions this top-notch?"

His shocked facial expression is emphasized by the pink pigment emerging to change the hue of his skin. He understands what I am doing but proceeds to coerce me. "Really? He sounds barking mad. Why did you agree to do such things with your therapist?"

"I'm a sexless divorcée looking to spice things up…and he's gorgeous. I'm not immune to his power of persuasion; he's seductively charming. I felt embolden to do something out of my conservative norm."

I turn away from him to see Mille's reaction. "In all fairness, he did warn me that his therapy was unorthodox."

"It's funny. When we went to dinner, he wasn't this uptight therapist, but a chill guy. He wasn't overly analytical or aloof."

I look at him dead in the eyes, "He's the type of guy I could fall for."

Our back-and-forth banter is interrupted by Millie interjecting, "Your first session sounds inappropriate, and your therapist sounds mental."

Entertained by her reaction, I jovially redirect my focus back to Mille. "Today, he took me to the Met. We spent the whole day comparing priceless art to my inactive sex life, and he told me how robust his sex life is. In fact, he gave me detailed instructions on how to get a guy into bed. Guys like aggressive, crazy women with bold-colored lips."

With the alcohol juicing the sarcasm in my veins, I ask, "Dr. Jameson, in your professional opinion, is this normal behavior for a therapist?"

Millie blurts out in horror, "Good God, I hope not! He sounds like a miscreant, not a doctor."

Ashley and I telepathically give each other a look before losing ourselves in laughter.

Enthralled, but not the least bit disappointed in my gag, Dr. Jameson retaliates with "I'm not familiar with his technique. It seems like his interest in you extends beyond just a patient. Maybe he's a sick pervert."

Feeling golden at the moment, I tilt my head toward him with a subtle smirk. "Maybe…he's both."

He constrains the conversation with a polite exit. "I would love to continue this discussion privately. I'm intrigued by your doctor's method."

Dr. Jameson excuses himself from his mother and Ashley and extends his arm out to me. Taking his cue, I loop my arm into his, like I am Shirley to his Laverne. He spirits me away from his mother and prying ears to find a neutral setting. Once out of sight, he lets go of my arm and slides his hand into mine with a guiding grip to lead me upstairs. We arrive at the balcony overlooking the dance floor.

Finding a quiet, isolated area for privacy, he lets go of my hand and faces me with a new fascination. "Is your therapist a pervert?"

My martinis give me diarrhea of the mouth. "Of course, he's a pervert. I'm waiting for him to fully expose it to me. Unfortunately, he is on some Hippocratic leash."

To my own delight, I hold my arms open to capture the view of the busy room. I proclaim, "I don't even think I need therapy. I just need to get laid. Which guy should I choose?"

"Actually, therapists don't take a Hippocratic oath, but I do swear to a therapist's oath, which does state that I shall be respectful."

He moves closer to me and places his hands on my bare shoulders. "I'm here to help you deal with sexual anxieties, not date you, or find you someone to shag. I'm here for your mind, not your body. In this short amount of time, your fears about intimacy have subsided."

Strengthening his posture upright, he says, "From my observation, you want a connection, not a random one-night stand. This will make sex more gratifying for you."

"Don't we have a connection? If being my 'fake' therapist is restraining you, then let's stop these sessions. What if we were just two strangers who met at a bar?"

He takes a long pause before speaking with absoluteness. "Alcohol enhances your honesty. Even though these sessions are a favor for Ashley, they are not fake."

He continues, "We were two strangers who met in a bar. I could've easily slept with you then, but I didn't. I left with someone else."

His stinging words hang in the air. Opening my mouth to scorch the earth, a lean, long-legged, auburn-haired British beauty cheerily sings out Dr. Jameson's name "Alexander!"

She grabs his hand and faces him to kiss his cheek. "There you are! I've been looking for you everywhere."

She eyeballs me up and down. She adds, "Who's your friend?"

Before he responds, she holds out her hand to introduce herself. "My name is Basil. I'm Alexander's date."

Basil's hand is an open invitation waiting for my response. She has one hand resting on Dr. Jameson's shoulder and her other hand extended out to greet me. I glare at Dr. Jameson with disdain.

Hesitant, I reach out to shake Basil's hand. "Nice to meet you, Basil. My name is Emerson. I'm here with

Ashley Livingston. Dr. Jameson was just telling me how he was here to help out his mum."

I make sure I give him a big, mocking grin to our inside joke. "Apparently, helping out his mum equates to something sexual."

Jealousy rages through me. Even with Basil's cheerful demeanor, she senses my tension and defends herself. "Sweetheart, Alexander is here for his mum. We always attend these things together." She grips his shoulder tighter to tug on it. "We need each other."

Looking over at Dr. Jameson, she points out, "She calls you Dr. Jameson, and not Alexander." She looks at him for an answer. "Is she a patient?"

I swiftly answer, "I'm more like a contestant on a game show, not a patient. I'm unable to reach the bonus round. I'll never win the grand prize."

Basil seems to enjoy my retort. "Well, sweetheart, many women have tried to win the prize, but they seem to walk away empty-handed. As for me, I'll be around with the cockroaches."

I conclude that spending two days with this man does not distract from his apparent history with Basil. "You're right. Everyone does seem to walk away emptyhanded. From the looks of the men in this room, he's not the only option…or prize."

She has a puzzled look on her face and stops herself from saying anything more. Patting his shoulder before leaving, she says, "I'm interrupting something intense. This looks like a good time to excuse myself. Don't take too long getting reacquainted. We have people to meet."

Before exiting, she chimes in with her superior British accent, "It appears Alexander has cocked up something with you. He can be a duffer sometimes. Maybe you shouldn't piss away the rest of the night on him." Then she turns away to leave.

"I'll be right behind you," Dr. Jameson assures her. She doesn't turn around, but waves her arm up as a physical dismissal, and sashays out of sight.

"I really am here for my mum. This isn't what it appears to be." He tries to soothe me over.

"She's right. I don't know what a duffer is, but I'll assume it's a dumb ass." I become comically animated. "Is Basil one of the sexually charged crazy bitches you enjoy? Or is she more like your rock?"

He is quick. "I've known Basil all my life. She is my rock."

In my mind, I feel so foolish. My belief was misguided by thinking he reciprocated my feelings. Revealing myself to him gave me misleading comfort. People waste time with games. But then, here lies the rub. We were being honest with no strategic mind games, yet he feels obligated to not cross an imaginary line.

I blankly look at him. "Everything I've been sensing between us has been a huge mistake. Meeting your girlfriend, Scary Spice, really cleared things up for me. Why am I pissing away the night on you?"

He gets a kick out of my description of Basil. "Scary Spice?" He looks at me with sincerity and speaks from the heart, "I don't think you've made any false assumptions. The situation in itself has made things complicated."

Spitefulness creeps up through my esophagus and out my mouth. "Let's even the odds. For tomorrow's therapy, I want you to take your clothes off. I'll be sitting in a chair, slobbering all over myself, with a shit-eating grin on my face. Your rating will be based on underwear brand, style, tightness of ass, and of course, your balls being manicured."

Amused by my veracity, Dr. Jameson stalks up to me. He maneuvers himself deliciously close by pulling my waist toward him. His hands slide down my lower back, drawing me into an embrace. I can feel his heartbeat, the rhythm pulsing with mine. I am aroused by his freshly spiced amber scent. Closing my eyes, I can only imagine the taste of his neck. The warmth of his closeness makes me want to pounce. His taunting mouth glides along my jawline, across my cheek, until his breath whispers in my ear, "Who says I wear underwear?"

I boldly position my hands around his waist, deliberately grabbing his ass, forcing him into me. He doesn't flinch but welcomes my aggressive forward pull.

Continuing his dalliance of tormenting me, he says, "By the way, you look enticingly exquisite tonight. But you don't really need a dress to look that way."

Opening the palms of his hands on my back, he firmly feels his way down, before stopping. He withdraws pressure after copping a sensuous feel of my body. He steps backward, leaving me wanting him even more. His flirtatious behavior is breaking me down to the point of consumption. I feel flustered with my body hot with desire.

I put forth an acidic smirk. "Is that all you got? You are just a snatch-tease. This playing doctor schtick is giving me blue balls, when you're supposed to be alleviating them."

He chuckles out loud at my analogy. "I have no intention of giving you blue balls. And to be clear, I've never slept with any of my patients. I'm not going to start now."

"Of course not, because that would be wrong. Yet groping and flirting with a patient is permitted, right?"

Making my scorned woman dramatic exit, I proclaim, "Later tonight, when your penis is marinating inside your favorite seasoning—Basil—just remember that when she consumes your penis, the aftertaste left in her mouth…is you being unemotional and bland."

CHAPTER 15

I find Ashley sitting at our reserved table with an attractive gentleman. Deep in conversation, her body shakes from hysterical laughter.

"Emerson! Where have you been?" she bellows. "I want you to meet Nolan Asher. He's a friend of Edmond."

Nolan stands up to greet me like a perfect gentleman. Intrigued, I cordially extend my hand for him to shake. He politely places my hand up to his lips for a kiss, and then professes, "Ashley knows all the beautiful people."

Inspecting him like a curious specimen, I respond to his charming confidence. "Her aura proves to be an irresistible beacon pulling people into her orbit."

Flushed by his charismatic personality, I mentally compartmentalize him as a romantic. I thank him for the compliment, and he offers me a seat next to him by pulling out a chair. He begins the typical inquisitive pleasantries of getting to know me. I try to focus on his questions, but my stomach needs sustenance. Responding with nods and simple answers, my eyes scan the table for food. Bingo. I spy a basket of fresh bread and butter nestled in scarlet velour cloth on the opposite side of the table.

Nolan must be following my eyes, which are fixated on the wire breadbasket. My intense desire for the bread must make me look like a stoned cartoon character. He walks over to where the freshly sliced loaves of bread rest and kindly asks if anyone would like a piece. Naturally, everyone declines this deplorable vice known as carbs. He returns to his seat with the basket in hand and politely asks, "Would you like some bread, Emerson?"

His actions trigger a laughter, filling my hungry belly with delight. "Nolan, you just made my night. If you really want to impress me, I think they have a dessert cart by the next table. How many cakes can you carry?"

They say karma works in mysterious ways. My disappointment with Dr. Jameson has been satiated by meeting Nolan. I wish Ashley had set me up with him as my blind date at TAO.

I shamelessly inhale the basket of bread like it was my last meal. Carbs and alcohol complement each other like mashed potatoes and gravy. The flakiness of the warm bread, served with little rose-shaped sweet cream butters was heaven. Every roll I consumed alleviates my alcohol buzz.

Nolan and I feel alone in our conversation regardless of being surrounded by mindless chatter. Unfolding this great mystery before me was easy. A divorced software developer, who made his money by investing in a variety of cryptocurrencies, untethered to an office, with the ability to travel the world at any given time, seemed perfect for me. Hearing him describe adventures in faraway locations was enthralling. He just returned from Paris, which sets my mind into overdrive, picking his brain for details.

My eyes watch his mouth speak. Not to hear him but sexualize him. I blame Dr. Jameson for these warped spontaneous thoughts. Surveying Nolan's physical appearance, I calculate he's in his late forties. His dirty-blond hair is wavy enough for my fingers to run through. His chiseled face is a sexually rugged version of Gary Cooper, accentuated with chestnut brown eyes, rimmed in darkness, and injected with a honey color like golden fall leaves. I wonder what's underneath all those layers of pressed formal garb. My dirty mind envisions him emerging from the ocean, like Daniel Craig in *Casino Royale*. Two days of sexual intemperance with my male tease therapist has reduced my temporal lobe to porn thoughts.

I wonder if his neck smells as alluring as Dr. Jameson's. Inadvertently snickering at my sexual prowess of the senses, I recall a scientific study regarding arousing odors for males and females.

Nolan is interested in the cause of my suppressed giggles. Shaking my head, I tell him, "I'm experiencing a brief moment of insanity." I reveal the contents of the article were about the correlation between scents and pheromones. A scientific study concluded that women are attracted to the scent of Good & Plenty candies.

"I don't smell like black licorice. I guess that makes me undesirable." Nolan surprises with his familiarity with the research in question. He states, "On the opposite end of that study, men are turned on by the scent of pumpkin pie combined with lavender." He jests, "Lavender reminds me of my grandmother, and pumpkin pie is disgusting…these two things turn me off sexually."

Laughing out loud, I respond, "Well, I find the smell and taste of black licorice is offensive. But if you tasted like dark-chocolate-covered Himalayan-salted almonds, I would be weak at the knees."

He one-ups me with his comparison. "There's this small bakery on Second Ave called the Two Little Red Hens. They make this amazing coconut cake. It's four layers of bliss separated by coconut buttercream frosting, and then topped with white coconut shavings. If you smelled or tasted like this particular coconut cake, love would be instantaneous."

I redress to his flirtation. "Sorry. Nothing is instantaneous with me." With a wink, I add, "Coconut cake sounds much more appetizing than the diarrhea-inducing pumpkin pie mixed with lavender. Men must really enjoy Thanksgiving and bubble baths."

He doesn't let my previous statement go unnoticed. "I believe there are things instantaneous with you. You just don't realize it."

I look at the dance floor wondering how bold I want to be with him. I glance back in time to catch him admiring me. This gift horse is looking right at me. Suddenly fearful, I relinquish control to my exploding hormones. Recalling *The Art of Seduction* by Robert Greene, it says you should never seduce your own type. Nolan is more than just my type. He represents an easy comfort I desire.

Smiling innocently, he asks me to dance. I'm hesitant, until Ashley nudges me to get up and move my ass.

Following Nolan's lead out to a secluded spot on the fairy forest dance floor, he pulls me into his orbit. Placing his right hand on the lower part of my back, he then gently slips my hand into his. I ease myself into this romantic moment. Avoiding long bouts of silence, I share how I impulsively bought a ticket to Paris, and how instantaneously gratifying it felt.

"Emerson, I know you're here for a brief time, but I would very much like to see you again. Would you like to join me for dinner tomorrow night? Maybe we can find coconut cake."

I immediately respond, "I would love that."

He catches me off guard with another suggestion. "I truly hate these society functions. I plan on decking out soon. Would you like to escape with me?" He seems nervous adding, "I'm staying at the Peninsula Hotel. They have this amazing rooftop bar called the Salon de Ning. You could join me for a drink."

Midway through my response, we are interrupted by a tap on Nolan's shoulder.

Dr. Jameson being suave says, "I don't mean to intrude. I was wondering if I may sneak in a dance with Emerson." Trying to avoid a cock fight, he sweetly assures him, "I promise to return her back to you."

Nolan affably obliges before kissing my hand, then releasing me to Dr. Jameson. I fixate on Dr. Jameson's raging blue eyes as if they are the darkest part of the sea. Drowning in the way he looks at me. His intensity is constantly pulling me in and pushing me away like angry waves, filled with pain, regret, joy, and love. At this exact moment, the direction of this current crashes back into me.

He gently asks, "I'm sorry for my interruption. May I have a moment?"

"Is this normal for therapists to dance with patients? Or are you here out of personal curiosity?"

He resolves, "Personal curiosity."

He positions me close. Sliding one hand around my waist, then weaving my right hand into his, our eyes lock. Moving around the dance floor, electricity hums between us. At this moment, Nolan doesn't stand a chance with me.

I try to keep things platonic by sympathizing with his past. "I'm sorry about your father. Ashley told me he died in a car accident." I hesitate but continue my condolences. "I'm also sorry about your stepfather as well. I had no idea you've dealt with this much loss."

He looks down at me with humility and woeful eyes. "Telling you about Victoria was cracking my emotional closet door open. Talking about my father and stepfather would've swung the door wide open, dumping all my skeletons out at once."

His hushed voice is somber. "Grief follows me like a shadow. Maybe that's why getting close to people is an acquired taste. It's hard to antiquate. Being alone is just…easier."

He studies my reaction by transfixing his eyes on my lips, then he shifts his gaze to meet mine. "Tell me why you're upset with me." He draws our intertwined hands against his chest causing me to step forward. He asks with discretion, "Or will you just insult my penis again?"

My eyes look away toward the pretty white lights decorating the trees. They remind me of the holidays. "I'm not upset…just frustrated." I close my eyes to pursue my thoughts. "There is this extreme attraction between us. The solution to our romantic equation is simple, yet you seem conflicted and confused. Life should be like a Buick commercial. Taking an easy Sunday scenic drive with the one you love."

He can't help but smile. "Do you see me in a Buick, holding your hand, driving along the California coastline?"

"No. I see us riding a unicycle around a bonfire. Each of us frantically peddling around this blazing circle. We never reach each other, because no one wants to fall and get burned."

Moving closer until there is no air between us. His weighted thoughts force his eyebrows downward. "Interesting analogy, but you're right. I don't want to get burned."

He takes a deep breath. "I'm sorry my behavior is confusing. You're truly the exception to my norm."

He opens my palm with his thumb, placing my open hand over his heart, pressing it firmly against him. The cold barrier keeping him from relationships has turned into warmth for me. Resting my head on his shoulder, we slowly sway back and forth to our own rhythm.

I lift my head to face him. "Why are you making this complicated?"

"Sex always complicates things."

I cross-examine his response. "I thought you were able to have sex without any emotional baggage. Why would being sexual with me be so problematic?"

Without haste, he responds, "If we had sex, you would factor me into the feelings you're currently experiencing. It's hard to solve the problems from your past when your focus is presently on me."

He plays devil's advocate. "Let's say we have sex. The following day, I return to our session like nothing happened. Could you handle this casual behavior? Or would you presume sex made us something more?"

I roll my eyes. "I'm so happy you have insight into what I would feel. It saves me the ability to experience anything. Pausing long enough to lash out, I say, "Believe me, I'm ready to let Jesus take the wheel."

Discombobulated by my statement, he asks, "What the bloody hell does Jesus have to do with driving?"

I want to laugh at his response, but I stay on track. "Forget it. It's a Southern thing."

"I have experiences planned for you; they don't require us having sex."

I wearily stare at him. "I'll factor your planned experiences into the sex I plan on having tonight. Then I can write a blog called *Single Sex Over 40: A Guide for Sexually Stagnant Dummies.*"

"Why is experiencing casual sex so important to you now, when it wasn't before?"

"Divorce has made me into a 'born-again virgin'. After spending all this time with you, I miss having sex; I'm primed and ready to go. Intimacy between us would be obvious, but I read you wrong."

The music stops. He becomes silent in his thoughts. Our conversation is taking a downward spiral, but we don't release each other. We maintain closeness while everyone shuffles off the dance floor. I feel like an infatuated teenage girl around Dr. Jameson. When I was with Nolan, I acted like a grown-ass woman. It is like wrestling with two versions of myself. In my need for clarity, everything feels topsy-turvy.

I tell him, "In our time together, you've made me feel self-assured and audacious. Just be a platonic therapist, and we will continue our sessions until I leave." I want him to understand that I am moving on. "I'm going to head back to my table now. There's a handsome guy over there who wants me to leave with him."

His facial expression reveals hurt and surprise as I add, "In fact, after our conversation about spontaneity, I purchased an airline ticket to Paris. Distance will solve any emotional dilemmas."

His emotions are kept on a short leash, until now. His responsiveness is significant. "Is your ticket one-way?"

"I plan on returning. I just don't know when. I've raised my daughter, ended a marriage, and now it's time to experience life on my own terms."

He holds up my hand tight against his heart. "I suddenly feel melancholy. Why is that?"

"I guess you underestimated the power of boring-ass beige underwear."

Releasing my hand from his, I step backward for space. "Thank you for the dance. I hope you and Basil enjoy the rest of your evening. I'll be enjoying my night at the Peninsula with Nolan."

At that moment, the charity emcee taps on the mic to get everyone's attention. He is about to auction off items to raise money for the benefit. It is a perfectly timed interruption for Dr. Jameson and me to walk away from each other.

CHAPTER 16

Ashley is ready to spend some money, but nothing being auctioned catches her attention. With all the ruckus in the room, Nolan sits within earshot. We try to verbally feel each other out quietly with lavish bidding going on all around us. Meeting Nolan was fate but leaving with him doesn't feel right. I resent Dr. Jameson for trying to be my Jiminy Cricket, by placing the "don't be rash" doubt in my head.

The emcee riles up the audience for the last round of items to bid on. My attention is redirected from Nolan to the stage. Commotion ensues when three eligible bachelors are put on the auction block for date night. My eyes pass over the first two gentlemen, immediately homing in on the identity of the third bachelor, Dr. Jameson. The ladies in the room become feverish. Each man is required to go up to the microphone and sell himself. I can't wait to hear Dr. Jameson's sales pitch.

The first bachelor is a smoldering Italian soccer player with rock-hard calves and a washboard stomach. He lifts his shirt to reveal his exquisite fitness. He has thick, wavy, wild tawny hair setting off his tan skin and perfect white teeth. No words are needed to sell off his perfectly sculpted body. A foaming-at-the-mouth young heiress immediately wins the bid at $10,000. Their date will be clothing optional.

The second bachelor is a delectable earth-brown-skinned gynecologist. His bright energetic smile, dark expressive eyes, and a powerful confidence, offset by his delicate features, is radiant. His thirty-year-old appearance screams "Boy Toy" for the older ladies who dismiss his education. A feisty Latina in a revealing low-cut evening gown screams her $15,000 bid in a drunken howl.

Leaning over to Ashley, I snicker, "Is she is looking for a date or a gynecological exam?"

When Dr. Jameson is handed the microphone, the ladies in the audience unleash construction worker cat-calls. Under the lights, his presence onstage is reminiscent of a dapper movie star dolled up in a Tom Ford tuxedo. Dr. Jameson's face turns scarlet from his built-in fandom. He doesn't even utter one word before a woman in the back of the room blasts forth a bid. "$20,000!" Everyone turns around to see that the bidder is Basil. She's sitting next to Millie with her paddle in the air. His look of horror settles into an ease of relief.

Ashley yells, "$25,000!"

Then she looks at me and says, "Merry Christmas, sweetie pie!" All the humiliation consuming Dr. Jameson under the spotlight has somehow entered my bloodstream. Everyone in the room directs their shock and awe to our table. Nolan's confusion pierces into me as to why Ashley would buy me a date.

Basil quickly responds, "$30,000!"

Basil wraps her arms around Millie, and they start laughing. She must be extremely close with the Jameson family. You can see her affinity toward Millie and Dr. Jameson with her astronomical starting bid.

Not one to be outdone, Ashley fires off a counter bid: "$50,000!" The crowd gasps in disbelief. Ashley leans into me and snickers, "Darlin', for this money, he better eat more than just dinner with you. He better be eating your—"

I immediately cup her mouth before she finishes the sentence. Cracking up, I start to wonder if women should bid on attractive single men while intoxicated. Dr. Jameson watches us both with eagerness. Perplexed by what Ashley is doing, his eyes sparkle looking directly at me.

The audience turns their heads around to see what astronomical bid will come next. It is like a tennis match. The ball is in Basil's court as Ashley scrambles to win double match point, with hopes for love. I watch Basil whisper into Millie's ear, give a look to Alexander, and then shake her head to indicate defeat. She gestures her hands to the emcee as if to say "No more."

The emcee slams the mallet down and with great enthusiasm and shouts, "Sold to the Texas beauty at table 7!"

Ashley proudly stands up like a homecoming queen waving to everyone perched up on her magical float. She giggles as she curtsies in every direction. Everyone vigorously claps for Ashley without realizing she just purchased me a $50,000 dildo.

The winning bidders are welcomed onstage to meet their prospective dates. Ashley walks up to Dr. Jameson with alcohol-incited satisfaction. She looks back at me, then hides what she's whispering in his ear. His eyes fix on me with a consuming lascivious grin.

Adrenaline hits me hard. I need to excuse myself. Telling Nolan I will be back in a few minutes, I walk up the stairs to the second floor, where Cipriani Club 55 is located. I exit out the terrace area and inhale the city air, lights, and sounds. I shut my eyes, and the fall breeze cools me down. As horns honk and people scurry down Wall Street, I meditate to the life of the city. The surrounding sounds of rapidness calm me.

A familiar hand strokes my lower back, with the pressure of two fingers skimming all the way up to my neck. His fingers push my hair off the side of my neck, and he puts his mouth to my ear. "Do you mind if I join you?"

I turn my head until we are facing each other. "Why do you want to join me?"

Dr. Jameson leans against a large Grecian pillar with his arms folded and a self-satisfying grin. The setting provides him with a mythological god's carved-out appearance. There is no denying his physical beauty draws me in, but it's just cake.

"Isn't Basil looking for you?"

He starts to chuckle at my question. "I was under the impression I am at your disposal, not hers." He slyly adds, "Ashley's instructions were specific. For $50,000, I had to fulfill all your needs." He continues with a provocative proposition, "What do you need?"

I let my mouth loose. "My neighbor never cleans up after her dog shits in my yard. Will you come over to pick up dog poo?"

He turns his head to the side to robustly laugh at my request. I stand silently surveying him while collecting my thoughts. There needs to be neutral space between us to rectify the tension. I walk toward the opposite pillar and replicate his demeanor with a casual stance. The breeze catches my dress and blows my high slit open enough to reveal my legs. Small sections of my spiraled hair sweep across my face. This is our sexual version of a Mexican standoff.

"You were clear about remaining proper with our patient/therapist relationship. Have you changed your stance on getting your sugar and bread at the same store?"

He fires off sarcasm mixed with a little propriety. "Yes. My intentions with you have always been professional. I'm doing this for charity, remember?" He pauses before adding, "Besides, your alluring smart mouth could be useful in a variety of other ways."

I challenge his cockiness with a cutting observation. "I see. I'm a charity case…as long as it's for a good cause, right?"

Calmly examining how to approach the situation, he starts tapping his finger against his chin. "There is a comfort in being with you. I haven't felt like this in a while."

"Just a few minutes ago, you were fine with my decision to be platonic with you." I roll my eyes and throw my arms up in frustration.

"It's simple. I changed my mind. First, you announce that you're leaving indefinitely. Then, you introduce me to a random guy you plan on having sex with tonight. Maybe I'm a dozy bloke who lost sight of reality until bitten with jealousy." His impromptu confession freezes me.

In a serious, self-assured tone, he admits, "I don't want to just show you pleasure. I want to give it to you."

With us standing isolated on a terrace overlooking Wall Street, our cards are on the table. In this romantic setting, a silly question leaves my mouth due to my nerves. "Do I get to call you Alexander now?"

He grins from ear to ear, his facial expression showing that he finds my request adorable. "Of course you can. You chose to call me Dr. Jameson, which made me think you wanted some sort of boundary."

The city lights dim to a dreamlike state. The throbbing sounds of downtown are muted by my internal pulse beating nervously. The night chill stops sending shivers down my spine. I feel anticipation. Anticipation can emote fear or delight. A blending of polar opposite emotions combine for just one moment. Suddenly, I feel vulnerable and inaudible. I close my eyes thinking this isn't real.

My eyes open to him standing right in front of my face. Our eyes intensely assess each other's mouths. The rambunctious vibration from city life is silenced by the thumping of my heart pulsing all the way down between my legs.

He interlaces our fingers, pulling my arms up and above my head, and pinning me against the pillar. I hold his restraint voluntarily, wishing I was tied up. Rolling my head to the side exposing my neck, I want his mouth on me. Accepting my invitation, he rubs his lips slowly up my nape. Soft kisses travel along my jawline, teasing my partially opened lips with his tongue. Our mouths could melt into each other effortlessly. He continuously torments me by not committing our tongues, making me want him more.

Stimulating and exploring forgotten nerve endings arouse my body hot. My breasts swell for attention. His fingers delicately slither down the tender parts of my arms.

Sensually mapping out my skin with his fingertips, tickling all the way down my arms, butterflies flutter inside my stomach.

I whisper, "How much pleasure do you want to give?"

Before I finish my question, his primal instincts take the air out of my last word. Our mouths powerfully devour each other. I taste traces of his peppermint seamlessly blending with the cinnamon gloss on my lips. Our wet kiss is minty sweet.

Our mouths move urgently in unison. Vigorously working his tongue deeper into me, our breathing becomes heavy and erratic. I return his passion with all that's been pent-up inside me. I feel dizzy and hot.

Gripping my curves until my head drops back to breathe, his hands work down my spine. He searches for the opening of the slit of my dress. Sliding his hand under my thigh, he wraps my leg around his waist. My hands cradle his ass to hold us steady. Feeling his hardness firmly against me soaks my panties warm. Burying his moans into my neck, he grinds up and down in a slow groove. My mouth salivates thinking about every inch of him.

Reaching down, I feel his restrained cock. He reacts by stroking his fingers between my thighs, then inside me. He gasps, "You are so wet."

Panting while desperately fidgeting with his zipper to release him, my blood is thrumming. "Fuck me. Right here. Right now."

Before I could undo his pants, we hear sounds in the hallway. Panic-stricken, all the blood rushes from our arousal back to our brains. I don't want to stop, but the commotion of voices is getting closer.

Satisfyingly distracted, we have lost track of time. The auction has ended, leaving revelers to fill into the once-vacant terrace. Our hot bodies primed for sex ease out of our intense embrace. We allow ourselves a few more minutes of intimacy. We end our moment with one long, deeply consuming kiss containing all the unspoken passion we've withheld.

Disheveled in appearance, we're like teenagers being caught by their parents. Wary of the people coming toward us, we humorously try to compose ourselves. Our arms swaddle around each other for one last squeeze. Nestling my face into his chest out of frustration, he laughingly kisses my forehead.

Leaning in to kiss my lips, he smiles. "I've been wanting to do that all day."

Shifting his eyes to meet mine, he affectionately adds. "I guess this means we're terminating therapy."

"We can still play doctor. But not in a professional sense." Looking up at the ceiling trying to conjure up a title for this, all I can do is laugh. "We're two friends having a romantic interlude. Friends who have deep introspective conversations, helping each other through pain…among other things."

His eyes widen. "Friends with benefits?"

"We are two adults allowing ourselves to explore our feelings without silly modern labels." Stopping for a moment, I snicker. "If we did have labels, then you'd be my man-whore for tonight."

Ashley's voice bellows down the hall calling out for me like a bullhorn, letting me know she's about to walk in on us. Alexander releases my pressed body from the pillar. I step to the side and try to straighten out my dress, fix my hair, and smooth my hands along my cheeks and lips to fix any makeup mishaps. Leaning his body up against the balcony rail, Alexander adjusts his jacket with precision to hide any conspicuous bulging. I wave at Ashley to get her attention.

She glances at both of us individually to survey our appearance. "What have you two been doing?" She sarcastically comments, "Is the doctor giving you…therapy?"

Grinning brilliantly, I comply, "You know me. I was just giving him some lip."

"I'm ready to go if you are…"

She reaches out for a hug in mid-sentence. "Alexander, could you kindly escort Emme back to the hotel? I'm going to hang out here for a little while longer."

She throws out a surprising proposal for me in front of Alexander. "Nolan asked me to give you his business card. He thought you left, so your night cap has been put on hold. He would very much like for you to call him…and maybe, treat you to some coconut cake."

Ashley begins tapping the business card against her chin. Speaking to Alexander directly, she devilishly cautions, "You aren't the only eligible bachelor in town interested in Emme. Don't hurt her with typical bachelor bullshit. If you do, you better give your heart to Jesus, because your ass is mine."

Nodding his head in agreement, delighted by her Southern colloquialisms referencing Jesus, he affirms, "Technically, my ass is yours. You just paid $50,000 for it."

"I have no intention of being typical with Emerson. She is pretty remarkable."

I reach out and accept Nolan's card and slip it into my purse. I can feel Alexander watching me acknowledge my options. I don't care. He told me once how physical connection is just pleasure. I'm taking the card as leverage.

******

Waiting down in the lobby for Alexander, I feel like a teenager about to have her sexual awakening. This forgotten euphoric emotion makes me giddy. I distantly watch Alexander affectionately say goodbye to his mom. Basil surprisingly reaches up to hug and kiss his cheek. I withhold my jealous appearance before Alexander finds me with his eyes.

Confidently walking up to me, he reaches out for my hands. Puzzled, I ask, "Does Basil know you're taking me home? Isn't she supposed to be leaving with you?"

Alexander bursts out laughing. "Yes, we did come together. She is very aware of our situation. I tell her everything."

He takes a long pause as his secret clings to the corners of his mouth. Auspiciously grinning, he reveals, "Basil is my sister."

Laughing at the silliness of his joke, but also knowing the underlining cruelty of my interpretation, he says, "We hate going to these events…she is always my date. Agreeing to be an auction item was for my mum. Basil bidding on me would ensure I wouldn't end up in some uncomfortable situation."

In my best English accent, I jest, "Well played, kind sir."

He tenderly surrenders. "It seems my predicament was beneficial to more than just the charity."

My facial expression is morphing into all the thoughts racing in my brain. His joke made me react like a jealous schoolgirl. My behavior toward Basil was like taking the Bullet Train to Crazy Town.

"I can't take you back to your hotel tonight. Your car is waiting for you."

Mysteriously, he suggests, "There is something I want you to try tomorrow. Part of the process is abstaining from sex. If I took you back to your hotel room, I'm not sure how much restraint we would have."

I feel terror-stricken at what he has in store for me. "Part of the process? What am I going to try?"

"Tomorrow, I want to take you somewhere to experience absolute Zen. Let's expand your personal exploration into pleasure."

He cradles my face in his hands to comfort me. "Please trust me. Your body needs as much release as your mind. It will give me great satisfaction to watch you do this."

We walk to my car in silence, I'm enveloped in thought. After opening up my car door, he faces me and wraps his arms tightly around me for reassurance. His sincerity is comforting. "Don't let your mind come to odd conclusions. There's no need to worry. You are in good hands."

CHAPTER 17

Day 4

Session 3

Alexander asked me to be hydrated and rested before I see him at 4:00 p.m. The effects of alcohol caught up with me once I hit my pillow. It was a blessing that he didn't take me back to the hotel. It wouldn't have been a great romantic first impression for Alexander to see me in my current state. I have dragon breath from my dry mouth, accompanied by the scent of sugary vodka seeping out of my pores.

Harley wakes me up with a morning call. She sounds breathless rushing to class, "How is your trip going? How was the date at Tao?"

"My date with Quinton was a disaster. Never fear…Aunt Ashley found me another date. We went to a charity auction last night. She bid on a hot doctor and won. I'm having another date today. And this one, I know I like."

I deliberately switched out the word *date* for *therapy* to avoid a long confusing conversation.

"You've been there for four days…and already planning another date? Your love life is more eventful than mine. Aunt Ashley has impeccable taste. I'm sure he's nothing like the Tinder assholes I've met."

Talking to Harley is the highlight of my day. Even if we speak for two minutes, I always hang up smiling. I can always juxtapose my married life with my life today. She needed me growing up, and now, I need her strength. My sexual adventure with Dr. Jameson will be an interesting story to tell later, but only the rated PG-13 version.

I add one more surprise, "Oh, and I bought a ticket to Paris. I don't know how long I'll be gone. This is scary for me, but in a good way."

Harley gleefully blurts, "Who are you? I love this side of you. This is a mental breakthrough of epic proportions. Maybe finding happiness with the hot doctor in Paris is next."

She tosses out, "Oh and don't forget your laptop! I've seen you dabble with writing. Get those stories out. You can research and write about an erotic romance set in Paris."

Her snickering vibrates through the phone. "You'll have to tell me more about this hot doctor, but I woke up late. Walking into class now. Love you!"

I send her my love and positive thoughts before ending the call.

******

Alexander texts me the address of a specific location. My driver pulls up to a town house on Manhattan's Upper East Side. It looks grand with five levels of beige brick walls. There are two front doors with a knocker fitted in the center of each side. Looking up to admire the architectural design, I notice the second floor has a terrace with a black cast-iron rail decorated with red-rose-filled flowerpots. The cozy home exterior disarmed me into thinking that nothing sexually sinister could happen here. I walk up the steps to the porch and use the brass knockers to make my presence known.

A beautiful Indian woman who appears to be in her late fifties answers the door. I graciously greet her. "Hi. My name is Emerson. Dr. Jameson gave me your address."

She welcomes me with a long affectionate hug. She oozes exuberance. "I am so happy to meet you, Emerson. Dr. Jameson is upstairs waiting for you. Please come inside."

I am startled by her jubilant greeting, but I reciprocate. "My name is Aakanksha Naran. My husband is a very successful fertility specialist, and I am a Tantric masseuse. I typically work with my husband on matters of fertility. Today, I am assisting Dr. Jameson."

"I'm not trying to get pregnant. I don't understand why I would need a Tantric masseuse."

She tries to soothe me. "Yes, my dear, I am not here for fertility reasons, but to enhance your need for intimacy."

In my state of confusion, I maintain a blank stare, but my internal dialogue is screaming, "What the fuck is this?"

Aakanksha gives me a tour of the downstairs area. This must be standard procedure to put her client's mind at ease. There are no sexual torture devices or an opium den. It is a culturally beautiful home with Hindu-inspired decor.

Aakanksha leads me up a regal spiraling staircase. Artistically lining the wall upward like a lithograph, it's unreal until you touch the banister. Looking straight up its center to the ceiling rests a clear window with a red lotus etched in the middle. The sun's rays ignite the color of the lotus throughout the house, making a majestic kaleidoscope.

Making idle chatter, while we climb up the stairs. She is sympathetic to my uneasiness, "All your questions will be answered soon." I know Alexander is waiting for me at the top of the stairs.

The top floor is a huge loft with numerous, vast, bright windows. The white furniture pops against the dark mahogany wood floors. In the center of the room is a massage table covered in white sheets. Extra folded sheets and massage oils are neatly organized at the end of the table. A divider in the room gives the illusion of privacy for changing or solitude. Placed behind the divider sits a large antique-style freestanding resin tub with a nickel-brushed hand spout and faucet. A tray of bath salts, oils, and flowers are placed on a try next to the tub. Vanilla-cashmere-scented candles flicker in jars lined against the wall. This is the perfect place for meditation and reflection.

Alexander is in the seating area, with two large white love seats opposite to each other. Freshly made tea has been placed in front of him. He sits comfortably with his arms sprawled out and legs crossed, looking fresh and clean in his charcoal-colored suit and pressed white shirt. His indigo-colored tie brings out the bold color of his eyes.

Once my presence is known, he stands up with a cat-that-ate-the-canary grin sprawled on his face. I stop in front of the love seat opposite him. Not knowing what our hostess might think, I proceed in a benign fashion to formally address him, "Good evening, Dr. Jameson. What does my therapy session entail today?"

Though he's curious about my behavior, he acknowledges my formality. He gestures me to sit. "I hope you enjoyed the tour with Aakanksha. Would you like some tea?"

"Yes, please."

I don't want to eat or drink anything, but it smells amazing. The spice and orange zest evaporating out of the steaming tea is aromatherapy for my jitters.

Alexander begins to pitch the point of this meeting, "Thank you for trusting me by being here. It is important for you to keep an open mind. Can you do that?"

I nod. "I think I've been keeping an open mind ever since I met you." I smile down at my teacup.

Aakanksha sits quietly next to Alexander as he speaks. She is observing me with a warm expression. "I have referred many clients here. Sexual frustration is at the core of most patients. I need them to let this frustration out. I need their bodies and minds clear in order to reveal their issues without any pent-up sexual aggression."

Alexander explains, "Tantric massage is great for couples therapy, but more importantly, it is fantastic for individuals." His pause is brief enough to develop the punchline. "Today, Aakanksha will give you a yoni massage. *Yoni* is the Sanskrit word for 'vagina,' your sacred space. This isn't a new-age way of getting fingered. It's about connecting with yourself, by awakening your sexuality. It is a spiritual experience, if you can just relax and let the weight of everything go."

There are a barrage of questions in my mind. How much sexual frustration comes out? Does massaging my yoni include my asshole? What happens once the frustration is released? I have about two years of sexual depravity. I'm about to release it on a table for a stranger to see.

My panic-stricken face focuses on Alexander and his description.

"Emerson, you don't have to do anything you don't want to do."

He ponders out loud to psychologically coax me, "When I asked you to show me your undergarments, your participation surprised me, especially after you told me to 'fuck off.'"

He leans forward to comfort me. "Once you did it, you felt empowered, and you were willing to try new things. The color or style of your lingerie never mattered. It was how bold you became by the end of the day."

In my mind, I am a contestant on some weird TV show, like *Sexual Ninja Warrior*. I need to overcome all these obstacles in order to ring my bell.

I defused the tension. "After a brief conversation with my yoni, we decided to participate. My yoni convinced me that she needs this before she becomes sealed."

Alexander swallows down his laughter with a cracked smile of optimism. He nods slowly at my decision, then he politely instructs me to follow Aakanksha to the back room. In an effort to appear professional, he remains seated, patiently waiting.

Aakanksha gives me a supportive hug, I appreciate her comfort. My bizarre thought process associates her with the Kathy Bates's character from *Misery*. She looks full of warmth and charm, but then she will bind me to a bed and break my clit with a sledgehammer. My nerves can't be hidden, and she keeps reminding me to clear my thoughts and to relax.

I follow her behind the partition, and she starts to draw me a bath. She explains, "Everyone must clean their bodies beforehand, plus it is good to just soak and meditate."

I am shown where to place my clothes after I undress, and where to grab a white robe once I am naked. The robe appeals to my insecurity, but I will eventually be completely nude.

Placing her hand in the tub to check the temperature, she remarks, "The water is perfect. Please undress and soak. I will return to add salts." Then she disappears behind the partition.

I find it odd that she would give me privacy to undress but has no issues tunneling through my ass crack. I keep telling myself, "Clear your thoughts. Serenity."

I do what was instructed, and within minutes she reappears to put flowers and bath salts in the tub. The pink flowers drift to my breasts like Mother Nature's bikini. I hold my arms out, grabbing the sides of the tub to recline backward. Trying my damnedest to meditate, I focus on Aakanksha arranging salts and oils onto a tray.

She starts discussing the different breathing techniques associated with Tantra. She explains how to breathe and begins showing me what to do. "Please try to mimic my breathing pattern. Once you get the hang of it, you'll start to loosen up."

She politely asks if I need anything else. I shake my head to answer no before dropping it back to enjoy the fragrant water. She picks up a remote to close the blackout shades on her way out. The room slowly drifts into candlelight. The natural sunlight is sucked out by the window panels moving down.

My mind is trying to catch up to all these ideas racing around. I applaud myself for taking Ashley's advice and getting totally waxed. Knowing I didn't want to appear unkempt while on display made me snicker. I groomed myself to benefit another woman.

I hear Alexander clear his throat. "May I have a moment with you?"

"Of course, if you don't mind the sound of me practicing my breathing exercises. I swear how can prenatal birth breathing and Tantric meditation be the same? Am I giving birth to an orgasm? Enlighten me."

He pulls a stool up next to the tub and then reaches for my hand. He inquires, "How are you doing?"

I release my fear by riffing on him, "Are you serious? I'm sitting naked in a tub in preparation for my sexual probing. My vagina is being marinated for some out-of-body Tantric sexual feast."

My hands splash the water forward in frustration. "Do they sell Groupons for a yoni massage?" Shifting the conversation to him, I ask, "Have you done this yourself?"

Reluctant to answer, he gives me a half smile. "Yes, I have. I've done it here a few times, and in London. Actually, I discovered this practice in London.

"After Victoria died, I had so much pent-up frustration. A colleague recommended that I try this technique. It was something new and unique, but worth a shot. I was surprised at how I felt afterward." He plays with my fingers, flipping my hand over and tracing all the lines in my palm.

Trying to make sense of his thought process, I say, "I can understand why you did this in London, especially after Victoria died. Why did you do it here?"

"I feel…sometimes…I need to be sexually purified." He looks at me deeply to read my reaction.

"Sexually purified? What does that even mean?"

My hands wave around creating ripples in the water, and I ponder, "Is this some kinky version of *Purple Rain*? You know…when Prince tells Apollonia she has to purify herself in the waters of Lake Minnetonka?"

Entertained by my analogy, his voice deepens to a sultry hush, "I know you're nervous. You turn into a comedian when you experience anxiety and uncomfortable situations. It's your defense mechanism."

"This massage explores your body in the most intimate way. Aakanksha will massage every inch of you. It might make you feel paranoid at first, but you need to relax. Your muscles need to release all the tension trapped inside you."

Swirling my hands around my propped-up knees, I confess, "The anticipation is making me tense. How the hell will she coax this tightness free?"

"She will externally, as well as internally, massage your vagina to stimulate your yoni." I hand on to every word in horror, yet he continues, "When your intimate parts are being touched, it is natural to hesitate and resist, but there will be a point where you just let go. The blood flow to your sexual organs will be in full force and awakened. When you orgasm, it will be more intense and drawn out. It's different from sexual intercourse."

He continues to explain, "Tantra is about having your body, mind, and emotions work together to give you control of yourself. It is a slow, enjoyable process that helps unblock all the stagnant sexual toxins by letting your sexual energy flow freely. This release will empower clarity."

"She's going to release my sexual energy? Is this like catching fireflies in a jar? Or will this be like flashing the Bat Signal in the sky?"

"Aakanksha will use pressure from her fingers and hands to stimulate your nerve endings, mainly focusing on neglected areas."

I scoffed, "Oh so this is a full body massage…everything has been neglected."

Totally unfazed by my sense of humor, he continues explaining, "Your imminent arousal will culminate sexual energy that will not immediately release it. Your orgasm will purposely be delayed—repeatedly. This builds up all the toxins, resulting in one epic climactic finish."

He examines my naked body in the milky water, before locking his eyes with mine. "You will love this."

Alexander's fingers touch my face to brush my hair away. "Believe it or not, I actually like just talking and spending time with you, not to mention, hearing your thoughts. This makes you unique. And your sense of humor is mental."

He creates this moment of quiet stillness. I digest his words. This is my romantic movie scene. He has no idea how elated I feel by his words.

I lean over to the side of the tub and grab his hand. "Are you going to stay or leave?"

I'm not sure how I feel about him watching me. I just know I don't want to be alone.

A devilish smirk emerges on his face. "I plan on staying. I have every intention of watching your happy ending."

He stands up to grab me a towel, places it on an empty stool where he was sitting, and then leaves.

I emerge from behind the divide wearing a robe. The room bathed in candlelight accentuated by a vanilla spice scent. I feel like I'm walking into a weird sexual sacrificial post.

Arriving at the massage bed, I wait for further guidance from Aakanksha. Alexander is dimly hidden in shadows stalking me with his eyes. Comfortably situated on the sofa, he sips on some tea and nudges the cup toward me like he's saying "Cheers!" He's about to see me in all my glory.

I take a deep breath as Aakanksha helps me up on the table. Catatonic from dread, I ease down slowly. I am instructed to open my robe and turn onto my stomach.

My knotted belt instinctively drops to my sides. Sliding my arms out of each sleeve, I prop myself up in order to flip over to my stomach. My body is now fully exposed. Alexander is probably taking all this in while sipping tea.

I rest my head to the side with my arms pressed against my body. Instinctively, I want to look the opposite direction from where Alexander is sitting. But I suddenly feel empowered. I turn my face toward him. Focusing on his eyes. I won't be intimidated by this experience.

He places his tea down on the coffee table and nestles back into the seat. The erotic peep show is about to begin.

Aakanksha begins warming oil in her hands by rubbing them together, then applies them on my legs and thighs. My legs are tensely locked together. With a slow, massaging motion, she eases them apart, just enough for her to work. Her hands slide up and around my legs, entering between my thighs. Her initial intentions are for my own relaxation. She doesn't stray into any crevices. She wants me to be disarmed before initiating intimacy.

Kneading my lower back with her knuckles, she edges out any tension. Slowly, her hands maneuver downward, gliding her fingers inside my cracks, and start rubbing around my yoni. These long, prolonged strokes delightfully awaken my insides without penetration. She encourages me to clear my mind with the breathing techniques she taught me.

The erotic motion of her hands helps me unwind. She can feel my trepidation diminish, as the tightness in my muscles alleviate when my breathing changes. She asks my permission before moving on to new areas. I respond with a weak, "Yes."

Aakanksha has insight on where to touch me. All my rigidness exits. She positions my arms outward and away from shielding my body. She advances upward, gently massaging the sides of my breasts, under my arm pits, then on top of my shoulders. I am a ball of mush ready to fall asleep. But I can't. My nerve endings are tingling all over making me wet with arousal.

Rejoicing in the physical hedonism happening in prone position, Aakanksha asks me to flip over onto my back and bend my knees. My tension creeps its way back into my muscles. Realizing what is about to happen, I initiate my breathing exercises.

She casually rubs oil on my belly button, then presses her hands up toward my rib cage, cascading around my breasts, and the arousal overtakes me. My breasts swell by becoming erect and hard. Sensing my body's reaction, she taunts my nipples—massaging then easing them in and out between her fingers, pinching my perked hardness with medium pressure. Resting my arms above my head, I perch my chest out. I'd forgotten how much I love nipple play. I crave her fingers to tantalize this area more. She complies.

I'm purring from pleasure. Taking advantage of my enthusiasm, her hands glide away from my oily breasts down to all my glory. She creeps her fingers down to my clit and emits a light flicker. Advancing the rhythm, she begins to play with me.

Aakanksha unexpectedly attempts to insert her finger into my anus while stimulating my clit. I clench up. My hesitation doesn't make her stop. She immediately continues to the areas that are reacting. The long broad strokes of her fingers mimic a man's tongue going down on me. I'm on the edge of erupting into orgasm. Aware of my readiness to climax, she eases the pressure to prevent release.

Aakanksha stirs my breasts and nipples into attention with her left hand. Her right hand moves down toward my clit, pinching, thumping, rubbing, increasing pace. I can't stand this repetition any longer. I need to come. The buildup is rushing straight to my sex. *Fuck. This feels so good.*

She thrusts her fingers inside me. Swallowing down every moan, I gasp for air. Her hands perform in unison. Her fingers play me like an instrument. Strumming my yoni. I'm primed to detonate.

For a brief second, my head turns to look at Alexander. Leaning forward engrossed in my performance, he smolders with delight watching live porn, patiently waiting to see me climax. He knows that I am at her mercy.

Grooving with her rapid circular rhythm, I want her to get me off. Arching my back forces her drenched hand to press harder. She curves two fingers inside me hitting my G-spot. My pulse races rampantly. I'm soaking wet and swelling for eruption.

Unable to abstain from exploding, she finally triggers a sensational release. An electric consciousness tickles all over me. My body quivers erratically, decimating my vagina to an uncontrollable vibration. I scream with delight. My legs continue shaking, until I breathlessly collapse. I'm rendered helpless. My skin feels sensitive to air. Bewildered, I lie very still.

Alexander was right. This orgasm is epic. Everything that was pent-up inside me has just left my body. I finally allowed myself to feel pleasure by just letting everything go.

Aakanksha gently covers my naked oiled body with a warm white sheet. She acknowledges Alexander with a happy nod, then leaves the area to give us privacy. Pulling the sheet up to my breasts, I roll over to my side to cuddle myself. My long spirally hair is sprayed out all around my head. This was an out-of-body experience.

Alexander approaches me. His fingers smooth out strands of hair dangling across my cheeks. His thumb wipes away any traces of tears, before tenderly asking, "How do you feel?"

I place the palm of his hand on top of my cheek, pressing down softly. I can't articulate what just happened. In a dreamlike state, I exhale, "Amazing."

I need a minute to collect myself. He tells me to take my time. Bending down to kiss my forehead, he brings my hand to his lips for another kiss before exiting the room. Content and exhausted, it would be easy to succumb to my drowsiness. I savor my metaphysical surrender with a long deep sigh.

CHAPTER 18

Alexander made dinner reservations at Daniel on 65th Street. I am pretty quiet on the drive to the restaurant. Feeling emotionally and physically spent, I'm not too keen on going out, but I need sustenance. Alexander opted for fine dining instead of room service or takeout.

He respects my silence, until my phone chimes. Looking down, I see a text from Ashley.

Ashley: There's a disturbance in the Force. I think an Indian Goddess just released some of your frustration. How was it?

Me: Very intense. Sexually exciting. Uninhibited. Alexander was right. This was something my body desperately needed.

Me: How could you possibly know what I just did? I didn't even know…until it happened.

Ashley: Edmond and I went to the "House of Tantra" to unlock our animalistic urges as well.

Ashley: Edmond and I both watched each other get off.

Me: You did this together? Her hand must have been sprained.

Ashley: I knew he would take you there. I'm glad you enjoyed yourself.

Me: I guess we were finger-fucked by the same chick. That goes beyond friendship bracelets.

Ashley: I love that you went through with this. Most people would freak out.

Me: The only thing I'm freaking out about is my growling stomach. I wish for a Spicy Chick-fil-A sandwich with extra pickles. I've got to go! Eating fancy tonight.

Ashley responds with an emoji blowing a kiss.

I glance up to see Alexander smiling. "Everything okay?"

I laughed. "I'm sorry. I'm not ignoring you. Ashley just needed to know if my vagina and I are okay." Gripping his knee, then looking up at his gorgeous face, I say, "We are great."

As we exit the car, he doesn't stick out his arm for me to grab. Surprisingly, he reaches for my hand, intertwining his fingers into mine, before guiding me into the restaurant. This sugary sweet gesture elicits a glowing smile from me.

Alexander reserved the skybox, a totally segregated area on the second floor. This private novelty is an intimate glass-encased room suspended above the kitchen. Once we enter the room, I notice a large table that could comfortably fit up to six people. The table has long, cozy-looking leather sofa-type seats on each side. The walls are peppered with photographs documenting the history of celebrities enjoying the skybox. I walk around impressed with the room's lineage.

I could've easily sat beside Alexander. His seat was large enough to accommodate both of us. I plop down on the seat across from him with a demure look on my face. He looks puzzled by my sudden shyness. The realness of everything trickled into my subconscious. He just saw me naked, having an orgasm, and now, we're seated in an exclusive room about to nosh on something I can't pronounce. Very surreal.

Alexander surveys the wine list and orders a bottle of Henri Germain Meursault 2010. I consider myself a connoisseur of martinis, not wine. I have never dined on upscale French cuisine. I want to utilize Google to translate fancy food names into simple words. I have never heard nor tasted any of these dishes, but every flavor seems to just complement another. I was famished enough to eat anything. This is sensual osmosis from Alexander. He's exposed each one of my senses to new pleasure.

I savor each bite of food and sip of wine. It's hard to comprehend how all this energy was depleted from my body. I pretty much just lay there while Aakanksha did her magic—the Tantric benefits of orgasm through masturbation. The massage made my brain high on dopamine, and now I have the munchies.

I concentrate on the topic of how Alexander stumbled across Aakanksha and her husband. I engross myself in every detail of his story. The tasty extravagant wine remedies any leftover tension. I am having a "Calgon, take me away!" moment in the most perverse way.

Noticing my flighty appearance, he asks, "What's going through your mind?"

I study him before asking my question. "Are we on a date?"

Nonchalantly sneaking in sarcasm, he asks, "Aren't I working off a $50,000 tab?"

"Oh, that's right…you're my man whore for a few days."

"Yes, this is a date. I'm sorry I didn't ask you out properly." He just grins at his profound revelation. "I didn't think asking you out before a vaginal massage was appropriate."

His coy response amuses me. "Yes, you just watched me orgasmically convulse on a table. I guess asking me out on a date afterward seems comical."

Overcome with happiness, I want to express my gratitude. "Alexander, today is incomparable to anything I've ever done. Thank you."

"I had no idea what a yoni or Tantric massage was until today. I would have guessed a 'yoni' was a new age Swedish musician, and a Tantric massage is most likely illegal in some states."

I pridefully acknowledge, "This is technically my first official date as a divorced woman. And no, I don't count Quinton. You really went all out for me."

"Thank you for letting me watch you tonight." He rests both of his arms on the table and leans in. "You are a beautiful woman. Your body is ravishing during orgasm."

Extremely flustered, my heated cheeks bloom to a light rouge.

"I have never watched a woman have a Tantric orgasm. It was very vulnerable…yet erotic."

I questioned his observation. "You didn't stay to watch Ashley and Edmond?"

"No. That was an intimate moment between a couple. They needed privacy."

A gentle sweetness softens his face, before he adds, "Even though this was your session, you welcomed me to watch. This was pure intimacy between us, without the sex."

I mimic his stance. Placing my arms on the table, I lean toward him. "It seems unfair that you have gotten to see every aspect of me in the most unconventional way. When do I get this point of view of you?"

"Sadly, it won't be tonight. It's suggested that after a yoni massage you abstain from sex. Your body needs a break. All your muscles were used to contract with control. Just relax." He hints, "I'm sure we can find other things to do."

I studiously remind him of his auction deadline. "Do you realize that I'm leaving in a couple of days?"

Downhearted, he responds, "Things are about to get interesting. Why leave now?"

He's right. I don't have to leave. I want to leave. My house is up for sale, Harley is away at school, and I am not working. Downsizing my responsibilities makes me feel untethered. Relocating to New York City and dipping my toes back into writing was already in the cards. I need to give myself the proverbial "gap year" to find myself before moving.

Trying to cultivate a response to soften the blow, I say, "Alexander, my life has always been a formulated timeline. I went from living with my parents and going to college to getting married and being a mom, all cumulating in divorce. Not only have I reached full circle, but I am truly on my own. Being alone and starting over is terrifying, but it's made me resilient. I am embracing this new phase. Things end only to lead to another beginning. I want to take advantage of all the things I've missed out on."

"Wouldn't you be missing out on seeing where this goes? I haven't felt this spark in ages. Do you feel the same way?"

"I do. But…I can handle a short-lived goodbye. I can't endure another heartbreak. This transient erotic fantasy of a vacation will never be obliterated from my memories."

Alexander is ambivalent in his words. "Every beginning leads to many more choices. Make the choices that bring you happiness."

"Would my choices bring *me* happiness, or you?"

We just sit for a second and analyze each other.

I tell him, "I believe you have choices to make as well. What would my relocating to New York City entail for you?"

Challenging each other with hypotheticals, he responds, "I would deeply regret not taking this chance with you. Maybe we'll fall madly in love or be a completely mismatched disaster. How will we ever know?"

I look down for a second, thinking of a million things to say, but the most poignant thought is our age. My brain thumps along with my heart.

I start with the obvious. "You are a gorgeous younger man. I'm an older woman." I shrug my shoulders. "Why are you interested in me?" I fold my arms to set up a barrier. "Age is irrelevant in terms of living in the present, but when you put age in the context of pubescent experiences or growing pains, the gap seems huge."

My persistence annoys Alexander. "Why are you fixated on age? I don't perceive our ages in this equation. We were both involved with people our own ages, and both of those relationships ended painfully. Age is irrelevant if we complement each other. Sometimes attraction has no explanation." He begs the question, "Why can't we indulge in this situation?"

Alexander continues, "Inundating myself with work has replaced my need for human companionship. I'm always surrounded by people. This doesn't mean I want to connect with them. It's ironic; if it wasn't for my work, I would never have met you. Your age is not a deterrence. You are completely lovely to me."

I sigh in defeat. "You've made your point."

He looks at me blankly, examining me as if I have just found a small black hair in his food. He slides out of his booth seat to scoot next to me. His fingertips tenderly brush my hair away from my face, placing it behind my ear, creating a magnetic shiver down my spine. His touch makes me crave something substantially more than kissing.

I gleefully point out an odd fact. "In the nineties, I was in college and you were in middle school! I was getting drunk and going into mosh pits; you were passing notes to girls."

Erupting in laughter, I gasp, "I feel like a pervert."

He responds, "What?! You are so mental."

He isn't going to let our different stages of puberty affect our current situation. "Your age has never even crossed my mind. I appreciate that you've lived a life. But more importantly, I've lived a life as well. Don't dismiss me due to age."

He pauses and gently runs his thumb across my bottom lip. "I'm sure there are a lot of new things I can teach you."

He's taught me a lot these past few days. I situate myself to be aligned with him. Placing my left arm on the back of the booth, I rest my head in my other hand. Smiling at our silly conversation, I selfishly admire his features.

"Alexander, I just want to lay everything out in the open."

I annoyingly tap my fingers on the table to conjure up something relatable. "It's kind of like when you're ordering food. You think you know what you're getting, until it's placed in front of you. The food doesn't look like it's description. You wished you had told to the waiter to tweak the ingredients to your liking. I don't want to order up something and realize there are hidden things, like red onions, mixed in. Red onions always give me bad gas. I want to avoid any ingredient that will give me some sort of physical reaction."

Alexander lets out a tremendous bellow of laughter. He copies my posture, before his eyebrows crinkle from concern. "I wouldn't want you to upset your stomach. What is the main food allergy in our so-called romantic dish?"

"You might regret dating an older woman when you factor in children. Didn't you want children with your wife?"

Confusion rapidly spreads across his face. "Who says I want children?"

"You don't want to experience being a father?"

I've known him only a few days. I'm already sabotaging a relationship that hasn't even begun.

"This may surprise you, but no, I don't want children. There was a time I was open to having children with Victoria, but that was ages ago. Having children may be embedded in most of us, but not me."

In full disclosure, he admits, "If I fell for someone who had children, then I would accept her children. It's a package deal.

"I've never dated anyone with children." Sudden shyness removes his confidence with pink hue. He quietly confesses, "I am curious about your daughter. Maybe, I'll meet her one day. Is she anything like you?"

His willingness to meet Harley catches me off guard.

"I love that bacheloritis hasn't made you rigid. You're still receptive to children."

I pull my phone out of my purse, and begin flipping through random photos of Harley. My face radiates pride. "She's an eighteen-year-old college freshman…and the epitome of an old soul. She's effervescent in positivity and drive. In a sense, it's like I'm childless. This must be ideal for you."

Speaking in a matter-of-fact tone, I say, "Even though she is an adult and away at college, if you weren't receptive to kids, this situation would not work. Harley is my heart, the love of my life."

He reads my openness. "Your love for Harley makes you even more gorgeous…if that's possible."

His words subdue me.

"I haven't been receptive to anyone, with or without kids. I have no intention of auditioning to be a father, but I wouldn't deny a chance at something great."

There is a languishing blue fire in his eyes. He emotes a foreboding sadness by revealing, "I'm willing to open once-closed doors, but you won't be here to walk through the door."

Alexander methodically leans in to kiss my neck to change the topic. I invite the affection by tilting my head, grabbing a fist full of his hair to draw him closer. He keeps taunting me by brushing his tongue and lips seamlessly against my skin. My open mouth meets with his, unleashing a wild hunger for each other. His wine-drenched tongue throbs in unison with mine. The taste of sweet berries makes me thirsty and breathless.

I reach for his jacket collar, jerking him closer to envelop me. He resists. Easing back from our embrace, he watches my reaction. Sliding his hand up my dress, skimming between my legs, I'm slick with arousal. I boldly reach my hand down to feel his hardness trapped inside his pants. Our mouths slow down as he teases my inner thighs. I hold his hand in place, feeling my warmth, giving him permission to fondle and enter me in this secluded skybox.

He apologetically denies me. "I'm sorry…it's not that I don't want to. Believe me. I want to. You need to rest your overstimulated body. Abstinence is proving to be extremely difficult tonight," he whispers, before reassuring me with a kiss.

Having his fingers so close to my yoni are equivalent to adrenaline jabbing into my heart. My turned-on body trembles from his recoil.

Alexander's lips soothe along my cheek and earlobe before sucking my bottom lip. Even with my eyes closed, I can feel him looking at me.

"I notice this is your plan of attack. Passionate kisses to divert the issue. If this is how you plan on shutting my smart mouth, there won't be a lot of talking between us."

He entertains the idea. "There are a lot of things I want to do with your smart mouth. Shutting it up isn't one of them."

CHAPTER 19

Day 5

Session 4

Today's session will be held at Alexander's apartment. Arriving at his address fills me with trepidation, curiosity, and a surmounting pile of knots in my stomach. He never speaks of money or acts holier-than-thou, but he lives an affluent lifestyle. Regardless of having a successful practice, he comes from old money. His home address is on Fifth Avenue, in the Upper East Side of Lenox Hill. This isn't going to be some cute bachelor pad with a fire escape. This address means having a doorman and people kissing his ass all day.

I look up at the self-effaced beige brick building. It doesn't scream wealth, but it's grand in stature. The stately exterior is manicured, and the sidewalks aren't peppered with construction.

The entrance is occupied by a smiling doorman and an elevator attendant. I tell the elevator attendant, "Hi. I'm going to PH14E."

Looking me up and down, he courteously replies, "Oh, you are a guest of Dr. Jameson, very well."

The attendant presses the button labeled PH. It suddenly occurs to me. The "PH" in his apartment number stands for penthouse. This isn't going to be a bachelor pad. The elevator doors open to the area known as the grand gallery. Alexander is standing there like Mr. Roarke from *Fantasy Island*, greeting me like a proper host. He gives the elevator attendant a male nonverbal thank-you nod. I silently stand in his entryway in awe. Alexander's appearance reminds me of an airbrushed male model in a European cologne ad. He's very fresh, polished looking, and sexually commanding in his tailored Tom Ford suit.

My inquiring mind is dying to see his personality through his home life.

"Did you have any problems finding this building?" he asks.

Engrossed in memorizing every detail, I shake my head glancing around. My head is screaming, "Holy shit, this is where you live!"

Instead, I opt for a more practical compliment. "I can't believe you've never had female guests. This is a ridiculous first impression."

"I've never felt the urge to impress anyone." He adds, "I thought since you've exposed so much of your-self to me, I should do the same."

He bends over to kiss my cheek, then lovingly my lips. He weaves his hand into mine to give me the grand tour. Alexander's design taste appears classical, with a modernized twist. The neutral colors of beige, grays, and dark blues contrast each other in a very sophisticated way.

"Did you pick all your own furniture, or did you hire a designer?" I wonder.

"I want everything to be a certain way. It took me a while, but I did this on my own." He goes on to explain how he kept the art Victoria painted for sentimental reasons, yet he doesn't want his new life to replicate his old life.

I grab both of his arms, and before giving them a light squeeze, with a sense of urgency, I say, "I need to see the most important room in your house." Enjoying the confused look on his face, I ask, "Where's your closet?"

He walks me into the master bedroom. Upon entry, I notice the bathroom to my left and then the main suite. The room is very elegant and simple, decorated with mahogany furniture, and the walls match the blue tone of his eyes. His nightstand has a stack of eclectic books, but the rest of the room is impeccably neat. There are two French doors leading outside to a terrace. My eyes zero in on the one place I am dying to see. His closet.

"May I go inside your closet?"

Puzzled, but graciously accommodating, he whips the closet doors open in one swooping pull. He moves to the side and watches me with a childlike fascination.

I dramatically deadpan. "Does James Bond know you stole his wardrobe?"

For a single man, his closet is insane. I'm awestruck by the organization, the amount of apparel, and its enormity in size. I run my hands over perfectly hung suits, formal wear, and crisp white shirts. They are lined up immaculately on each closet rail. His shoes and ties rest neatly on built-in mahogany shelves.

His closet puts most female closets to shame. "Do you even own jeans? Maybe a T-shirt?"

With his arms folded, pretending to look insulted, he proceeds to walk over to the built-in dresser. Each drawer holds neatly rolled T-shirts, socks, and underwear.

He taunts my observation, "I am very normal, and yes, I do wear these clothes. If you are done analyzing my sense of style, I would like to show you my favorite part of my house."

He leads me to the French doors and opens them up, exposing me to an entirely different version of New York City. An enormous terrace with a view of Central Park and parts of the city is revealed. Large potted plants and impressively shaped bushes line his terrace without obstructing the city view. This is his own private island.

A very comfortable living room is set up outside, complete with two oversized chairs, two fluffy stuffed sofas, and a Grand Stone firepit table in the center. On the other side of his terrace sits a large patio dining table for six covered with a large umbrella. Even though this area is outside the house, it is an extension of his cozy home.

I simply whisper, "Magnificent."

The breathtaking view combined with the illuminated city's pulsing sounds makes me wonder, "Do you spend a lot of time out here…alone?"

He senses the look on my face is one of pity. "Please don't think of me as a lonely person. I'm always working or going to functions for my mum. I'm constantly with people. My guilty pleasure is being alone."

"I see." I stand next to him by the terrace rail to take in the view. "Where would like you do my session today?"

He puts his hand on the lower part of my back to lead me out of the terrace. He guides me through another set of French doors and into the main gallery, where I notice the formal dining room has a table that seats eight. There is a crystal teardrop chandelier over the table, a large painting of the English countryside on the wall, and a bar with rows of sparkling glasses lining the shelves.

"Do you host dinner parties? This room looks untouched."

"No. I'm not one to throw parties. I use this room when my mum and Basil join me for dinner, which is rare. This is our family dinner table."

I'm in full-blown curiosity mode. "Who cooks for you?"

I have a housekeeper, Sophia. She does all my shopping and cleaning. If I need her to cook, she will do that as well. I never ask her to cook though."

"Did Victoria cook for you?"

"She was not domesticated, but she tried. When her depression started getting worse, we had a full-time housekeeper and cook."

He adds an astonishing revelation. "I can live off cereal if I wanted to."

I could live off Progresso soup and bagged salad. Who was I to judge?

We enter the dining room and walk through a door leading into his office. His desktop is empty and neat, with a Tiffany lamp resting at the corner. Located a few feet in front of his desk is a large leather seat ample enough to fit two people. This is a basic no-frills office—a minimalistic version of the rest of his house, with no photographs, just scenic art hung on the walls.

Ready to plop down on the leather seat, Alexander asks me to sit at the chair behind his desk. I oblige with his request.

He sits with easiness in the leather seat and instructs me, "Today, I want you to reverse roles with me. I want you to be my therapist."

I sit back behind his desk with a monumental smirk on my face. I feel power over him. I wonder if this is how he feels toward his patients. People lean on him to solve their problems.

I relish in this role-playing. I begin with a simple question. "Why do you think you need therapy?"

He doesn't hesitate in his response. "I've dealt with a lot of loss in my life. Lately, I've realized I am not living a full life. I've isolated myself to the point I can't reciprocate human connection."

"Why are you realizing this now?"

He can see my amusement, but reiterates, "I've always felt that being busy with work and various other activities would keep me satisfied. These past few days, though, something inside me has switched on. I haven't felt this way since I pursued my wife."

"What are you feeling?"

With a smug look, he responds, "Happiness."

My heart thumps rapidly, but I remain stoic and in character. "What do you miss most about your wife?"

"She was a passionate person with a unique outlook on life. I miss hearing her tell me about why everything has a deeper meaning. I miss seeing things from this exceptional point of view."

His voice becomes solemn. "I never imagined I'd find this unique idiosyncrasy ever again, until recently."

Trying to stay in character, and not reduced to sentimental gooey mush, I stay professional. "Please enlighten me. What happened recently?"

His twinkling eyes unleash a beguiling smile. "I met a beautiful woman who has this unusual knack for describing moments perfectly. Her smart mouth evokes emotional responses from me. I tend to be the one galvanizing thoughts from people, yet her views are remarkable to me."

He continues, "Meeting her was supposed to be typical. As the day progressed, it turned into something more. I didn't want the day to end, but more importantly, I couldn't wait to see her the next day."

His words crawl up my spine.

He continues, "I'm somewhat smitten by her."

My heart is rendered powerless with his undeniably sentimental disclosure. "Does she know how you feel?"

"I just found out she's leaving for Paris." He leans forward to ask, "How should I convince her to stay?"

"You should assume her leaving has nothing to do with you," I speak from the heart, "but her return has everything to do with you."

His pursed lips expanded upward into a brilliant smile. Relaxing himself into the chair, he asks, "So, how does this therapy work?"

I invoke our past first encounter. "During this session, you might interpret my flirtatious behavior as me being interested in you sexually. This might prompt you to have intimate urges toward me. Please set these emotions aside for the sake of propriety."

Carelessly shrugging my shoulders and waving my hand at myself, I say, "I am a professional, after all."

Alexander's handsome face glowingly responds, "What would you like me to do?"

I fold my arms on top of his desk, then instruct, "I need you to stand up."

He obediently complies.

Tapping into my dominate sexual side, I order, "Now, pull down your pants. Let me see your underwear." Insidiously smiling, I add, "Pretty please… with sugar on top."

"Are you the 'every man' type who wears boxer briefs? Or do you feel well-endowed enough to rock traditional snugly fit briefs? Maybe you're edgy and hip in colorful trunks? Or are you a hang-loose guy who sticks with boxers, even though they ride up your ass."

I egg him on with my cavalier demeanor. "In order for me to give a full assessment, I need you to take off your clothes. I don't have a lot of time with you, and it helps to get the basics out of the way."

Playfully engrossed in our role-playing fantasy, he asks, "What do you think I'm wearing?"

Embracing my porn-esque character acting, I evaluate him. "You look like the type who wears black briefs. Black representing seduction and power, and briefs to show off your package."

Alexander's tactile demeanor keeps his eyes locked on mine.

Standing up to slide his jacket off, he then neatly places it on the back of the chair. I prowl up to him, close enough to feel his breath. My overzealous heart is about to burst from adrenaline.

His arrogant confidence creates feverish shockwaves between my legs. Watching him unravel his tie, I take control. Weaving my hands on top of his working fingers, I patiently unwrap him like a gift. Taking my time in undoing each of his buttons, I sense him leering at me in wonderment. Feeling anxious like a virgin on prom night, I press my hands against his exposed skin. I edge my way down his shirt down, until it tumbles onto the floor. My eyes shift up to meet his gaze before I begin to undo his belt.

Unzipping his pants for entry, his invitingly seductive voice taunts, "What makes you think I'm wearing any underwear?"

"I'm hoping you're not."

Easing my hand inside his pants, I playfully stroke the length of his arousal. Tugging his pants down enough to sneak a peek, I grab his ass tightly, forcing his hardness against me.

I bat my eyes at my discovery. "It appears that you wear boxer briefs."

I peer down once more with a twisted smile. "And they're black. You're always powerful…and in control. Who knew our underwear was our introspective mood ring."

I organically respond to what is in front of me without a second thought. My fingers coast along his chest before shifting down to his abdominal area. My hands motion around each groove carved out by muscle. There is an erotic simpleness with just touching his unseen physical beauty.

His austere beryl-like eyes lock onto mine for direction. I calmly instruct him to sit back down. He submissively sits and then reclines backward. I remove the rest of his clothes in a controlled manner.

Kneeling before Alexander's arousal, I surrender myself completely. My lips purposely move up his inner thigh. Slipping his erection in my hand, I pace my stroke. His moaning pleases me. My tongue slowly licks from the bottom of his shaft to the tip, swirling my tongue around his cock. He watches me massage him farther into my mouth. He tosses his head back to catch his breath. Gripping my hair to control the pace, he gyrates deeper in my mouth. Sucking him wet and hard, I alternate my speed to ensure every inch is tasted and savored. Feeling him in my mouth makes me feel powerful.

His voice is commanding when he says, "My turn, Emme."

I seductively stand up, then walk over to the desk. Bending over, facing down, I grip the sides of the desk and invitingly spread my legs wide enough to fit him behind me. Creeping up against my backside, he brushes my hair onto my shoulder to unzip my dress. His kisses ravish the back of my neck, while stripping me down. My dress topples down to the floor. Revealing my Agent Provocateur black lace lingerie set, I keep my red LouLou platforms on and kick my dress to the side.

Spinning around to face Alexander, he props me on his desk. I automatically wrap my legs around him. My platform heels clank together when I lean backward. His fingers patiently trace the shape of my panties. His ever-so-slight touch makes me tremble, until his animalistic eagerness yanks them off for entry. My black lace push-up bra is the only barrier between us.

Reclining my body flat on his desk, he spreads my legs to taste the insides of my thighs.

Burying his face inside me, I gasp, "Oh my God… yes!"

His tongue playfully strokes in a circular motion. My panting enthusiasm makes me breathless. He enjoys tasting me by pushing his tongue deeper. His mouth humming and vibrating against me soaks me wet.

I plead with desperation, "I want you inside me."

Alexander brings me to the edge of the desk by pulling my legs forward. Teasing me by rubbing his cock against my slickness until he enters me, his pumping action escalates deeper and harder. My hands grip the desk to take it all in.

I want to erupt all over his desk. Alexander suddenly scoops me up and maneuvers us onto the leather seat. I situate myself on top with a wide-open straddle. Slowly I mount him inside me. Cradling his face, we are transfixed on each other. Feeling his way up to my bra, he eases the straps down, spilling my breasts into his mouth, softly suckling each nipple, gauging my sensitivity. He nibbles and sucks my pinkness hard. My elated body rides him rigorously, bouncing up and down. Finding my pleasure spot, Alexander placed his hands on my hips to manipulate the rhythm and intensity. A radiating sensation washes over me. I crumble to the energy discharging inside me. Unable to contain it anymore, I explode. My legs shake with every part of me tingling. I scream with delight.

Watching me orgasm pleases Alexander. "I want to be on top of you."

Alexander secures my legs around his waist, and then carries me into the formal dining room. He gently lays me down on the elegant mahogany table. I scoot myself back to the center and invitingly spread my legs. Climbing on top of me, he thrusts harder with each drive. He steadies his hands flat on the table to strengthen his stride. The table shakes vigorously from our grooving bodies. Drenched in sweat, drowning into each other, we need to resurface for air. His grinding vibration creates a ticklish heat at my core. We gasp with delight when our bodies pulsate. We are consumed by seconds of ecstasy before collapsing.

Our lifeless intertwined bodies resemble modern pieces of art. He holds me tightly in his arms. My fingers stroke his skin to the cadence of his chest. In a moment of Zen-like clarity, I'm apologetic, "I was wrong, Alexander."

Perplexed at my statement, he nods, "What were you wrong about?"

"Your penis isn't bland, and that was not unemotional."

He sweetly nuzzles his face next to mine and then kisses my forehead. I feel safe. We lie gazing up at the beautiful chandelier illuminating over us. The sparkling twinkle of giggling at something he said earlier. I mocked, "Apparently, you do use this dining room for entertaining."

In jest, he quickly responds, "I guess we should entertain here more often."

CHAPTER 20

I lather myself up in Alexander's shower gel to wash the sex off. The smell of lemon, mandarin, and bergamot steams with his scent. Alexander opens up the shower door to join me. I put my arms around his neck to greet him with a long, soapy kiss.

Looking down into my eyes with remorse, he says, "I need to apologize about your panties. I had no idea I was going to rip them off."

I throw my head back in laughter anticipating something more dramatic. "No need to apologize. Just make sure you toss them out before Sophia comes to clean."

Refreshed and clean, I exit the shower. Alexander reaches out for my arm to stop me. He flirtatiously asks, "Where are you going?"

"I know exactly what will happen if I stay."

I give him a meaningful kiss before stepping onto the cool tile. Drying off with a huge, fluffy white towel, I notice he laid out a pair of drawstring sweatpants and a T-shirt for me. Looking at my reflection in the mirror reduced me to giddiness. His clothes hang on me, but looking like a tomboy is better than being naked.

******

I venture off into the kitchen to find something to eat. My body feels drained after our sexual Olympics. After surveying his kitchen, I locate the pots and pans. I rummage through his refrigerator to find ingredients to make something tasty, yet practical. I pull out items to make a one-pot Parmesan Alfredo, and set them on the counter.

Silently approaching me from behind, Alexander slips his hands under my T-shirt, wrapping his arms around my waist to hold me close. Tenderhearted kisses pepper along the back of my neck. I turn around to find him disheveled and dressed in a T-shirt and sweats. Seeing him dressed casually startles me.

"Where's Alexander…and what have you done with him?" I fawn over his appearance. "I love seeing you like this, not suited up and professional. This is a Kodak moment."

His deconstructed relatable inception makes him look exceptionally sexually rugged.

"What are you doing in here?" he asks innocently.

"I'm making us something to eat. I feel like a contestant on an episode of *Naked and Afraid*…famished. I haven't burned off this many calories in a very long time."

"We still have all night. There are more calories to burn," he corrects me with a wink.

"While I'm cooking, please find my panties…and feel free to disinfect your dining room table too." My "mama bear" instincts emerged in full force. The idea of Sophia finding the house in a mess makes me feel like a bad guest.

I finish mixing the pasta just as Alexander enters the kitchen. He comes in holding up my ripped undies like the birth of Simba from *The Lion King*.

I peer at him in disbelief. "Please toss them out. No sex souvenirs."

He takes one last look at them before commenting, "You have great taste. Please let me replace them."

We look like a normal couple making dinner together. I've missed certain aspects of being in a relationship. Moments that appear simple and mundane can be extremely intimate. Observing Alexander in the kitchen makes me think this is unusually domesticated for him. He probably only came in here to warm up food or grab a snack, but not to cook.

I divide up the pasta into two bowls while Alexander pulls out a 2006 Marcassin Vineyard Chardonnay from his wine closet. Picking out wine is the extent of his culinary knowledge. He feels a bottle of Chardonnay will pair well with the pasta. I take his word for it. I'm the type who would drink wine out of a box.

Watching him uncork the wine, I ponder, "Is this strange for you?"

Handing me a glass of wine, he responds, "Strange?"

"Being domesticated…with me."

He just grins. "Oh, I thought you meant is it strange for me to have sex on my formal dining table."

Playfully slapping his arm, I point out, "No! I mean having me here in your home."

Alexander sweetly notes, "Actually, it feels nice. I'm very comfortable with you in my house, in my clothes, and on my table."

My contained happiness seeps out by turning the apples of my cheeks rouge.

Alexander suggests we eat outside on the terrace. He hands me Sherpa throw blankets to swaddle my legs while he kindles a fire. The dark sky peppered with stars is outshone by the city's lights. The fire set ablaze replaces the warmth from the missing sun. We huddle into each other under the cozy blankets to shield us from the autumn's chill. We remove our empty bowls of pasta from our laps and watch the sputtering ash and dancing flames crackle in our comfortable silence.

The delicious Chardonnay makes my toasty insides drowsy with sentimentality. "My life has changed immensely in just a few days. I've always been confined to my own expectations of how to be a daughter, wife, and mother. For once, there aren't any expectations. I can do whatever I want; it feels fantastic."

I turn toward him to ask the all-important cosmic question, "Why do we worry about fulfilling everyone's expectations, rather than what we want for ourselves?"

I philosophically bask in the moonlight. "I never expected to have mind-blowing sex twice this week. I've never been sexual with a woman or a younger man. I guess my bucket list is almost complete." I take a deep breath. "All that's left is Paris."

Alexander finds my bucket list amusing. "Having a yoni massage is not lesbian sex."

I confess, "I consider a woman fingering me to the point of orgasm as same-sex sex."

He counters, "I don't agree, because what you're stating isn't therapy, but a backroom illegal massage."

He changes the topic with an enticing offer. "Emme, your time here isn't over yet. Who says you'll only have sex twice?"

Placing my arm on the back of the sofa, I rest my head on my hand to completely focus on Alexander. I steer the conversation back to him, not sex. "What expectations do people have of you, especially your family?"

"My father was a successful businessman and heir to a large fortune. He seemed to have it all. A beautiful loving wife, doting kids, a large estate in the countryside, but making money meant more. He never reaped the rewards of his hard work by actually taking the time to enjoy it, which meant never being home. In a cruel twist of fate, if he would have just stayed home that Sunday, instead of going to his office in the city, he might be alive."

I try not to pry, but I had to ask, "What happened?"

"The day he died is foggy to me, but I remember how badly it was storming. The rain camouflaged everything white. Regardless of the tumultuous weather, my father chose to go to work, instead of spending a lazy Sunday with his family."

Taking a sip of his wine, he continues, "While driving home, he lost control of his car, skidding off the road, before striking a tree head-on. The impact killed him instantly. I was ten years old, and Basil was eight years old."

His voice was toneless and factual in describing his father. "My father was an emotionally distant workaholic. His preference of work over family left Basil and me with this empty void in our hearts."

"I am so sorry, Alexander. How was life with your stepfather?"

"I was fifteen years old when my mum remarried. My stepfather, Carlisle, was a good man. He didn't have any children of his own, but he loved us as if we were biologically his. Even though we were teenagers, his interest in our lives saved us.

"When he died of leukemia, it was a devastating loss for all of us, especially my mum. He was the love of her life." Hearing the fluctuation in his voice, I could sense the death of Carlisle hurt more than losing his father. The derivative of most of his pain was watching his mother suffer through loss again.

"I can't imagine dealing with so much pain at that age." Intuitively curious, I ask, "Why aren't you in England running the family business?"

"I have no interest in the family business. Basil is more suited for the cutthroat aspects of the corporate world. She successfully modernized the company, all her own."

He glaringly smirks, "My daddy issues are one thing, but don't even get me started on Basil's daddy issues. Running the business is her way of staying connected with him. He would be very proud of her."

I'm riveted by the hidden personal side of him. His life story explains why he always appears controlled and serious. The old adage about money not buying you happiness comes to mind. When we first met, he corrected me in assuming he had a perfect life. After hearing him speak, I understand why.

Delving deeper inside his closet of emotional skeletons, I ask, "Why haven't you dated anyone since Victoria died?"

"My mum and Basil have sadly attempted to set me up on dates. They always ended up being more sexual than emotional."

My mouth was agape knowing these were family acquaintances. "Do you still run into these women?"

"There are sexually driven women in all social circles. Yes, I see them on occasion. We are always cordial, but they found what they needed from other men. They found stability and marriage."

In therapist fashion, he examines my thoughts, "Do you think I'm some sort of heel?"

"I think sex seems to come to you so easily." I shrug. "Don't look a gift horse in the mouth, right? I am not going to judge you for living your life."

Trying not to come off as insecure, I asked with confidence, "Would you consider the sex we had similar to one of your one-night stands?" Giggling like a schoolgirl, I add, "For me, it was fuckdiculous!"

Touching my cheek, his eyes are hypnotic. "No. I wasn't fucking you. Everything with you is emotional. This wasn't a one-night stand or anything casual. Giving you pleasure was import to me, and I'd like to do it again."

I place my hand on his face. My fingers trickle down his neck in spider-like precision. "Thank you for opening up to me."

I look away to watch my fingers trace his body, before skittishly asking, "Have you ever opened up to any of these women you've been with?"

"Women in those casual situations are there for sex. There is no emotional connection. Stop comparing yourself to basic encounters." He sweetly admits, "Nothing about you is platonic to me."

He pulls me in for a stimulating love-induced kiss, insatiably craving his taste on my mouth and all over my body. I shudder. *Why does he have this power over me?*

Sensing something is amiss, Alexander pulls away from my lips, "What's wrong?"

My question startles him. "Was our first kiss more powerful than our first sexual encounter?"

I further explain, "I was watching *ABC News*, and they did a story about how people find kissing more intimate than sex. Most people remember the most details of their first romantic kiss over having sex with that person. In your professional opinion, is that true?"

"Emme, you have a knack for saying the most bizarre things at the most unusual times. I truly enjoy this about you." He begins chuckling, before he answers my question. "From a clinical standpoint, I have to agree with that opinion. Usually, the first kiss is the first impression of intimacy."

He starts to rub his thumb on my lip. "I can remember our first kiss vividly."

He devilishly recalls, "I remember you tasted like cinnamon, smelling hints of vanilla on your neck, and I felt helplessly aroused. It wasn't just a sexual response. I just wanted you."

I respond to his sentiment with a kiss. Deep and breathless, I break away to whisper against his lips, "So my beige bra and panties didn't do it for you? It was our witty banter?"

"Yes, your wit seems to keep me on my toes. For example, we were having a lovely kiss, until you had to stop to ask questions." He laughs, "I love this about you."

I feel flustered by his honesty. I wonder, "With all these women you've been with, what impression did their kisses leave on you?"

I sense his defenses come up. My inquiries make him look like some whoring lady-killer, which isn't my intention.

"No, I don't remember kissing any of those women. They didn't leave an emotional impression on me. I can probably tell you more about their sexual fetish, but nothing else. They were all very smart, attractive women who wanted nothing more than sex."

Alexander appeases my insecurities by explaining the difference to me. "When you are looking for casual sex, kissing can be meaningless. It is a technique to sexually arouse someone. Your brain isn't telling you it's love, but more of an enticing mechanism."

His body turns to align with mine. His eyes twinkle with sincerity. "A long, passionate first kiss is different from any other kiss. It can render you weak and selfish. A meaningful kiss is an emotional investment in that person."

I shiver, watching his mouth move. "How does it make you selfish?"

"You don't want to share that person with anyone else. It disarms you into wanting more."

I feel shook hearing him add, "This is how I feel about our first kiss."

I respond with tenderness, "I'm not afraid to admit that I feel lost in you. Sometimes this feels unreal. I've unknowingly given you the power to break my heart."

"If I broke your heart, it would be unintentional. You should just live for the moment and not question everything. Every day is a clean slate, a new discovery, so let's see what happens."

"I'm sorry. I seemed to have ruined a perfectly romantic moment…with questions. I assumed emotions and desires are without a hidden agenda. They aren't mechanisms for my brain to trick my body into having sex. I'm so naïve."

Suddenly befuddled by my inadequate sex life, I add, "I've lived a good life, but it seems like I didn't live a full one. Why is that?"

"Sexual experience doesn't equate to one's quality of life." He quickly points out, "No one expects the life that is given to them. You just need to appreciate what you have, build on it, or change what you don't like."

His statement compels me to sit up straight, provoking my mind to wander off to left field. "When my husband left me, I read a lot of self-help books and contemplated online dating. *Contemplated* is the key word. Modern dating and relationships as a middle-aged woman is depressing. The last time I dated, Blockbuster video and dial-up internet was fashionable. Holy hell…I'm as antiquated as a VHS tape."

Referencing the past made me feel like a grandparent contrasting their life with youth. I audaciously laugh out loud. Pulling myself together, I conclude, "Nothing is simple anymore. Everything seems staged and technically driven. It's like being tethered to a device to meet another human being."

"Maybe you think it's weird, but it works for a lot of people. It's hard to meet people under normal circumstances. Look at us. We didn't meet under normal circumstances. We all need a little help."

I steer our conversation to deciphering modern romance. "I've read a few stories about people wanting to dress up like furry animals to fuck, electrifying butt plugs and vaginal inserts, and people who find trees sexually arousing. In your line of work, have you dealt with this?"

My hands flail in dramatic fashion emphasizing my curious nature. "Did you know some men ask women to shave their balls? During my marriage, I was never asked to shave Dylan's balls or even his asshole. When did sex become complicated?"

I conspicuously look at Alexander. "Are you into kinky stuff? I'm all for exploring my sexuality, but shaving you, fucking trees, or dressing up as a plush toy? I'm just not that girl."

Alexander held my hand up to his mouth to kiss it. He gently gives my hand a squeeze before placing it against his heart. "I promise never to make you shave my ass or balls."

He tries to contain his laughter, but it is uncontrollable. This is the first time I've seen him laugh hysterically. He usually smiles, winks, or gives a chuckle, but this is something truly hilarious to him. I hit him with a pillow on the sofa.

He regroups to become clinical. "These are very normal people living responsible lives, but they have a fetish. It's actually natural to explore your sexuality and find a partner willing to complement those needs. It makes their sex life fulfilled."

I suddenly look like I am filibustering Congress to change dating standards for divorced older women. "I know you're a sexual encyclopedia, but this stuff is so new to me. Dating and then having to meet some modern expectation of sex at my age is not only cumbersome, but scary. I have no idea what men want now. I'm just now figuring out what I want."

Alexander explores my statement. "What do you want, Emme? Do you have a fantasy you want to live out?"

"The sex we just had was a fantasy. It was something natural and erotic at the same time. Maybe my fetish is spontaneous combustion without props or scenarios."

Alexander pushes the pillow off to the side to pull me onto his lap. I straddle him and look at him for reassurance. I feel shy in regard to admitting my inexperience at my age. Lacing my fingers with his, he brings both my hands against his chest to pull me forward. He questions my previous statement with sensuality, "Why are you so worried about sexually connecting with other men? When you are with me?"

I want to avoid eye contact, but those deep blue eyes are transfixed on me. I confess, "None of this seems real. This whole week has to be some fluke. The one time I venture outside myself, I find you. You are the epitome of sex. For someone like you to be interested in someone like me seems cosmically unfathomable."

Pausing enough to remind him, I say, "I hope you didn't forget that I'm leaving for Paris. Visiting Paris is at the top of my bucket list. I want to do something for just for me."

He squeezes my hands to show he is serious. "I am beyond fascinated with you. I don't want this to end. It's time for you to try something new; stay with me."

I reply, "Leaving is not as easy as you think. You've opened my heart and mind up on so many levels. I have to wonder. What else have I missed out on? I don't want to ask myself that question anymore." Without sounding authoritative, I affirm, "I am going to Paris."

I cradle his face in my hands, in hopes he will understand. "I am in no way rejecting you. For once, I'm choosing…me."

I spontaneously ask, "Why don't you come with me?"

"Why not let me show you the world here?" he counters.

"Alexander, this really isn't easy for me at all. I came here to release my past. I found you. We both have damaged hearts, not to mention, loads of other issues. These feelings I have for you are irrational. We literally just met, but I can see myself falling madly in love with you. I need for you to understand that my needs go beyond sex. My happiness shouldn't be defined by having a partner."

He brushes my hair out of my face and twists it onto his finger. "I think you are avoiding the obvious. You're afraid if you choose to stay, I'll eventually be bored, or leave you. The sense of abandonment your ex-husband gifted you, my wife did that to me as well."

My eyes are heavy with shame. "Everything you said is true. Falling in love is easy. The actual act of love is difficult. Loving someone unconditionally means you are choosing to love them every day, forever."

Reeling me in close, he whispers in my ear, "*Que será será.*"

Whatever will be, will be. We put our foreheads together for a moment of reflection. He slides his hands inside my shirt and soothes my lower back. Massaging his fingers into my skin—I know what he is doing. He is physically changing the subject.

Gliding his fingers around my waist, he creates circular motions with his fingertips unleashing chills throughout my body. My shyness subsides by instinctively reacting. I watch his fingers explore me. He knowingly turns me on with a sleight of hand up and around my breasts, shifting around my nipples, with temperate pinching. Forcefully pulling my shirt up, he sucks my nipples with a hungry intensity.

Breaking his mouth away, he gazes at me with a sexy dreamlike stare. His blue eyes unravel me. Tilting my face to lean into his mouth, we greedily devour each other. He grips my thighs and presses me down. I moan feeling his hardness between my legs. Rubbing against each other in unison, I grind my waist rousingly down, his hard cock soaking me warm. I meet his mouth with intensity while trying to untie my bottoms.

I exhale in his ear, "I want you inside me…now."

I want to wildly ride him under the sparkling night sky.

In the midst of our arousing foreplay, we hear a female voice clear her throat, "Ahem."

We immediately freeze at the sound of a female voice. Ceasing our foreplay, we look up in a paralyzed state of shock. Basil is standing behind us with her hands over her eyes. "Let me know when you both are finished."

CHAPTER 21

Flustered with embarrassment knowing Basil was watching us, I dismount off my British stallion. Alexander will not let me climb off. He holds my hips stationary. I can't move. I silently mouth to him, "Let me go."

He shakes his head and mutters, "No."

He unleashes a burst of laughter to hide his red face. Absorbing his laughter against me, I realize he doesn't want his sister to see his protruding erection. Immediately covering displayed boobs, I maintain my straddle out of consideration for his dignity.

Basil removes her hands from her eyes when she hears us laughing. "Sorry for the interruption. I see you have your hands full, Alex."

Alexander snaps, "What are you doing here?"

"You were supposed to pick me up for Mum's dinner party. When you didn't show up, I thought I was supposed to meet you here."

He places both hands over his face remembering his plans. "I am so sorry. I totally forgot. I was having such a great day."

Even though I am awkwardly mounted on his lap, Alexander doesn't forget his manners. "I don't know if you recall meeting Emerson at the auction. Emerson, this is Basil, my darling little sister."

She raises her eyebrows and, with a snappish smirk, says, "I see my brother is giving you the full auction package."

Feeling his blood leaving his penis and heading back to his brain, I crawl off Alexander to sit next to him. I try making myself presentable, but there is no hiding the obvious. "It's nice to see you again."

Basil just giggles and plops down on the sofa across from us. "Don't worry, sweetheart."

Her next comment catches me off guard. "I've rarely seen him look this relaxed. All is forgiven. I'm just pissed I'll be sitting with these manky wankers all by myself."

"For what it's worth, you look beautiful." I admire her beautiful Armani tulle sleeveless black halter gown. She looks stunning with her hair pinned up, accented with pearl drop earrings.

Alexander finally stands up to greet his sister. He walks over to give her a hug, then kisses her cheek. "I honestly forgot about tonight. I'm sorry."

He returns to sit next to me before concluding, "But I'm not sorry for being here with Emerson. Tell Mum I'll call her later...groveling for her forgiveness."

I look at Alexander. "I can leave if you need to go. You still have time to change and make the dinner."

Basil is, by far, the unfiltered version of Alexander. In her superior British accent, she tells me, "If I were Alex, I'd stay put. Even though we both promised to never leave each other alone with these old vampires, I don't want to feel the wrath of taking him away from this. For once, Alexander looks...happy."

Alexander jokingly acquiesces, "My sister is everyone's favorite for a reason."

I stand up to excuse myself. I want to give them time to talk privately. I need to make light of the situation before heading inside. "Basil, regardless of our uncompromising position, it is lovely to see you again."

Basil slyly replies, "Likewise, sweetheart, I'm sure we'll be seeing more of each other, but without the naked tits." She giggles. "Cherrio."

I enter the house through the French doors leading into his bedroom. I can hear them talking and snickering on the balcony. Entering into his master suite, I head toward the bathroom. I crack open a new toothbrush, then wander around his room brushing my teeth. His room is stylish but empty. There are no personal photographs on display just a large painting above his headboard. The painting is of a castle with a beautiful garden of yellow, purple, and red flower bed maze with manicured trees. I zero in on the image of a little boy sitting by a fountain looking at the castle. I can't make out his face. He looks so diminutive, but noticeable.

Trying not to drip toothpaste out of my mouth, I sit on his bed to scan over the stack of books on his nightstand. I turn the book spines toward me to read the titles. He has an eclectic mix of reading material. He has books on psychology and sex, relationships, an unusual book about sexual fetish, and then there is Neil Gaiman's novel *Norse Mythology*. I wonder if those sexual books are enjoyable reads before sleeping. He is such a mystery to me. Every new fact discovered is a small gift of insight.

After cleaning up, I meticulously survey his bedroom. I don't feel comfortable crawling into Alexander's bed. It is like inviting myself into his personal space. I grab two pillows off his bed and head toward the living room. There is a large enough space on the floor in front of the fireplace for me to set up a makeshift camp. Situating my blanket and pillows on the floor, I grab pillows off the sofa to complete my soft pallet.

I kindle a fire to create warmth and light in the room. I examine all the framed photos on the fireplace mantel. It is heartwarming to see him as a child spanning physical and emotional changes into manhood. Most children are silly and smiling in photos, but not Alexander. He is a stoic, proper gentleman posing with his dad. In the photos of his mother and sister, he is debonair and suave. The photographs with him and Victoria seem natural and playful. They were a young couple in love.

I settle down on my homemade bed laid out on the floor. Fluffing out the pillows before resting my head down, I am swallowed up by its comfort. Alexander's pillows release a drug-like aromatherapy for my senses. His intoxicating scent soothes my heart. With the crackling sound of the fire, a flickering warmth puts me to sleep.

My siesta subsides with the touch of Alexander's hands sliding under my shirt, encompassing my belly. I don't open my eyes. A natural grin of delight emerges hearing his voice, "Are you falling asleep on me?"

I murmur, "Is this where you tell me our session has ended? Are you forcing me to do the walk of shame back to my hotel?"

He moves my hair away from my neck to trace my skin with kisses. He suckles my ear lobe before answering, "On the contrary, darling, I would prefer you in my bed versus the floor. We've kind of been everywhere tonight." I laugh when he adds, "I'm actually getting to know my house better."

My body wakes up feeling his closeness forcing me to prop myself up. He follows my sight to a painting hanging over the fireplace. It is of a young woman sitting in a grassy field. The field is filled with vivid yellow flowers. The bright yellow flowers speckled all over the painting complement the dark green grass. In the middle of the field, a pretty young lady sits wearing a red dress. Her dress is off the shoulders and fluffed out like a Renaissance ball gown. Her brown hair is pinned up with little spirals dangling around her face. She has crimson red lips visible against her ivory skin and blushed cheeks.

"Who is that girl in the painting?" I ask.

Alexander perks his head up to answer me, "That's my mum when she was younger. Victoria found this old photo of her. She enjoyed how innocent and youthful my mum looked and painted this gift for me."

"Victoria was immensely talented. Her attention to the details and the color choices are mesmerizing." I roll over on my back to see him looking down at me. "Besides the obvious beauty in the work, why does it captivate you?"

He looks up to study the painting before his gives me his interpretation. "It relaxes me to see home, to see my mum so young, and it represents a joyful time for Victoria. It was an exquisite moment of her being brilliant and happy."

I stay on my back but turn my head to examine it again. "If I didn't know it was your mom, I would have thought she was some young temptress. You once told me the color red is alluring to men. She looks like she's up to something."

He looks up again to absorb my observation and snickers. "I never viewed my mum as a Lolita before."

"Since we're on the topic of paintings, who is the little boy in the painting in your bedroom?" I wonder.

"That would be my dad as a child visiting the Hampton Court Palace's gardens. Victoria found an old black-and-white photo of his visit there. She brought it to life with color and detail."

I point out, "You seem to have your parent's youth embodied in art on your walls. Both paintings gorgeously reveal a special moment in time. I can understand why they are nostalgic to you."

Alexander soothingly kisses up and down my neck, teasing my mouth with flickers of his tongue on my lips. I grip my hand behind his head, consuming his kiss deeper into my mouth. I aggressively roll myself on top of him. I support myself by pinning his hands down. My hair dangles on his face.

He brushes my hair away, then surprises me with an unwavering proposition. "I want to show you how to pleasure yourself."

"Why would I want to pleasure myself if I am with you?" I reply.

"You are leaving. I want you to know how to pleasure yourself for my own selfish reasons. How will you ever know what you want sexually if you don't explore yourself?"

I wonder how his block of instruction will subjugate me. I've never truly explored intimacy with myself. He sits up against the sofa positioning my straddle on his lap. Pulling off my T-shirt over my head, my exposed breasts are alert. I await his instruction. He responds by pulling off his T-shirt, leaving us skin on skin. My fingers wander around aimlessly, trying to memorize his physical beauty.

Wide-eyed with innocence, I ask, "What do you want me to do?"

"I want you to lie back."

I nervously recline myself. My legs are open with him as the centerpiece. Resting back on his knees, he senses my tension while tugging off my sweatpants and tossing them to the side. He doesn't remove his pants. He kneels between my open knees to spread my legs wider.

"Now give me your hand."

He places my hand on my stomach. Placing his hand on top of mine, he starts to guide my movement.

"Just relax. You know what excites you physically. Find a spot you enjoy, then I'll let your hand go. You set the intensity. I want to watch you pleasure yourself."

My apprehension subsides with his tongue arousing my breasts. He fiercely suckles my nipples into swelling arousal. His kisses travel down to my stomach. Opening up my legs wider, he pauses long enough for us to lock eyes. Rubbing his mouth around my inner thigh, he injects his tongue inside me. He holds my thighs apart to push his tongue deeper. I can feel my wetness all around his mouth. I can't stop moaning. Arching my back, pushing his head down further inside, his tongue flickers harder.

He pulls back before I explode. "I can't let you come yet."

He suspends himself over me. My face is flushed from no release. He smolders sex as he leers down at me. "Give me your hand again."

I follow his movement around my breasts. At first, I feel like I am giving myself a breast exam. I start snickering.

Like clockwork, Alexander finds a way to physically change the subject. He subdues me with a deep romantic kiss. I can taste myself on his tongue. I wrap my legs around his waist, rubbing up and down against each other.

My giggling subsides once our bodies rhythmically move against each other. I beg him to take off his pants.

He quickly responds, "No."

He denies my hand from going inside his pants. "I need you to sit up, turn around, and lean back on my chest."

He props himself back against the sofa and pillows. I sit up, putting my back against his warm chest. Alexander seizes control of both of my hands now. It is time to map out my body. He smooths my hands over my breasts until my right hand reaches my pubic area. He instructs me to open my legs wider, directing my index and middle fingers. Stroking them inside me.

As much as I want to enjoy it, I prefer staying outside myself. I form a V-shape with my fingers to fondle my erogenous zone. My blood flows as my hands boldly flicker in every direction. Alexander lets go of my hands. I willingly play with myself until I'm drenched. Rearing my head against his chest, my raging body work my fingers faster.

Alexander's arousal from watching me masturbate makes him eager to participate. "I want you to turn around, and climb on top of me."

I deny his request. "No."

I sprawl my hands out on the sofa in front of me. Gripping the sofa, with my ass up, I glance back over my shoulder. I playfully ask, "What are you waiting for?"

Enthusiastically driving into me, he takes me from behind. Pulling my thighs apart, he slides his cock up and down my sex, then slides inside. His forcefulness makes me gasp. Smacking rapidly back and forth with unrelenting force, he wraps my hair in his fist and grips it back to hold me steady. He pulls out long enough to teasing my anal area. I clench up.

"Don't worry, darling. I will behave." His hips fiercely crash into me with robust exertion. He groans, "Do you like this?"

My body constricts with each thrust pushing inside me. "Yes…harder."

I cry louder with gratification. He grips my hips to rhythmically pump every inch vigorously deeper. Clutching the sofa to absorb each thrust. I edge on orgasm. My fingers move down to stimulate my clit to heighten my climax, flicking myself until my hand is drenched.

Feeling waves of pleasure reverberate all the way down to my toes, I breathlessly yell, "I'm going to come."

Losing myself to internally exploding with energetic release, I feel him trembling. We shudder inside each other until we can't move.

I collapse backward onto his chest. Breathlessly, we lie on each other. He affectionately wraps his arms around my stomach, squeezing me closer.

Kissing my neck, he inquires, "I felt you tense up. Were you afraid I was going for anal?"

I sway my head back and forth, laughing. "I'm not ready for anal. I know some people enjoy it, but I can't even eat shrimp if it hasn't been deveined."

******

Alexander enters the room holding a tray of food. I smile seeing the domesticated side of him. The impromptu buffet is composed of chocolate chip cookies, black-and-white cookies, and slices of German chocolate cake, coconut cake, and carrot cake.

Each item looks sinfully tempting. Alexander explains how Sophia likes to pick up bread and desserts from the bakery Amy's Bread on Ninth Avenue.

"Do you have a sweet tooth? This is a huge assortment for just one guy."

He just shrugs. "I believe you can have anything you want in moderation."

With a smirk, I respond, "Really? There is nothing moderate about these past two days. I think you broke my vagina."

He leans over to kiss my cheek before handing me a fork and napkin. "I'm sorry to hear that. I was hoping for a go at it again later."

I roll my eyes at him as I taste the carrot cake. It is so moist, and the flavors ignite my taste buds. This cake is perfection. My sexually exhausted body is in heaven consuming sweet sustenance.

I watch him take a bite of the German chocolate cake. Then I ask, "Is this typically what your sex life is like?"

"No, this is not what my sex life is like. This is what I'm like with you."

My inner teenage girl melts at any flirtation from him. The youthful spark dimmed down from middle age was burning brightly. Guarding myself is becoming impossible. Emotional preservation tries to kick in, but not around him.

I start thinking of Basil alone at their mom's dinner party. "Is Basil seeing someone or is she a workaholic too?"

He breaks a black-and-white cookie in half and hands one part to me. "Basil is a very strong woman with an intimidating personality. She's had the worst luck in love. She seems to attract those with avoidant personalities, or they like to cheat. She needs to find a man who is secure in himself. She would very much love to have a family, but things just haven't worked out for her. And before you ask, yes, she is a workaholic just like me."

Awestruck by his description, I gush, "Women like me are amazed by women like her. She's beautiful, successful, and smart. How can someone like her be alone? Maybe she should meet Nolan."

He raises an eyebrow at hearing that name. "Are you being cheeky?"

"What's wrong with Nolan? He is very sweet, interesting, and handsome." I egg him on for a reaction. "I would have fucked him."

"You are definitely being cheeky."

His reaction interests me. I'm not trying to make him jealous, but I wonder if he is. "He's good friends with Ashley, and I trust her judgment. Is this some masculine territorial bullshit?"

I bring up last night to test the waters. "If Ashley didn't have the winning bid, we would have kept playing 'Catch and Release.' And I would have left with Nolan. In fact, I would've been camping out in Nolan's hotel room last night, as well as tonight."

He is pretty sure of himself. "There was no way you were leaving with him."

In true bitchy fashion, I pompously respond, "Really? I'm pretty sure I walked away from you on the dance floor."

He responds with an affirmative, "When we were on the dance floor, and you walked away, I had no intention of letting you go." He pauses. "You belong with me, not him."

His honesty leaves me defenseless. Switching conversational gears back to his private life puts me back in my element.

I look up at the painting of his mother. "Why do you have paintings of your parents embodied in their youth? I don't see any pictures of them together."

"I can't recall ever seeing them together. I wouldn't find it natural. These images capture their simplicity."

Before I take a bite of the German chocolate cake, I stop to ask, "Do you still grieve for your father and Victoria?"

He responds, "It's hard for me to miss my dad. I really didn't know him. Psychologically, you want two parents. Most children are affected greatly by parental loss, no matter the age."

His eyes shift from the painting of his mom to the photos on the shelves. "As for Victoria, the pain will always be there, but it's not like a ball and chain being dragged around. She was my first true love."

Eyeballing me sideways, he smirks, "And if you're wondering if I think about Victoria, while I'm with you...I don't. She creeps up on me, but never while I'm with you."

His words are doused with sadness, but not regret. The roaring flames contained in the fireplace are hypnotizing.

My eyes transfix on the dancing persimmon hues. It made me think of the song "Hurt" by Nine Inch Nails.

I convey my random thoughts to Alexander. "There is beauty in everything. From how people live and suffer to the cruelty of humanity. In the end, we are all equal—dust blowing away. We all have a way of hurting each other regardless of our intentions."

Caught off guard by my words. Alexander looks at me deeply. "Do you foresee us hurting each other?"

"We are in the infancy stages of romance. This is new and exciting. There's no way we can ever guarantee each other pure bliss. Life is full of uncertainties. I don't think either of us would intentionally cause each other pain, but love and pain go hand in hand."

Alexander places his hands over my hands. "Even though it's only been a few days, I will really miss just sitting and talking with you, even when you're mental."

Placing his fingertips on my chin to lead me into his lips, he stops. With convincing eyes, he becomes serious. "When you leave, the pain will be unintentional, but I will feel it."

He leans over the tray of delightful edibles to kiss me. An unfathomable feeling of love enters my soul. This fantastical kiss is emotionally unequivocal to anything I've felt in a while. My internal butterflies tickle my very existence to happiness. This is my Molly Ringwald moment. In the movie *Sixteen Candles*, when Jake leans over Samantha's birthday cake to kiss her, it is an uncomplicated romantic moment. I had no expectations of feeling this way in my forties. All my doubts are lifted by a madly deep, stupendous kiss.

CHAPTER 22

We end up crawling into Alexander's bed to sleep. The sound of a vacuum cleaner humming in the hallway shakes me to wake up. Sophia is here. The mom side of me shudders thinking of the mess I made. I left dishes in the sink, a camp site wreaking of sex, and not to mention the dirty plates left on the tray. I feel like a rude house-guest. I don't want Sophia's first impression of me to be a wanton woman.

Sleeping with Alexander was the opposite of my marriage. He liked to cuddle or touch me in some way as we slept. His constant need for touch reassured him I was there. I'm used to sprawling out alone in my bed, but this is surprisingly endearing. Trying to sneak out of bed like a ninja, I roll on to my back to see him soundly sleeping. I ingest his beauty in the radiant light, before testing the depth of his sleep. My fingertips glide like a feather on his arm, which causes him to react. He pulls his arm around my waist tighter. Without disrupting his peaceful stillness, I slither out of the bed with stealth precision. Once I hit the floor, a loud thump echoes in the room. Trying to conceal my laughter, I bite my lip and cup my hands over my mouth. Tiptoeing to the bathroom like a thief, I quietly shut the door to survey myself in unforgiving lights. My reflection confirms how I feel, like just I competed in a sexual triathlon.

In the early stages of dating, there is a certain level of deceit and illusion of being natural. The true, stripped-down version will eventually appear as the relationship evolves. I frantically brush my teeth and pull myself together before going back to bed. It dawns on me that my bra and dress are lying on his office floor.

I panic knowing Sophia will find our clothes dispersed everywhere. I sprint out of the bathroom wrapped in a towel. Alexander is not in bed. He laid my bra and dress across the footboard, next to a folded fresh T-shirt and a pair of sweatpants. Once I start dressing, the reality of my missing panties hit me. I can hear Sophia's robust laugh coming from the kitchen.

"Oh shit! I have no underwear!"

Even with a bra and Alexander's baggy clothes on me, I feel exposed. I enter the kitchen to see a casually dressed Alexander with bedhead. He is leaning against the kitchen counter and enjoying a cup of coffee. Sophia is putting away dishes. They both stop everything and look at me with a different expression. Alexander's smile is happiness, and Sophia's is one of curious delight.

I have stage fright, but I muster up the courage to walk in, and be awkwardly polite, "I'm Emerson. It's so nice to meet you."

"*Bom dia!* Emerson"

Her hazel eyes drenched in golden caramel ecstatically glisten. Reeling me into her motherly affection, she throws her arms around me for a colossal bear hug. Her unrelenting affectionate welcome means she's considered family.

In her flavorful voice, rich in texture, she welcomes me. "It is so wonderful to meet you too. Would you like some coffee? Breakfast?"

I shyly respond, "Coffee would be fantastic." Then I add, "I'm so sorry about the mess we left you. I had no intention of leaving you dishes and food to clean up."

Sophia just waves her hands at me as if I am being ridiculous. She startles me by asking, "Did you both get to use the dining room?"

My face turns crimson thinking we left something obscene behind. I blurt out, "Why?"

"You left your shoes in there, Miss Emerson. If you were wondering where your shoes were, I left them by the dining room entrance."

Alexander's crooked grin unleashes a hearty chuckle. "Yes, Sophia, I entertained her in the dining room. Emme fully enjoyed using the formal table. She's never experienced anything like it. She found the table to be sturdy and large enough to lay on."

Alexander wants to play a game of sexual innuendo. I quickly return a verbal volley. "Alexander is exaggerating. He prefers to eat on top of his office desk."

I begin tapping my finger on my lips, pretending to recollect the night. "The flavors and complexity of our meal were pretty intense. At one point, he whisked me away to the dining room table, so we could pound out the last course."

Alexander's immediate laughter causes him to spit up his coffee. Sophia knows we aren't talking about food. She walks over to hand him a kitchen towel. He cleans the dribbled coffee on his mouth and around his mug. She reverts to her Portuguese native tongue, "*Eu não quero saber de nada.*"

Her disapproving Brazilian motherly glance toward Alexander was deafening. She immediately turns her smile back on, as she hands me a cup of coffee. She radiates warmth in my direction but reprimands Alexander with a chilling glance over her shoulder.

Expressively shaking her head in disbelief, she repeats her prior statement, "I don't want to know anything."

Once she turns away from us to resume putting pots and pans away, Alexander and I lock eyes and telepathically share our embarrassment. I covertly mouth the phrase, "You bastard." He just winks at me and continuously giggles while cleaning up his coffee mess.

Alexander stalks up to me in a delightfully sunny disposition. He leans in to kiss my cheek, then softly speaks into my ear, "Good morning, darling. Did you sleep well?"

Trying not to let Sophia eavesdrop, I whisper, "Out of all the places in your house, I enjoyed your bed the most."

He affectionately pulls in for a morning squeeze, then nuzzles his face with mine. Kissing my forehead, he releases me, then proceeds walking backward down the hallway. "I'll be right back. I have to check my work email and phone calls."

Sophia welcomes me into the kitchen with a hot cup of coffee. Her natural instinct is to feed me. I grab a warm croissant and enjoy its buttery flakiness. She sets a bowl of beautiful red strawberries next to my coffee. Our introductory chitchat is of the pleasant variety, but I want to know what Alexander is like as her boss.

"When I first started working here, Mr. Jameson was not social. He was always working, reading, or outside on the balcony. He only interaction was with me, his family, and patients."

She explains, "Mr. Jameson has always treated me like family, not his housekeeper."

She grips my arm for a slight squeeze, before revealing, "Dr. Jameson has never introduced me to any female friends. Every morning, he is always here…alone."

The golden sparkle in her eyes flicker with a mother's approving grin. "You are the first person he's ever brought home, Miss Emerson. I guess you must be important to him."

Sophia continues her observation, "He reminds me of sunlight now, bright and happy."

My heart feels like an 808 drum thumping, turning into confetti, and bursting out of my chest.

I thank her for the pep talk accompanying breakfast. Once again, I express my sincerest apologies about the mess we left. Walking down the hallway to Alexander's room, I think of Sophia. She has no idea what we did the night before, and I hope to God she wore gloves while cleaning. Spotting my red LouLou dancing sandals in front of the formal dining room entrance, I scoop them up with haste.

I enter Alexander's bedroom quietly. Shutting the door behind me, I hear hangers clanking and shifting around in the closet. Standing in his closet entryway, I perversely watch Alexander inside the closet, dripping wet, with a towel wrapped around his waist. My lips twitch with a hungry grin observing him in front of a row of pressed shirts, shifting each rejected selection to the left.

In true cocky fashion, I clear my throat to announce myself. "Let's see, Mr. Bond. Should we go with the first white shirt? How about the fifth white shirt to accompany your array of Tom Ford suits? I'm sure there's a distinct difference to the untrained eye. Let's be bold and go with white shirt number three."

He doesn't turn around immediately. Instead, he holds up white shirt number three and mockingly observes, "I don't know if this shade of white brings out my eyes."

He shrugs and scoffs at me. "It's a good choice…for a beginner."

He hangs the white shirt back on the bar and turns toward my direction. Devilishly grinning, with his body gleams with dampness. His delicious pheromones entice me from his freshly scrubbed skin. Just looking at him makes me thirsty. Even with space between us, electricity draws us in.

In lascivious fashion, he requests, "Why don't you come over here and help me pick out a tie?"

Tilting my head against the door frame while innocently batting my eyelashes, I jokingly respond, "Alexander, I'm staying right here. Where it's safe."

I slap my hand on the door frame indicating it is some imaginary time-out from sex box. This is my illusion of safety from his erotic space–time continuum. His sexual relativity pulls me up/down, left/right, forward/backward, and of course, wherever he feels like penetrating me.

Alexander angles toward the doorway. Movement doesn't budge his tightly wrapped towel. Stopping right in front of me, he teases, "Who says you're safe by the door?"

No barrier, real or imaginary, could shield our magnetic pull toward one another. Once we let sex out of the cage, it has been this uncontrollable entity between us.

He propositions me, "Forget the suit. Why don't we stay in today? We can both wear nothing."

Touching the drying beads of water on his chest, I counter, "That is a tempting offer. But I already have plans. I'm meeting Ashley for lunch. Plus, I would love to change into some clean clothes…and put on some panties."

Knowing I'm commando perks up Alexander's libido. Working his hands around my waist and into my sweatpants, he cradles my ass in his palms. "We shouldn't waste this fortunate opportunity."

Pinning my body up against the door frame, his fingers skim down to my waist. Untying my drawstring, my oversized sweatpants drop instantly. I forcefully kick them off and away from my ankles. Pulling me toward him, he lifts my T-shirt over my head, exposing my breasts. I stand in front of him naked with bedhead. My aroused nipples, pink and swollen, press up against his chest. In one swift move, he rips off his towel, hiking up my right leg securely around his waist.

Without even looking down, I feel his erection teasing me.

I gasp. "How can you be so hard? We haven't even done anything."

"Just being this close to you makes me hard," he growls, before ravaging my neck. He hungrily reaches my chin.

Breathlessly enjoying him suckling from my neck to my nipples. "I'm naked with one leg wrapped about you. I think that has something to do with it."

The wet heat from his body skims against my skin. Disarming me with his stormy eyes, he reveals the obvious. "Maybe…I love being inside you."

Hearing him say "love" sinks me into a dizzy spell. The soreness from the night before suddenly diminishes. I want him now more than ever.

"You'll be the death of me, Alexander Jameson."

Our flirtatious banter ends with him propping me up against the door frame, furiously devouring each other. Taking a moment to catch our breath with an approving grin, there will be no foreplay. Just raw uninhibited sex. I want him to fuck me.

His fingers smooth over my stomach before placing them between my legs, massaging up and down along my sex, before inserting two fingers inside me. I ride his hand soaking wet.

Grabbing on to his working hand, I surprise him by pulling his fingers out. Chocking down my excitement for being in control, I say, "Playtime is over. Fuck me." I stroke his cock before sliding it in, slowly, feeling every of inch of him pulsing through me.

His kissing tongue mimics the forcefulness of his thrust. My greedy mouth opens wider needing to feel more of him. Dropping my head back, unable to breathe, my hips groove to his pumping rhythm.

His eyes shift downward, watching himself drive in and out of me. Gripping the back of his head for balance, I latch my leg around him, bracing myself by clinging to him. The creaking door frame absorbs every thrust, slamming me backward. I lose myself, feeling his hot breath quicken on my neck. His upper body strength uncontrollably bounces me up and down, smacking our bodies loudly from wetness.

I command, "Harder!"

Alexander tightly grips both my thighs to elevate my pelvis higher up against the door. I submissively wrap my legs around his waist in a stranglehold, fastening him steady against my sweet spot. My nails dig into his back, anchoring my position, while he vigorously swivels his hips in the same motion, dripping my thighs up and down. He is animalistically slamming into me, and our sweat-drenched bodies make him hard to grip. I can feel his back muscles contract with each grunting thrust.

His unwavering forcefulness is punishing, pushing me to the brink of explosion. I inhibit my need to release.

Unable to hold out any longer, I beg, "Come inside me."

Unhinged from vibration, his outburst of groaning is muffled by my neck. Feeling him pulsate inside me sends shockwaves throughout my core. My muscles convulse into biting shivers. Looking up toward the ceiling, my eyes roll back from screaming ecstasy.

We quietly cling to each other, holding each other tightly until we need air. My body is rendered helpless. Alexander cautiously releases my legs down to earth. I quiver adjusting to gravity.

Our loving embrace is interrupted by my sudden fit of giggles. Trying to sound gracious, I jest, "Thank you for giving me such a memorable tour of your home. I really enjoyed your closet."

Suddenly horrified, I ask, "Do you think Sophia heard us?"

We both stand in silence, monitoring Sophia's location in the penthouse. We focus on each other like two children playing hide-and-seek in a closet. It sounds like she is vacuuming in the dining room.

Alexander answers me in jest, "I think we are safe."

Laughingly, he asks, "Which would be worse? Sophia hearing us or finding your torn-up panties?"

His comical assessment makes me grin profusely. I enjoy his devil-may-care attitude. Glancing over my shoulder, I nudge my head toward the bed. "I'm glad we only used your bed for sleeping, because using it for anything else would've been weird."

He squeezes me tightly. "I will miss you tremendously. I still have other rooms to show you."

His words punch me in the throat. In the midst of consuming each other, Paris is waiting for me. Being lost in this romantic cocoon of sex, I had pushed it to the side and forgot. I'm leaving in a couple of days. I wonder if whatever is evolving between us will diminish or flourish in my absence. It will be a testament to the old adage that absence makes the heart grow fonder. Then again, my absence might create a lonely void that needs to be filled instantaneously. I begin to doubt my choice, but caution myself that if this is meant to be, then nothing will change. I think of the quote by Irina Dunn: "A woman needs a man like a fish needs a bicycle."[1] My constant motivator in self-love.

I lean my head to the side, examining his beautiful eyelashes, the lines around his mouth, the shape of his eyebrows, and all those details I need to see up close. I trace the outline of his smile with my index finger.

"You don't have to miss me. You can always come away with me."

He kisses my forehead and explains, "I wish I could, but I can't right now."

---

[1] Phrases.org, The Phrase Finder, "Irina Dunn," https://www.phrases.org.uk/meanings/a-woman-needs-a-man-like-a-fish-needs-a-bicycle.html

I quickly quote Ferris Bueller's famous line: "Life moves pretty fast. If you don't stop and look around once in a while, you could miss it."[2] In a smart-alecky tone, I make clear, "A popular quote from my teen years, which places you in middle school at the time."

He rubs his chin like he is trying to recall a lost memory. "Ah. Yes. I'm deficient in the teachings of 1980s American cultural mantras. I was still wearing nappies."

He succumbs to my humor by snickering. "You are humorously mental to me."

Cracking a wicked smile, I ask, "Is that what you tell all your patients?"

"I have never considered you a patient. If you want me to play therapist, I will. In fact, after your lunch with Ashley, let's do a session. I want to take you shopping to buy some parting gifts for your travels. You can pick out anything you want."

His eyes illuminate sneaking in the therapists' clause. "Promise to keep an open mind."

"For Christ's sake, Alexander! I'm assuming the disclaimer 'keep an open mind' means you aren't taking me to Nordstrom."

He tries to contain his laughter by nuzzling his face in my neck. "Not unless they sell sex toys."

I turn into a sarcastic mime. Motioning my hands dramatically, trying to recollect all these hypothetical disclaimers. "I've kept an open mind from the moment you analyzed me in my panties...to right now, where I'm literally naked with door frame markings on my back."

---

2 Rotten Tomatoes, "Ferris Bueller's Day Off," Quote, https://www.rottentomatoes.com/m/ferris_buellers_day_off/quotes

I give him the "go fuck yourself" eye roll, before sputtering, "There's fine print attached to everything."

Thundering with laughter at my reaction, he clarifies, "You didn't get the disclaimer coming to my house."

Enthusiastically ranting to plead my case, I say, "That's just semantics. You wanted me to keep an open mind as you guided me into masturbation. Open-minded, my ass!"

Playing along with my sarcastic tantrum, he responds, "Hmm. Your ass? They do have a wide variety of butt plugs at this particular store. Did you know the anal region has many erotic stimulation points?"

He smugly continues, "I want you to fully explore all your sexual options. I'm amazed at how open you were to masturbating last night. At one point, you hesitated and didn't follow through with your fingers. I want you to feel comfortable with your body. It's about discovering what you like, because it feels good."

Even though I'm giving him a hard time, the concept of self-pleasuring would be a delectable instructional lesson. I've never been inside an adult toy store with my lover. It's actually sidesplitting stupid fun with my friends. I presume he's taking me there for specific items. He must have a mental shopping list of stimulates for every orifice of my body.

I concede, "I will always keep an open mind with you. At this moment, you are psychoanalyzing me."

Motioning my hands and looking down at myself, I add, "I'm standing naked in your closet doorway oozing sex down my leg. Let's have this conversation later when we are decent."

******

Instead of having the chauffeur pick me up from Alexander's penthouse to drive me back to the hotel, we opt to walk. It is a beautiful morning for a casual stroll. Regardless of the bustling populated surroundings, it feels like we're alone. My arm tightly loops around Alexander's arm with a self-satisfied grin.

I delightfully reveal my secret to him. "I'm walking down Fifth Avenue with no panties on. I probably look and smell like a hooker."

"Bollocks!" He laughs and leans over to kiss the side of my head. "You smell like vanilla to me. Maybe that's why I want to feast on you."

I squeeze his arm with my hand. "Why, Alexander, you truly are a romantic. I remind you of vanilla ice cream, cold and sticky."

"Even now, I am gobsmacked by your sarcasm. Who will make me laugh when you leave?"

I realize he's brought up my leaving, accompanied by the notion of loneliness, frequently. I suddenly stop and face him. "Then come away with me. Show me Paris."

He looks at me with sincerity. "You are genuinely tempting me in so many ways. But I have too many commitments to just leave on a whim."

"You seem to bring up my leaving a lot. If it bothers you, then come with me! If you can't come, then don't look like I kicked you in the balls."

I nudge his arm and reassure him, "I will return to New York." I sneak in the offer again. "I feel Paris would be a million times better with you."

"If I'm the romantic, then you are the wordsmith"—he chuckles mid-sentence—"who kicks me in the balls." He pulls me toward him to clutch me closer. He kisses my forehead, reassuring me everything will be okay, before we commence with our lazy walk back to the hotel.

An unusual fear creeps over me when the hotel comes into view. Alexander's large sexual appetite invades my insecurities. Once I am gone, I wonder if he will resort to his usual ways of seeking out aggressive women. We literally just met. Placing demands of exclusivity seems premature. I decided to test the waters even though his honesty might break my heart.

"When I'm gone, will you resort to your usual takeout of pad Thai, with a side of oral sex? Depending on her aggressiveness…and full lips?"

My question lingers unanswered, until we arrive at the front of my hotel. My doubts seem silly, but they have serious implications for my heart.

He knows what I'm asking, yet remains coy with his resolution. "No, Emme. I'll have no desire for 'takeout' while you're gone. You can FaceTime me at night. I can watch you use your new toys. Maybe, I can join you by masturbating in some unusual part of my house."

He pulls me in close enough to feel his body quaking from rambunctious laughter. "What about you? Will you be seeking out crème brûlée at the phallic-shaped Eiffel Tower?"

Playing along with our double entendre, I say, "No, I don't eat crème brûlée. Custard gives me diarrhea."

The truth of my statement makes me bite my lip. Trying not to crack up, I express my terms of endearment with food analogies. "While I'm in Paris, I would love to be this French apple tart, but unfortunately, my heart won't be into it. I seem to be enjoying my 'Eton mess' more than any French desserts."

Alexander leans in for an extraordinarily heated kiss in front of all the walking New Yorkers, tourists, the hotel doorman, as well as the exiting patrons of the hotel. I look like a hooker kissing her john goodbye at the forefront of the Four Seasons. I am panty-free, unruly from sex, and I probably smell like old pancake batter, and it doesn't bother me. His kiss sweeps all over me, empowering me with happiness, unleashing my internal butterflies. I want to remember the stripped-down emotional simplicity of this moment. Every one of my nerve endings is saturated with sentiment.

CHAPTER 23

I enter my penthouse and stop at the doorway to survey the elegance of the sunlit room. I regret not enjoying all this luxury, a swank slice of heaven overlooking the city, but there are more pressing things. Unstrapping my shoes, my barefoot arches lay flatly on the cool buffed floor. My hand effortlessly runs along the dazzling inanimate objects, while I walk along the room feeling weightless and carefree.

I hear Harley's ringtone chime with a text.

Harley: How was your date with the hot doctor?

Me: It was beyond anything I've ever imagined. It was perfect. I'm afraid to jinx it by talking about it.

Harley: Are you still going to Paris?

Me: Not you too! Yes, I am.

Harley: I was just checking. Don't stay over some guy. Love is like whatever. I find it to be inconvenient.

Me: Are you currently being inconvenienced by love?

Harley: Love is this label I don't want to conform to. I love pizza more than men. I just need to focus on self-love.

Me: Okay "Deep Thoughts," by Jack Handy. I'll hold your hippie existentialism advice to heart.

Me: Maybe self-love is about trusting someone with your heart.

Harley: Trusting someone with your heart is a huge deal. This doctor better be legit. Or excellent in bed.

Me: I'm not having this conversation with you. I have to go. Having lunch with Ashley.

Harley: Your avoidance screams that he is. Good for you, Mama. A doctor prostitute. Just kidding. I love you!

Shaking my head from the absurdity of our conversation. I walk into my bedroom to find a large gray box, wrapped with a big pink bow, sitting on my bed. I immediately recognize the packaging from Agent Provocateur. There is a card tucked underneath the ribbon. I open the card on the box and read:

> "You are beautiful regardless of what you're
> wearing. —Alexander"

I'm a grown woman reduced to schoolgirl giddiness. I press the card against my heart to absorb its words. His grand romantic gesture flushes me with adulation, knowing he's thinking of me.

I lay the card down next to the box and untie the bow with precision. The contents reveal a replacement pair of black panties, along with some other new sets to his liking. Alexander's selections indubitable favor delicate intricate designs with lace. He must have made arrangements for my gift this morning. I remind myself to enjoy the femininity of the lingerie gift, because perversity will be given later.

******

I'm meeting Ashley at the Gotham Bar & Grill for lunch. The restaurant looks luxurious and bright from the outside. The inside is just as impressively upscale. Upon entering, I notice Ashley sitting at a round table draped in a clean white linen cloth. Her appearance is always stunning in any setting. Regardless of clothes, she is bewitching with just her body. Wearing a black plunging neckline lace dress, which accentuates all her curves, she dazzles. A divine teardrop diamond necklace nestled in between her partially exposed boobs, scream, "Look at me!"

While strolling to our table, I look up to admire the lighting. There are two long rows of ivory-draped lights situated on the ceiling. They gather into a bunch at one focal point, with longs strands of cloth flowing downward. It gives the appearance of a huge jellyfish swimming to the surface. The restaurant is humming with chic patrons noshing and socializing. My eyes can't help but admire everyone's plates as I walk by them. All the food looks like delicious works of art presented on porcelain canvas. My stomach growls in hunger with each passing table.

Ashley stands up to greet me with, as she would describe it, a "big-ass hug." Every time we see each other, there is this blanket of comfort that cloaks over me. There is this unbreakable bond of understanding and compassion between us. The deep devotion we share for one another is irreplaceable. She is a blessing to me.

We both place an order for a Belle Dog, before diving into conversation. I need a vodka-induced citrus libation before Ashley interrogates me about sexcapades with Alexander. With knife-like precision, she deviates from the normal pleasantries to get to the details.

Delving into her curiosities, she asks, "Was Dr. Jameson worth every cent?"

The pink-as-a-kitten's-tongue that is shading my face answers that question. Warm with embarrassment, my forehead must have the "I got laid" stamp on it.

Trying to contain some amount of dignity, I turn pragmatic as if I am being deposed. "Yes, he was worth every cent. And I'll be tipping him tonight."

I don't shy away from revealing all the dirty details. The hot sex doesn't surprise her; it was the emotional connection. I welcome her third-party's point of view. I tend to forget that she's a therapist because we act like sisters. She digests all the particulars of our night before formalizing her opinion.

She asks the simple question, "Are you falling in love with him?"

I take a long sip of my Belle Dog. The Grey Goose and Brut champagne swirl around my taste buds while contemplating my answer. Her question is so simple, but my answer is complicated. It's not a matter of yes or no but more of an explanation of what's filling my heart and head.

"I've never believed in love at first sight. It's too far-fetched of a concept for a rational person to comprehend."

I sighed out, "When I was at TAO, I saw him looking at me from across the bar. I was mesmerized from the get-go. It wasn't the way he looked at me. It was how he made me feel...disarmed. Just from that one look, he could have had me that night. Even if it had been a one-night stand, it would have been worth it."

I continue my introspection, "At first, my attraction to him was physical. He's pretty remarkable looking. Women fantasize about these types of men but are rarely approached by one. It's like encountering Sasquatch out in the wild…or a plot in a romantic comedy."

Ashley's burgundy-colored lips slowly stretch into a stealthy grin of delight. "I believe it's called falling in love, because it's rapid and beyond your control. Don't dismiss the sentiment of love at first sight."

She reevaluates what she said by jokingly adding the obvious, "On the other hand, maybe it was more about what clicked in your pants." Her revelation releases a big, hearty, contagious laugh.

Ashley raises her glass to me and toasts, "It's about fucking time, honey pie."

Feeling happiness for me, she veers forward and needles, "How is sex after divorce?"

I sit there considering what to say, while the waitress places my food in front of me. I dive into my seafood salad knowing once I start to answer her question, my food will remain idle on my plate. My indulgence of this dish supersedes gossip.

Letting my food absorb and settle, I put down my fork, then answer her million-dollar question, "It was amazingly dirty. It's like having some prostitute fantasy where you're this uninhibited sexual person. Anything goes. Your curiosities are answered without judgment." Looking at her dead on with delight, I say, "I loved it."

Ashley's sparkling eyes are accentuated by her approving smile. "Sweetie, there's nothing wrong with that!"

Ashley suddenly reels in her emotions by becoming quiet and stoic. She processes her words before speaking. "I have to be honest with you about something. Don't be mad at me."

Here it comes. The big kick in the nuts proving this is a figment of my imagination. I gesture my pointy finger for her to wait one minute, then proceed to slam my drink. Liquid meds are needed to ease whatever is about to follow. Placing my glass down, I'm ready to hear anything.

Before Ashley could speak, we're both shocked to find Basil standing right beside me. Unsure about seeing Alexander's sister at this very moment, I feel flustered. The basis for our lunch is to talk about sex. Sex with her brother.

We both stand up to greet Basil with hugs and kisses. She is having lunch a few tables down with her attorney. As their meeting ended, she noticed us from across the room engrossed in quiet conversation. Not one to miss out on gossip, Basil asks if she can join us for a drink. Despite our topic being about Alexander and me, there is no way we would turn her away.

Basil takes a seat and asks the waitress to bring her a dirty martini. She observes our sudden heavy silence by her interruption. She reclines in her seat with the appearance comparable to the cat that got the cream.

Basil directs her question toward me, "Sweetheart, you all look like you were having a serious conversation. Are we talking about my brother?"

Ashley responds, "I was just about to explain things to Emerson."

I am so confused. "Explain what?"

Basil chimes in, "One night at a charity dinner, Ashley talked about her job as a therapist. The topic of sex therapy came up."

She glances at Ashley. "Not wanting to be fodder for gossip regarding her marital problems, Ashley pretended that one of her patients needed a referral. She asked for a recommendation. Naturally, I recommended my brother."

Ashley injects, "Alexander's credentials proved him to be highly recommended. Without hesitation, Edmond and I sought out his help. The counseling sessions with Alexander proved to have resounding results."

Blushing like a bride, Ashley admits, "Like any normal red-blooded woman, I noticed his physical appeal. I thought he would be an ideal match for you. Before I let my imagination get the best of me. I had to discover if he was married? Gay? Single?"

She concluded, "Once I had those questioned answered, I decided to play matchmaker. I suggested to Basil that we find a way to set you both up."

She sweetly adds the cherry on top. "He seemed like the quintessential sexy, rich doctor most women would love to meet."

Basil interjects, "My brother hates blind dates. Ashley and I decided to use both of your issues against you. Alexander is a workaholic sex therapist." Glancing at Ashley for approval, she continues, "And you're sexually frustrated. You both just needed the right circumstances to meet."

Ashley explains, "When I hired him to treat you, exclusively for at least one week, he found this to be… as he put it, 'mental.' But he agreed to meet you for an assessment."

Ashley shoots me a smirk. "He was surprisingly candid about his first impression. He found you to be not so typical. He was willing to clear his schedule to treat you exclusively for five days."

Basil straightens up. "The charity event was a perfect foil. Alexander agreed to put himself up for auction, only if I outbid everyone." She crossed her fingers over her heart and said, "Well, I lied. But he wasn't the least bit angry knowing I lost to Ashley. He saw this as a serendipitous opportune circumstance. He would have a moment to romantically interact with you as a red-blooded man, not a therapist."

Trying to digest every sorted detail, I don't react. I'm befuddled that Alexander seemed so uncharacteristically timid about me.

Basil explained, "Women flock to Alexander, but he is particular in his tastes. He can go out with fifty beautiful women and not be interested in any of them. Yet he will notice a woman sitting on a bench engrossed in her sketchbook. He is captivated at how she translates her version of reality onto paper. He has always been drawn to women with an abstract thought process. Stunning women with no substance do nothing for him."

Basil bats her eyelashes at me. "I guess you have that *je ne sais quoi* that gets him off."

Ashley elaborates on her observations. "Alexander didn't know how to convey his interest in you. He didn't want to seem like some pervert therapist taking advantage of a patient."

Basil's face appears innocent with childish delight. "Last night, he seemed gratified and unrestrained. He looked like he just consumed the best meal of his life, savoring every morsel. I haven't seen him emitting this amount of happiness in years."

Ashley shares one particular conversation with Alexander. "At the end of your first session, he told me that he couldn't be your therapist. His approach to you was professional. As the day progressed, it evolved into something else. The session was very unconventional and unguarded. He felt attracted to you but knew it was wrong. It would complicate his ethics if he continued seeing you as patient."

Ashley places her hands on top of mine and smiles. "I didn't want him to stop seeing you. I convinced him to give it another day. He agreed. Even though he wanted to keep things platonic and professional, the magnetism between you both are a foregone conclusion."

Even though I want to explode with psychotic-cartoon-like laughter, Basil speaks up to soothe things over. With surprising tenderness, she wants to expound on the circumstances. "I love my brother more than anything. When Victoria died, it was like he died too. He was this vivacious, charming guy who loved life. He dated girls before Victoria, but she completely stole his heart. Granted, she was lovely, but she tapped into something intellectually with him. She basically saw things outside the box and that beguiled him. He was madly in love with her, and he disregarded the evolution of her depression. The depression was always there in bits and pieces, but it was a slow process. Over time, it came out erratically, and then the episodes got worse. Coping with her illness truly sucked out his effervescence. He changed when she died.

"At first, when Ashley thought you would be a good match, I sniggered at that notion. I've tried to set my brother up with many lovely women. He was not interested, well not with their personalities, but then again he was on the pull. You know, just fucking around."

Basil is ballsy and blunt by informing me about Alexander's indiscretions. "When I saw him getting off with you on the terrace the other night, he was not the brooding serious big brother I was accustomed to. He looked so blindingly happy."

She shakes her head in disbelief. "He was laughing."

My pale facial hue transformed to a rose red. Basil must have seen more than my tits, but hopefully, not his erection. I sit still, trying to absorb all this information.

Giggling at how ludicrous this all sounds, I ask, "Basically, this is some six-figure blind date?"

They both enthusiastically boom in unison, "Yes."

The dam of laughter breaks. Unable to speak while cracking up, I ask. "What the hell Ashley? You rented me a penthouse and bought me a night with him. You are like a high-class pimp. Why did you invest so much money?"

"You are two forces of nature who needed a little push into the same direction. By coming here and opening yourself up to everything it, ironically, helped heal both of you," Ashley replies.

I find her phrase "opening yourself up" comical. It must be some sort of therapist catchphrase. I can't even fathom how many new experiences I've undergone, as well as the ones I'll be encountering later. I'm not about to tell Basil that her brother is taking me sex toy shopping.

Reaching over to Ashley's hand, I gently squeeze it. "I truly love you, but this was not necessary. All this scheming seems insane. You should have just sent me a photo of him, and then asked if I would go out with him. My answer would have been, 'Hell yes!' You didn't need to spend anything on me. Thank you for giving my heart carte blanche to your checkbook." I reach over to hug her by pressing our foreheads together.

"The money is insignificant. You needed to realize you are beautiful, desired, and fearless. You needed to step away from your safety zone of yoga pants, scrunchies, and nostalgic '80s romance movies to experience this," Ashley whispers.

I sigh. "I will truly miss you when I leave."

Basil almost spits up her drink. "Oh bollocks! Did you say you were leaving? Where the bloody hell are you going? For fuck's sake! My brother fancies you."

Her reaction startles me. "Basil, your beauty and obscene language are an absurd combination. You are physically elegant, but your mouth is a British Porta-Potty. This discovery has made my day."

I place both my hands on Basil's wrist. "I would never do anything to cause Alexander pain. I'm going to Paris for an indefinite amount of time. It might be a week, but then, I might hop on a train and go somewhere else. I've been suffocated and deprived of the world. I just want to see it."

There is this unwavering inclination to plead with her, "I did ask Alexander to come with me. He said he couldn't leave due to obligations."

Smiling apologetically to her, I reassure her, "We will find each other again."

CHAPTER 24

I switch gears by putting the focus on Basil. "What about your love life? Is there someone special?"

Basil swallows the other half of her dirty martini in one gulp. Before settling the glass, she pauses long enough to unleash a ferocious laughter that mocks my question. "I've dated every fucking high-class nob across the pond. Then I came here and decided to try online dating, to meet people locally. What a cock-up!"

Ashley and I look at each other in disbelief. Trying to restrain my peeking grin, I ask, "Wait a minute! You dated online?"

Looking like I just won a five-dollar lottery scratch off, I tease, "I'm sorry for appearing giddy. I'm somewhat shocked you were online."

"Yes, I was online! How else can I meet men nowadays? Believe me, I regret it."

Basil looks me straight in the eyes and delivers me a warning. "You didn't delve into the gormless world of modern romance. It's like an online merry-go-round of cocks 24/7. Weeding out the fuckbois among the interesting men is like some full-time job. I lack the mindset and the continuance to invest in this type of courtship."

Someone as beautiful as Basil having dating issues had me horror-struck. I have to ask the million-dollar question. "What was online dating like for you?"

"At first it was fun and very flattering, but then, it evolved into being bloody daft. Most of these men were mental in some shape or form. A lot of them were seeking out a vaginal Band-Aid. It's like looking through this huge bag of turds and hoping you pull out the most polished one."

Basil gives us the schematics of the online dating culture. She explains how it's like a voyeuristic window of singles in every zip code. "Everything is based on split-second glances of photographs. If I get one hundred messages in one day, then that's one hundred pounds of shit I have to go through. And yes, it stinks!"

Basil stuns me with her observation. Raptly staring me down, she shares, "You are in the worst age group. Women in their forties have their shit together, but most are mums. Men in their forties crave youth."

Basil continues, "Don't take it personally, sweetheart. Men would definitely swipe on you." She starts tapping her fingers on the table, like her brain is in hyperdrive. "They aren't all crypt-keepers. There are a lot of sexually inexperienced younger men. Younger men would love to shag women your age, especially since you're a MILF. They don't want a relationship. They want your sexual expertise to tutor them."

Hearing that women my age are regarded as either submissive for old men or a teacher for young men enrages me. "I'm a MILF to millennials, but not to men my age? That's fucked up! You'd think they would want someone they can share life experiences with. This is cuckoo for Cocoa Puffs!"

My life only affirms Basil's hypothesis. "Maybe, you're on to something. My ex regressed to the needs of his eighteen-year-old penis."

I continue with disdain, "He didn't want anyone like me, middle-aged, but you say I'm a MILF. What does that make his girlfriend?"

"A trolloping village bicycle!" Basil snaps with sass.

Not to miss out on a whore analogy, Ashley responds like a true Southern belle, "Honey, she's a box of assorted Hostess cakes. I wouldn't call her a Ding Dong, Twinkie, or even a Whoopie pie. She truly embodies a Ho Ho. She's like a log filled with thick cream and a flat ass. Indulging in sinful treats is not a healthy lifestyle."

Basil seems flustered by the terminology. She fixates her eyes on both of us. Her lips are pursed in a frown. "Are these American desserts? Or are they American sexual innuendos?" She just unloaded a deluge of British slang for us to interpret, yet she is stumped by Hostess snacks.

The muscles on my face are quivering with delight at Basil's innocent question. I hold myself together in an effort to politely answer her. "They aren't normal desserts, like cheesecake. These are cheap treats you could grab at a gas station. I used to love Ding Dongs as a kid, especially when they've been in the fridge and the chocolate is hard."

Basil does an about-face and throws her hands up in defeat. "What in bloody hell are we even discussing? Whores or snack cakes?"

The nonsensical turn in conversation has me in stitches when I respond, "I was whining about why men my age wouldn't click on my fictitious dating profile. I was being overly dramatic. Yet, here I am, dating a younger man. I smell the paradox."

The obvious predicament challenges me: "If my age, ovary usage, and keen ability to detect bullshit disqualifies me, then why in the hell is Alexander dating me?"

Suddenly frazzled, I gasp, "Is he going to be hitting that biological clock as well?"

Basil throws her head back and laughs out loud. She pushes herself forward to ensure I hear her. She speaks slow and clear, "Alexander positively does not want children. This will never be an issue for you." She holds her hand up to her heart to show her sincerity.

"Basil is right, Emme. Some people know what they want and find that person who wants those same things. I knew I didn't want children. Edmond didn't want children either. I know it's encrypted in our DNA to mate and have families, but for some reason, it bypasses some of us."

I say, "Forget Alexander's urge to not bear fruit. Let's get back to discussing age."

Trying not to boast, Basil sits up to inform us, "I've been out with a few divorced forty-year-old men. There are consequences in dipping into certain age gaps. There's an immaturity that creeps up on men. It's called 'having a midlife crisis.'"

Ashley perks up and challenges her. "Excuse me? I'm madly in love with an older man. His age never bothered me, because he's handsome, charming, and romantic. He is everything I've ever wanted. I'm happier than a pig in mud."

Basil defends her view with a compelling argument. "Edmond is not some geezer trolling the internet for women half his age. Your age is just a circumstance to your relationship. Edmond is a catch, and you are lucky."

Basil can't let this discussion go by without identifying the obvious. "Let's be truthful. You are much younger than Edmond. But Edmond has probably never dated a woman his age. Has he?"

Knowing Basil is right, Ashley concedes, "Edmond has always dated younger women. Regardless of our ages, we are compatible in every sense. Age never really mattered. We were meant to be together. Maybe he's youthful, or I'm an old soul. We are much happier than couples who are the same age.

"I've always known what I wanted in a man," Ashley confidently answers. "I never felt the need to try all thirty-one flavors offered online." She winks at Basil. "Knowing what you want versus searching are two different things. You are still young and exploring. Just don't settle for anyone. Respect your grit."

Ashley calls attention to Basil's circumstances. "You might want to quit focusing on your age group. The guy you're looking for might be older. Emme just found herself a younger man. Age is irrelevant."

Basil speaks with much resolve. "These online dirty geezers do not remotely resemble your debonair husband. They resemble a bag of smashed assholes. A few men tried pursuing me like Buffalo Bill from *Silence of the Lambs*. It was like eating ass pie."

"I've never eaten ass pie, but I do love a deep-dish apple pie with a golden crust. It's best served warm. Is ass pie more delicious than that?" Ashley's Texas drawl is a stark contrast to Basil's British accent.

With one raised eyebrow and a deviant glare, Basil is quick-witted in her response. "Ass pie might be a good side dish to a tossed salad, but in the end, they all taste like shite."

Basil snaps, "Online dating is this tedious process that sucks a big bag of dicks. Technology has made people into conversational dimwits. If it's not the emojis replacing words or abbreviations substituting for phrases, it's texting replacing voices on the other end. In a world where you can reach anyone anywhere, people are shockingly good at ignoring you."

Ashley holds up her hand like a notepad and pretends to transcribe a prescription on her palm. "As a doctor, I think you are suffering from anal glaucoma. You can't see your ass with anyone." Ashley has to ask, "What gives, sweetheart? You didn't go out with any of these jabronis?"

Basil snaps back, "Codswallop! Most of the men on these sites are pervies into fast-food fuckery. The quantity doesn't liken to the quality of the person. It feels like a job pilfering through the unexceptional."

Basil lifts her freshly filled martini glass and uses it as a prop to toast us. Painting a picture of a typical first encounter. "This is the daft part placed on females. We prepare ourselves like the perfect martini. You are three parts perfectly divided. You transform into a sexy, yet beautiful woman, with intellect and a deep interest in them. It's an illusion of self-perfection created for some chap you've never met. Yet it all boils down to the initial first four minutes."

"What's in the first four minutes?" I ask.

"I've been told, by men and women, that your fuckability is determined in that first impression. Within that first few minutes, you imagine if you are attracted enough to shag this person. If the answer is yes, then you feel relaxed and enjoy yourself. If the answer is no, then you're stuck there in misery. You force yourself into a Botox-like happy facial expression. The events leading up to the first encounter have no bearing over the first few minutes of meeting them."

I immediately recall the first time I laid eyes on Alexander. I was willing to fuck him within those first few minutes, and he wasn't even my date.

Basil startles us by clapping her hands together in exuberance. "I have to tell you about this one corker named Theo. He was this charismatic and funny guy. He wasn't even my type physically, yet his quirkiness made him enduring."

I watch Basil's face when she tells her story. A smile washes over her facial features when she speaks of him. This will not be a dating horror story, but a fond memory. Her cheeks have a rosy bashful hue, as if shyness is inching into her psyche. Basil reflects on one particular date with Theo.

"It was romantic because he thought about all the little details. He brought me flowers, pulled out my chair, but more importantly, he listened to me with complete interest. It was flattering to experience something you only see in movies."

Basil's voice becomes demur in revealing her made for Hallmark TV romance. "After this whimsical dinner, he asked me if I wanted to go back to his apartment. So why not? I needed a slap and a tickle." In dramatic fashion, she adds a soap-opera cliff-hanger. "I noticed something was amiss. There was something wrong."

In unison, we lean in closer and pry, "What was it?"

I imagine this as an episode of *Scooby-Doo*. Basil pulling off a mask that hides Theo's true self. The big reveal is his disguise. The handsome gentleman isn't Theo, but Old Man Winters with saggy balls.

Basil's demeanor intensifies, like someone telling a campfire horror story. "Theo is grinding between my legs, and there is no friction. I put my hand on his pecker to stroke it. I couldn't feel anything."

She shrugs off her confusion as a moronic act of naïveté. "I thought maybe I was grabbing the wrong area."

Ashley loses herself in boisterous laughter in the absurdity of that statement. "The wrong area? Honey, the shaft is still located between his two balls, which are warmly tucked between their legs. You could be blindfolded and find his boner."

Basil simpers, "I was just randy at the moment, which made me confused. We were still fully clothed, but things weren't progressing…normally."

We stare at her, trying to comprehend her unfortunate juxtaposition.

Basil mimics a teen recounting their first sexual rendezvous. She innocently confesses, "I couldn't feel his stonker rubbing against my fanny."

Ashley reads my mind. We both need a translation from her British slang. She inquires, "Honey, I'm from the South. I have no idea what a stonker is. Are you saying he was like a Ken doll?"

Basil sighs when she translates her words. "You know…his twig and berries. He lacked a stiffy. I couldn't feel it pressing on my pink bit."

Ashley gasps. "Oh! He couldn't get an erection? Or did he have a micropenis?"

Agitated by this new terminology, Basil exclaims, "What in the blazes is a micropenis?"

Ashley educates us in the topic of teensy phallus. The physician in her becomes clinical and not satirical with her answer. "A micropenis is a penis that is 2.5 inches erect. It functions like any other penis, but it's diminutive. Unfortunately, for these men, most straight women need a normal-sized penis to climax."

"I wish he did have a micropenis. I wouldn't have felt so humiliated. Theo just wasn't aroused. No matter what I did, he couldn't get hard. He even asked if I could give him a cock meat sandwich to arouse him."

She shudders, then shakes her head and waves her hands from side to side. "When a bloke is limp, I'm not sticking his todger in my mouth."

Ashley quickly adapts profane British vernacular into a sarcastic menu of Southern cuisine. "Cock meat sandwich doesn't sound tasty. I do like a smoked brisket on a potato roll covered with a tangy BBQ sauce. Serve that up with some ass pie, and you might have one hell of a meal."

Like a little girl disgusted after being served peas, Basil squinches her face. "He had me half-naked on his bed. He was pressed between my legs, and he couldn't pop a chub."

Basil places her hands on her breasts and motions them down her body. She traces out an imaginary chalk outline of herself. She emphasizes her hands underneath her bra cup. "I'm no *Sports Illustrated* model, but my nakedness should get most men hard during foreplay. He should have had a loaded gun in his pants the moment he felt my boobs.

Ashley nods in agreement and identifies it with her own predicament. "Edmond suffers from erectile dysfunction. I thought he was having an affair because he couldn't get hard either."

A faint twinkle of amusement in Ashely's eyes indicates her compassion for Basil is about to end. She mischievously lobs an observation about Basil's breasts, "No offense, but my hooters are way more impressive than yours. I'm built like a brick shit-house. I get porn-star-type attention from men. Everyone looks at my boobs. Hell, you're looking at them right now. I proudly show them off because they are amazing."

"You're right. Your tits are spectacular. I'm getting hard just admiring them."

One would presume the men seated close by are staring at our table. It looks as if we are having a showdown between tits and ass.

Basil looks at us as if she shrewdly closed a lucrative business deal. With a self-satisfied grin, Basil reveals, "My consolation prize was letting him give me the iron butterfly. Fortunately, his kisser worked well on my vertical bacon sandwich. This was the first time I'd ever experienced an orgasm from oral sex."

Gripping the table and balling the linen cloth in her fists, she bites her bottom lip for dramatic effect. "I literally lost control of my legs."

Ashley quickly points out, "Sounds delicious! Vertical bacon sandwich, arse biscuits, and ass pie, your dating life resembles an unhealthy meal. You should become vegan."

Basil deeply reflects on Theo and what happened afterward. "Oddly enough, he pursued me. I gave in to his charms and ended up liking him. Regardless of one bad sexual encounter, the intimacy between us turned out to be intense. It wasn't love, but I grew fond of him."

She postulates her time with him in a low defeated tone, "Out of the blue, he emails me to say I'm not the girl for him. He politely thanks me for our time together, offering me friendship as a form of comfort. He likes keeping people in his life."

Ashley interjects, "Theo's friendship is about as worthless as tits on a bull. Men only offer friendship as a way to make them feel less of an asshole, or when they are lonely and looking for sex."

Basil shrugs in agreement. "I've never wanted a friendship with any man who dumped me. He doesn't need to be injected into my life. Friendship means we can talk about anything. I didn't want to listen to him unload his dating vagina monologues on me."

Ashley states the obvious conclusion, "Honey, never assume the problem is you. Don't change who you are to accommodate any man. You will come out of all of this knowing what you don't want. You don't want the lethal combination of a huge ego and ineffective penis."

Basil shares her wisdom with a big smile, "Love will come at me when I least expect it. Isn't that how life works? When you stop giving a fuck, something amazing happens."

Ashley shoots me a look that reads, "I told you so."

She then gives Basil some of her middle-aged wisdom. "When you get to be our age, you have fewer fucks to give. There is this great freedom in not caring about every single thing."

Basil informs us the most important connection she's made is with herself. She uses her love for Coke Zero as an anecdote for her expectations. "Every day at lunch, I look forward to one can of Coke Zero. I open the can, put a straw in it, and revel in sipping it. It is a delightful simple pleasure. I will stop everything and enjoy that one can of soda."

This is Basil's stripped-down version of romance. Someone who takes one moment out of a busy day to slowly drink in time with her. Actions always supersede words.

I've only known Basil for a few days, but I find her tactful charisma refreshing. I know she portrays a Teflon-skin exterior, but she has a soft side. The Eden Ahbez quote comes to mind: "The greatest thing you'll ever learn is just to love and be loved in return."[3]

Basil's portrayal of being savored like a Coke Zero makes my idea light bulb blow up in my mind. I suddenly remember the unusual scent combination of pumpkin pie and lavender. And of course, the delicious taste of moist coconut cake. I scoop up my purse and pull out a business card. I eagerly slide it over to her.

Basil curiously picks up the card, and reads "Nolan Asher" out loud.

I suddenly become earnest. "At the auction, I met this dashing thoughtful gentleman, Nolan. I believe he might be your unicorn."

Basil stares at me in confusion. She examines his business card as if there are hidden clues waiting to be solved.

"This is karma thanking you for your clandestine love connection between your brother and me. Now you are this force that needs to be pushed in the right direction. Consider me the compass shoving you north, toward him."

---

[3] The Quotations Page, Quote #33530, lyrics written by Eden Ahbez in the song "Nature Boy," sung by Nat King Cole, http://www.quotationspage.com/quote/33530.html

Ashley convincingly joins in on the Nolan bandwagon. "Sometimes taking a risk is scarier than being alone, but it all might be worth it in the end."

This would be a true blind date based on Basil trusting our instincts. I convey my logic, "You know if I didn't end up with Alexander at the auction, I would have, without a doubt, went out with Nolan. He is most likely everything you've been looking for. A guy like that would never be found online, because he's the real deal."

Ashley contrastingly takes on the sexist approach. "I know you have your hang-ups about age gaps. Nolan is more our age. I'm willing to bet within the first fifteen minutes of meeting him, your mind will be objectifying him."

I shine a spotlight on another angle. "Nolan commented to me how Ashley knows all the beautiful people. By introducing you, this ideal would remain absolute." I give her a playful wink, before adding, "He won't be disappointed, especially when he sees your tits."

My compliment has embarrassed Basil into a loss for words. Basil leans toward me with a generous grin showing her acceptance. She and Alexander have the most startling, penetrating blue eyes. Her blushed cheeks remind me of the shade Orgasm by Nars.

Teetering on concession after our sales pitch, Basil confesses, "I am so glad we wasted this entire afternoon together. And I know you both wouldn't set me up with a nob. I'm looking forward to experiencing your matchmaking skills."

******

Sometimes the best moments in life are simple and unpredictable. It's like a rainy Sunday morning in the fall. You stay inside. You're warmed by your PJs, engrossed in a good book, and the sound of your stomach growling is the only indicator of time. The three of us laughingly hug each other as we say our goodbyes. Basil is the first to leave.

When her cab pulls up beside her, she abruptly stops. She turns back around to look at us. After a brief pause, she raises her voice to compete with the city's hectic sounds.

"Emerson… Paris is full of savoir-faire. All your senses will explode from the city's visual brilliance. But your heart might want something that's tangible and fulfilling. Once you are thousands of miles away, you'll realize your journey to self-discovery was never about leaving, but staying."

I place my right hand over my heart to reflect my love for her words, then close my eyes for a split second to search my mind for a response. Her authenticity stuns me because I wasn't expecting such wisdom without sprinkles of blasphemy. As with most hard decisions, I'll realize the right choice when the wrong one punches my gut.

Buzzing and feeling like Han Solo, I mouth the words, "I know."

We both understand each other in that succinct bustling New York minute. Basil slides her oversized jet-black Prada sunglasses over her alcohol-glossy eyes. Looking like a fashionable stone-cold bitch, she transmits a nod with a huge boozy grin and bellows, "Cheerio!"

She ducks into the cab and rides off into the rapid flow of traffic. Even though we've known each other only a few days, I am looking forward to seeing her again.

Ashley gestures to her driver to pull up, and I squeeze her warmly. "I know this is corny. I miss this life. I miss you, the city's energy, salacious discussions, and—"

Ashley finishes my thought, "Sex! You miss sex!"

"Yes! I miss that too." I throw my head back, laughing at her statement.

She places both hands on my arms and exudes positivity by telling me, "I love you. Have a safe trip to Paris."

Ashley's driver stands there, holding her door open. Trying to fend off a tear-jerking goodbye before my trip, she throws her arms around me and pulls me in for another overzealous bear hug. I whisper, "I'm about to pick out sex toys with Alexander. Wish me luck."

Her eyes widen with delight. "Honey, I can't wait to hear what he put in your goodie bag. What a fantastic way to end this afternoon! An alcohol-induced toy shopping spree with a sexy doctor. Now he gets to see what kind of freak you are and vice versa."

I can only imagine how my vodka-glistening eyes appear staring back at her. I think of the movie Who Framed Roger Rabbit. My eyes probably resemble Judge Doom's eyes popping out of his head.

I wonder out loud, "Me? What kind of freak is he?"

I start envisioning us walking into the sex shop. The sales associates would look up and greet him as if he were Norm from Cheers. How often does he shop at these stores? What does he have in his house? I can't imagine sweet Sophia using her own special blend of cleansers for his exotic display of cock rings and dildos. My mouth and mind are racing to all these conclusions about his research and fetish.

"Have you lost your ever-lovin' mind? I wouldn't set you up with some sadist. Enjoy the shopping excursion, and if he makes some suggestions—"

I sarcastically interrupt, "I know. I know…keep an open mind."

After all this time, I'm beginning to learn who I am. Being single has nothing to do with being alone; it's a symptom of the situation. I spent most of my youth with one guy. I had never approached sex as a way to connect with myself but more of a way to connect with my partner. My evolving sexuality is beyond self-pleasure. It's more about figuring out personal growth in my forties.

CHAPTER 25

Day 6

Session 5

Alexander asks me to meet him at the Pleasure Chest at 3:00 p.m. I quicken my pace down Second Avenue to avoid being late. A steel-gray-colored store with welcoming bay windows comes into view. They are taunting you to peer inside. This is not what I envisioned. The store doesn't resemble something scandalous. It doesn't have a male mannequin wearing a gimp suit displayed out front. It looks like a posh boudoir. It stands out from the surrounding stores, not because of gaudiness, but due to its elegant exterior. As I watch, I notice how people stop to glance inside and see the display—the natural perverse curiosity of the passers-by wanting to survey the items hidden inside.

I suddenly have a hankering for a big hat and a pair of sunglasses to make me incognito. I am about to enter a store famous for their sex toys! Alexander catches my eyes before I even pull the long gray door handles open. He is standing in front of the big display window. A neon sign lighting up the phrase "Sex Is Back" is perfectly situated behind him. He looks dapper in his charcoal-tailored Tom Ford suit, accented with a clean white shirt and maroon tie. He watches my hesitation curiously.

Welcoming me with a hug and a kiss on the cheek, he politely asks, "Are you ready for a bit of shopping?"

Out of personal interest, I wonder out loud, "Is this the store for all you rich Upper East Side perverts? More importantly, how often do you come here?"

Amused by my directness, he calmly replies, "This store is not exclusive to rich perverts. It's for people who want to experiment with their partner or even with themselves. Curiosity is natural. Discovering new things sexually keeps life interesting."

He then answers my other question with a devilish grin. "Yes, I have been here, but only for research. I promise."

Once Alexander opens the front door, I gingerly step inside. My eyes are trying to process what I anticipate versus what I am actually seeing. The refined interior belies the perversity in plain sight lined neatly upon shelves in diverse sections. It's posh with various levels of perversity divided up into sections of interest. Every square inch of the shop is utilized to present the items uniquely. I imagined walking into a convenience-type store with aisles of perversion hanging on hooks or just sitting on shelves. But the toys are not presented in a demeaning or cheap way. Rather, each particular item has all its variations cataloged by different brands and styles. If you are looking for a cock ring, every version in all colors is represented.

The Pleasure Chest is very bold, but tasteful in presentation. The name, Pleasure Chest, is in big platinum letters centered on a painted brick wall. The seductive red color of the wall has a luster reminiscent of the *Rocky Horror Picture Show* poster. When the light hits the lacquered brick wall, an unintentional wildfire effect emerges around the words.

One section of the store is lit with a beautiful circular chandelier. Light reflects off the glossed floor like sunlight sparkling over water. Under the chandelier stands a glass case with various sexual tools inside. Each encased apparatus is foreign to me. Clamps, whips, restraints, and cuffs lie beneath the glass under lock and key. They remind me of tools you'd use to fix a car engine. But the shiny metals and black leather make clear their kinky purpose. A sign catches my eye: not only do they sell every sexual gizmo, but they hold classes to promote product usage or to enhance your sexual experience in general.

My mind is lit like the Fourth of July night sky. Ideas are popping off in my brain as soon as my eyes catch sight of the array of goodies. The word *sex* is eye-catching throughout the store. The "Sex Is Back" theme is propped up in the center of each glass display in the aisle, as well as the art settled on the walls. The phrase follows me around like subliminal propaganda. Shopping here with friends would be fun, but not with Alexander. Whatever I choose will be used on me by him. I have no idea what experience I want.

Trying to contain my inner thoughts from spilling out of my mouth, I absorb my surroundings objectively. My immediate reaction is to start laughing. Some of these items are not realistic to me. They appear cartoonish, not sexual. Every uniquely shaped product is designed for stimulation. I am a grown-ass woman trying to revamp my libido in the most abstract way. At some point, I will orgasm from a product in this room. My mind stews with contradictions.

Alexander is mindful of the sexually charged optics laid out before me. He seems to enjoy introducing me to all the things I consider taboo. I need to play this out like a game of poker. His version of therapy is equivalent to losing my virginity daily to new sensations. I confidently begin walking away from him, freely strolling around with a confident shit-lock smile.

Alexander silently shadows me with constant supervision. He is waiting for me to communicate my feelings. I stop myself in front of the large selection of dildos. My initial thought is, *How can this be possible?* I had no clue dildos were this abundant. There are so many colors, shapes, designs, and sizes. The variety of materials composed to form each dildo ranges from crystal to plastic to carved wood. Each one offers an array of features. They are categorized from beginners all the way to the more advanced luxurious players. Not only could you pick out your favorite color, but there is length and circumference to decide on. Shopping for shoes seems so much easier.

Alexander walks up behind me and whispers in my ear, "Do you see anything you like?"

Trying to be respectful, by not laughing, I shrug my shoulders. I have an awareness of the people who are shopping there with a purpose. The store is busy with couples looking for particular items and asking the salesclerk serious questions. My eyes are fixated on a section of dildos rights in front of me. My smart-ass mouth can't be contained. Without haste, I grab two boxes from the shelf, then whip around to surprise Alexander.

I hold up one box right up next to my face. With a stupid sweet smile, I quip, "At last, my childhood dreams have been transformed into erotica. I have found the illustrious fabled unicorn-horn dildo. Let me ride my way into a magical orgasm by poking myself with a twisted, thick rainbow-shaped penis."

Without skipping a beat, I hold the other box up to the other side of my face. It is another unicorn dildo but with a more realistic design. I cheerfully continue, "I will call this one, Mr. Pointy. It resembles a horn's natural color, style, and shape. It's even sharp and elongated like a magic wand. Women love a good bone, right?"

Alexander tries to stay the course as a prim and proper Englishman. He plays along without breaking character. "Do you want to fantasy role-play?"

I will win this battle of frivolity, by digging down deep to tap into my inner Meryl Streep. Conjuring up a reaction so genuinely amazed, I should have won an Oscar. I exclaim, "I am hoping we can play My Little Pony. You can show me your 'element of harmony' by unleashing your magical powers on me."

Overly gleeful with a more pronounced explanation, I jest, "Unicorn magic isn't let loose without a good reason. Each pony must use their special element to defeat evil. The evil in this case is sexual repression."

Flipping the box to my face, I speak to the clear plastic covering, "I will name you Ham Shank, the Masturbation Pony."

Alexander tries his damnedest to refrain from laughter, but he finally lets go. "You are holding up two unicorn dildos. I cannot contend with this."

Feeling crazy like a bag of cats, I'm horrified, curious, and humored. Intrigued by what Alexander himself wants to test on me, I place the unicorn horns neatly back on the shelf, slide my hands on his chest, and with seriousness ask him to clarify his intentions. "Alexander, I have no idea what would interest me or what you think I need."

I glance around the room before my eyes meet his. "There is a difference in needing toys and wanting toys," I point out. "We've had sex three times in the past twenty-four hours. We did it without assistance from any appliance."

He opts for the professional answer. "Sex toys are used to enhance a couple's sexual experience. Sometimes they are needed. A lot of couples achieve higher levels of arousal, excitement, and orgasm using a toy. Women particularly benefit from sex toys, especially when they don't have a partner."

He concludes his pièce de résistance. "When you are away, I don't want you to stop experiencing sexual gratification."

I consider his words with a silent stare, place my hands on his shoulders, then do an about-face. I take two steps before reaching over to an adjacent shelf for an item, suddenly turning back toward him in humorless theatrics. "You're right. Maybe I should use Belladonna's Magic Hand instead of my own."

I hold up a replica of a woman's hand and obnoxiously rub it on his cheek. The plastic hand has the thumb folded in and the index and middle finger positioned outward. This hand position is meant to stimulate the clitoris. Moving the plastic hand off his face, I place it against my right shoulder, like a baseball bat.

Alexander grips the dainty wrist of Belladonna's Magic Hand to disarm me. He takes the plastic hand and places it back on its display shelf. He gently squeezes my shoulders. "I'm aware this all seems inconsequential. Just consider it a fun shopping experiment."

I nod in agreement. I intend on being mature. Yet, I feel the urge to scrutinize the toys in front of me. The shelf next to my hand is dedicated to a large display of butt plugs. I immediately grab a particular box that renders me speechless.

I exaggerate my interest in purchasing this one particular toy. "I just found what we need for tonight."

I face the package toward me in order to read the box's description verbatim. "I found this black XL humongous butt plug for you." The wheezed laughter escapes from my belly. I can rationalize a normal butt plug, but one sized as humongous makes me cringe.

How in the world is this designed to go up someone's rear end? It is ginormous! I agonize over the amount of force used to push that in. The variety of butt plugs rival the selection of dildos. There seem to be a stopple created for every hole in your body. The variations of plugs could be compared to all the different flavors of Jelly Belly jelly beans.

I maintain my sassy pace. Noticing the hedonism of the luxurious toy items next to the butt plugs, I grab a behemoth brown dildo.

I loudly advertise my intended purpose, "While you're wiggling that humongous thing up your ass, I will treat myself to a high-end penis made of VixSkin Buck. This is six inches of the highest quality soft toy material."

I gasp in disbelief and place it up to my eyes for a closer look. "It's so realistic that it has veins protruding! We can have family game night at your penthouse. Instead of contorting our bodies to a game of Twister, we'll play plug up the holes."

Alexander is quick to point out, "I know it is in your nature to be a smart-ass. For some people, sex is part of their evolution. It can be about enjoying yourself alone. In order to break the pattern of monotonous expectations of sex, why not embrace what is in front of you?"

I feel disappointed in myself. I want to be balls-out sexually liberated in my midlife, but I'm in a room full of things I don't understand.

Not wanting to come off as hopeless, I try putting my mental anxieties into words. "In all fairness, I have wholeheartedly embraced everything. I can't imagine myself with clamps on my vagina, gyrating to a 3D plastic hand, or placing things up my butt. I don't understand how this will make me feel fulfilled."

He mocks me, "Maybe I want you to place things up my butt. During game night, let's play quid pro quo. You do me; I will do you."

I roll my eyes at him with overly dramatic disdain but secretly applaud his comeback. There is an advertisement on the wall that catches my interest. A seminar is being held in one of the store's back rooms. I tap his shoulder and redirect his attention toward the sign.

In a joking manner, I ask, "Did you want to sign up for tonight's class on advanced anal play? That might come in handy for our game night."

"Would that interest you?" he inquires.

I grimace out of frustration by shaking my head. "We haven't been together long enough for you to toss my salad. No matter how amazing I think your ass looks. I'm not ready to give you a rim job…or stick anything labeled 'humongous' up in there."

I cup his face in my hands and whisper, "Baby steps, Alexander. Baby steps."

He challenges me, "What makes you think the anus isn't pleasurable? The anal walls are full of sensors. Have you ever inserted your finger in a man? Has your anal area ever been fondled?" He questions my resistance, "How do you know that you won't like it?"

I respond, "Since I've arrived in New York City, my body has been the *Giving Tree*; let me ease into this."

Needing to redirect my nervous energy, I automatically reach out and fidget with his tie. I don't want to meet his eyes, but I feel them searing into me. He wants to explore our discussion about anal euphoria. I do not.

I speak softly enough to let my words soak in. "The more time I spend with you, the more sexually inexperienced I feel. My enjoyment of everything you've introduced has been this surprising revelation."

He bores his wondrous blue eyes into my eyes. The way he looks at me is reminiscent of the sun's warmth on a chilly autumn day. I can feel my skin singing into a flushing glow. He is quietly reading me, in order to reconcile my misgivings.

"I promise to abandon my inhibitions, but I need you to do something for me. Try walking in my high heels. Heels look sexy, but they hurt like hell, and you occasionally fall on your ass. But you need a sense of balance before you strut the catwalk."

My romantic prose is lost when my eyes rest upon the boxes bumping against my shoulder. I'm trying to be thoughtful and analytical in front of the Femme Funn Turbo Baller. Nothing says "inspiration" like rows of realistic vibrating cocks.

I check my attitude at the door and surrender to participation. "I promise to browse and embrace your adventure." I begrudgingly add, "I will try to keep my sarcastic diarrhea from flowing out of my mouth."

I cross my fingers over my heart to emphasize my sincerity. Before Alexander can respond, a clerk approaches us to inquire if we require assistance.

Alexander quizzically looks at me and asks, "Emme, do you need assistance?"

The kind salesclerk is a lean, youthful-looking man named Gary. He can sense I am in a dither by my body language alone. His expertise in sex toys of all kinds could never be classified as normal. He must answer crazy questions all day. The inquiries probably range from stupid pranksters to those truly needing his know-how on usage. His poignant knowledge is likely achieved by reading tons of manuals or testing out most of these products himself.

In a presumptuous tone, I ooze friendliness, "Nice to meet you, Gary. My name is Emerson. This is my sex therapist, Dr. Jameson. He wants to unlock my inner whore. My virtue has been hidden away after years of missionary sex. I am entering into this vortex of sexual contraptions."

I suddenly feel like Princess Leia asking Obi-Wan and Luke Skywalker for help. "Help me, Gary. Help my vagina find her voice."

My eyes shift around the room of colorful foreign objects, slowly ingesting all this sex with facial shock and awe. Without making a mockery of the situation, I just spit out my thoughts. "I feel like I'm on a game show called *Sexual Jeopardy!* I'm seeing all the answers, but I don't know any of the questions. It appears every sexual desire is answered here. What do I need?"

I hold up a box containing pasta-shaped penises. Shaking the box in the air like maracas, I ask, "Let's say this is a Daily Double question. What kind of male organ do you put in your mouth that never gets hard, and it's okay to chew on it?"

My sense of humor can't be contained. I flip the box toward my wry expression and pick Gary's knowledgeable sex brain, "Do men like a nice bowl of cock covered in marinara and freshly grated Parmesan cheese?"

Alexander shockingly responds with upmarket wit. "I am confident enough in my sexuality to enjoy a bowl of penis-shaped noodles in pesto. Naturally, I would pair it with a Bella Luna Gross Stiletto Vineyards Sangiovese."

Impressed by his response, I compliment him, "Touché, Dr. Jameson. You are an evolved man. Some women wouldn't enjoy a guy's limp noodle in her mouth. And yet, you know which wine to pair it with."

"Most limp noodles expand in size once they get warm and wet." Alexander's quip pairs science and satire seamlessly.

While we discuss the ins and outs of cooking penis pasta, Gary glares at both of us. He seems to be mentally calculating whether we are condescending his craft or serious toy shoppers. He takes the box of pasta from me to examine the written description on the back.

He remains polite and professional. "I've never tasted the penis pasta, but a lot of women love it for parties. I do know from personal experience our yabbo cupcakes are delicious."

He divulges an interesting tidbit about their top-selling confectionary, "Our most popular candy is our 'Let's Fuck' lollipops. They come shaped as penis or nipples."

Puzzled by Gary's word choice, Alexander asks," What are yabbos?"

Placing my hands on Alexander's shoulders, I curtail my giggling to explain, "Yabbos is slang for boobs. I learned this word while watching the Disney movie, *Hocus Pocus*. Imagine explaining that at a tween slumber party."

I look at Alexander, then bit my lip. You would never hear a clerk at Whole Foods rave about their cupcakes decorated like breasts. I examine the shelf full of explicit sweets. I can't believe there is a factory somewhere producing candy-shaped nipple tassels, cock rings, and pecker sprinkles, not to mention the irresistible BJ Blast Oral Sex Candy that mimics pop rocks. The crackling in your mouth while giving head makes it explosive!

Alexander wants this store to trigger my sexually adventurous side. I just can't see myself wearing a leather mask and getting into bondage. There is a stimulant for every nerve, whether it is delicate with vibrations, or painful for adrenaline. I'm making this too cerebral when it is supposed to rouse my pleasure senses.

Alexander approaches me closely. I can feel the warmth of his chest radiating into my breasts as he inches closer. With a soft voice out of Gary's ear shot, Alexander snaps me out of my sex coma. "I'm not judging you. Humor is your defense mechanism."

He gently continues, "We all have fantasies. I want you to live out your deepest dirty thought."

"Really?" I shake my head in disbelief.

I test the waters by revealing my desires without discretion. "What if I want to have uninhibited sex with a stranger? Let's say I want to pick up a random guy in a bar. I don't even want to know his name. I don't want to know anything about him. It's about being casually irrational without having feelings involved."

Alexander doesn't find my revelation earth-shattering. "Is that what you want?"

Wanting no confusion, I clarify, "My fantasy is with a man, and not some USB insertion toy."

In the midst of our conversation, our soft voices have grown louder, and we forget there is a third party present. Regardless of what his profession entails, I sense a minuscule amount of discomfort from Gary.

He clears his throat and asks, "Do you both still need my assistance? Or do you need time to try to figure things out?"

The corners of my mouth turn up in mischievous delight. I turn toward Gary with self-assurance and promptly respond, "I believe we are trying to figure things out. In more ways than one."

I turn back to Alexander to fixate my eyes on his face. I want to see his reaction as I bluntly call him out. "Dr. Jameson seems to think I'll be gratified from purchasing an item from your store. But my deepest fantasy might consist of being irrational and spontaneous. I've envisioned myself having combustible sex in a public area with a stranger. I want him to dominate me, because I am sick of being in control all the time."

Gary's face lights up when I mention being dominated. He instinctively chimes in with a recommendation. "We have a vast array of bondage paraphernalia. I don't know the level of domination you want, but the basics are usually handcuffs, wrist ties, and bed restraints. Would you like me to show them to you?"

Without taking my eyes off Alexander, I cheerfully acknowledge him, "Thank you, Gary. That would be lovely."

Gary, our sex toy guru, seems unfazed by our unusual banter. He directs us into the more advanced paraphernalia. My breath quickens as I take in my surroundings. The extreme kink and bondage culture catches me off guard. It's the medieval equivalent to a Toys "R" Us store. Gone are the silly colors of the sex toys. Blacks and reds are the primary colors of submissive pain. Various implements of bondage with an array of restraints lies before my eyes organized by degrees of restraint.

I pull him close by his collar lapel, then slide my hands over to his tie, gently adjusting the knot. I know Gary is lurking somewhere close by, but I want this conversation to be private. Deliberately moving closer, I place my cheek against his. "Why would I want just an appetizer of a sex toy? The fantasy in itself is all three courses, and my needs being met is the actual entrée."

He studies my face before addressing my proposition, unsure if I am bluffing. He politely requests, "Where would you like to go to fulfill your encounter with a stranger?"

"I've already met him."

His eyes widen. "You have?"

"Yes. His name is Gary."

It may seem cruel to say something so asinine, but he wants to stick a B-Vibe Rimming Plug up my back door to instigate anal arousal. Alexander deserves all my sarcasm.

"Bloody hell, Emme, you are just being cheeky with me?"

"I'm being exceptionally cheeky. The fantasy I revealed earlier was very true." Pretending to be coy by tracing his jawline, I inhale courage, then submit, "I have always been proper, not promiscuous. I want to tell you what I want."

CHAPTER 26

I take a step back and boldly tell Alexander what he wants to hear, "This is my fantasy.

"Picture a club scene out of any movie. The place is dimly lit but vibrant in sound, lights, alcohol, and voices. The room is filled with scantily clad people dancing and breathing in the pheromones in the room. There is a sexiness to everyone that makes them magnetic."

I close my eyes in an effort to tap into muscle memory. Recollecting something that's never happened pushed forth by my dirty mind. I want Alexander to feel my details.

"I'm standing at the bar admiring my surroundings. I lock eyes with the most striking male specimen. He's the cliché: tall, dark, and handsome. There is confidence in his tough exterior, displaying his need to dominate. He nonchalantly walks over to me to initiate conversation. I don't care what his deep voice is saying. I just watch his lips move. In this instance, I feel gorgeous, because he's with me. In mid-conversation, I nix the small talk and pull his face to mine. He gladly reciprocates by driving his tongue hard and deep, opening my mouth. Our bodies passionately pull into each other, feeling each other's arousal. I allow his hands to openly feel every curve of my body. His hands travel under and inside my dress to feel wetness in my panties. He smiles down at me while he flickers his fingers, making me gasp. He commands the situation by grabbing my hand. Purposely, he guides me through the sea of dancing bodies to find seclusion."

Locking eyes with Alexander, I weave my hands into his, powerfully gripping him close as if to intimately seal ourselves together.

"He leads me down a hallway, and we walk into the men's bathroom. He locks the door. Impulsively embracing me, then he pushes me toward the sink. He props me up on the cool porcelain vanity. I feel his body heat against mine when I peel his shirt over his head. I lift my arms to invite him to slide off my dress and then toss it on the floor. No words are spoken. My body syncs with his. He is in complete control. I pull his chiseled waist into mine, feeling his hardness dripping me wet on the sink."

Smiling to take a deep breath, I continue, "Without haste, he reaches around to unsnap my bra to savor my nipples. I grab his hair to nuzzle his mouth harder into my chest. My chest is salty with our body sweat and saliva. He bites at my hard nipples to create a flash of enjoyable pain. I welcome him with gyrating pleasure. I lean back on the mirror, gripping the edge of the vanity for balance. Unzipping his pants, he slickly thrusts inside me with intense momentum. People are pounding and yelling outside the bathroom door. Hearing the strangers' voices outside the door excites me. The fear of someone walking in intensifies my arousal. I invited him to punish me. He holds my legs out to thrust with gasping force. The fierceness of our sex makes me out of control. The shuddering between my legs keeps escalating until I can't resist. Tremors of screaming delight convulse throughout my body."

My face softens to an innocent grin. I conclude, "There is no shame. No judgment. I can walk away without feeling any guilt."

Alexander stands quietly and digests every word, like I just read him erotica from *Cosmo* magazine. Allowing him insight into my own perverse imagination, I wait for his response.

He charmingly responds, "Thank you for being vulnerable and open. Believe it or not, a lot of women crave this type of scenario. You want to release your sexual repression on a stranger as a means to avoid shame or guilt."

The Sex Kitten Mask and Cuff set I stand next to emboldens me. "You could have had me that night at TAO. The moment you singled me out and spoke to me. You could have taken me to some isolated corner and completely violated me."

"Am I less appealing to you now since you know my identity?"

I respond by yanking his necktie forward to draw him to my lips. Alexander welcomes me with a lustful embrace. Having him fondle me in the "Kink for Couples" section is within its own realm of enterprising visual spectacles.

A familiar voice interrupts us and jolts us back to reality like a bucket of cold water. Despite Gary's presence, we linger momentarily, our tongues slowly easing out of our delectable kiss. We wrap our arms tightly around each other and bury our faces into each other's necks to muffle our giggles. For a moment, we forgot where we were while enjoying nonchalant public foreplay.

Gary is a dose of reality. He waves in front of him an item labeled, "The Little Black Box Kink Kit."

He apologetically hands the box over to me before adding, "Sorry for the interruption, but I thought this might interest you both. It's popular for those who want to dabble in BDSM. This kit has everything for beginners."

I examine the box and its contents. Inside the black package are four items: nipple clamps, a blindfold, a slapper, and "premium leather handcuffs." "Thank you, Gary. This is perfect! I was looking for leather that could be easily washed with soap and water."

There is a mischievous twinkle in my eye. "Gary, you have been a tremendous help. I think we can take it from here."

Bashfully he decks out, before asking, "Let me know if I can help you with anything else."

I nod and simper, "Of course we will."

My gaze follows Gary as he scurries away to a group of young women planning a bachelorette party. I laugh as I hear him pushing the edible penis products.

Alexander breaks my trance with his wisecrack, "My, my, aren't you full of surprises today. You already have a strategy of how to wash up your playthings."

"Yes, every woman's innermost desire is sterilizing toys after sex, especially our beaded nipple-to-clit clamps." Sassily responding, I give him a complacent smile.

I turn away from him to visually sweep the area for more products. Glancing over my left shoulder, I see him captivated by me. Satisfaction creeps across his face. A storm of conflicting feelings churn inside me at the thought of him. Alexander, this remarkable hurricane of ecstasy, intelligence, and elegance, is admiring me.

Arms crossed, I try to conceal our box of bondage by firmly pressing it into my chest. I am transported to being thirteen years old again, and buying my first box of tampons, trying to camouflage my obvious intentions as to why I went to the store. There was no need to be ashamed. Everything here serves a purpose. The moment I laid it on the counter in front of the register, it would be in plain sight. But here I am years later hiding my purchase again.

I keep my eyes locked on the shelves in hopes of finding something else. One item stops me dead in my tracks. I have no idea what it is, but it appears straight out of a science fiction movie. It reminds me of a black flashlight with a parasite living inside it, like it has an appetite for penises with an unsightly flesh-colored mouth. I need both my hands to fully investigate this device. I quit guarding my bondage kit and place it down on a shelf.

Picking up this unconventional device, I hide it behind my back and walk back over to Alexander. He knows I am up to something, and his eyes light up as he asks, "Emme, is the object behind your back something you want or something so profoundly shocking it's funny?"

"Well, it's both."

"Both?" he asks.

"Since you want to get me a going-away present, I should definitely get you something too. You can use this when we do our naked FaceTime."

"Naked FaceTime?" he says with intrigue.

"Yes, naked FaceTime or Skype. Whatever you prefer to make this long-distance relationship work."

Knowing this will end with me making fun of something, he humors me by politely asking, "Okay…I'll bite. What's my gift?"

I hold the box up next to my self-serving stupid grin. "This is the Fleshlight Original Masturbator. Pink lady model," I loudly geek out, and then add, "I guess she's like one of the cool chicks from *Grease*. The box says the mouth-like opening of this contraption is modeled after a porn star's cha-cha." I gasp at my discovery like I just discovered fire. "This is the essence of her vagina!"

I read the description out loud twice, wanting to ensure I read the packaging correctly. I turn the box back around and examine the rendering of an adult film star's pootie-tang.

"A mold of this lady's vagina was made to enhance the realness of male masturbation. She must be as smooth as a bowling ball down there. Someone has a job to spread that molding cast on her va-jay-jay and then pull it off." I shake my head imagining this being an episode of *Dirty Jobs*.

"You want me to toss off inside a plastic mold of a porn star's vagina? You are the epitome of romance."

I soak in his lighthearted response, before he becomes clinical. "I have had some male patients who have used this device. They found it very satisfying. I know a lot of these things don't appear to serve a purpose, but there was thought put into it."

I shrugged off his response, "Just like you've put thought into what I need."

"I don't think you need anything per se, but I think a human body needs release. Maybe I'm being selfish, but if I can't be the one to satisfy you, then I want you to do it."

His suggestiveness quickens my pulse. His concern for my sexual well-being exposes his affection for me. I put the Fleshlight Original Masturbator box back on the shelf. My body is relaxed as I look at his scintillating blue eyes.

"What would you like me to try?" I ask warmly. "I promise…no jokes or laughing. If your taste in toys matches your taste in wine, it must be pretty good. What do you suggest?"

"I did buy you something, but I was hoping you would choose something as well."

He hints, "Believe it or not, it's very pretty, and you can wear it out. I wasn't going to pick out something cartoonish knowing how daft you think everything is."

"I accept your generous gift…without even knowing what it is. Are you my secret Santa?" Flirtatiously, I point out, "I'm sure Christmas won't be coming just once a year."

I step forward to wrap my arms around him. We squeeze each other while shuddering from laughter. "Whatever you got me will be fantastic. I trust you."

"Does this conclude our shopping excursion?" he asks.

"Yes, we are done."

A smirk crawls up the corners of his mouth. "We can incorporate your fantasy with your gift. I would very much like to use it on you tonight, in front of everyone. It will be a memorable parting gift…"

Doing my rendition of a saucy Elizabeth Bennet, I butcher an English accent. "Why, Mr. Darcy, I bet that's what you tell all the ladies."

Alexander robustly chuckles, "Yes, Miss Bennet, I aim to please…even if that means shagging you in a public loo."

Sliding his hand into mine to lead me out of the sex den, he lovingly kisses my cheek.

"Thank you for meeting me here. I could tell this was way out of your comfort zone, due to the sarky remarks."

Grinning with approval, he admits, "I haven't laughed this much…in a very long time. But we did have a breakthrough. You communicated your fantasy in great detail. A few days ago, you were too closed off to share anything that intimate."

He leads me past rows of sexual contraptions for adventurous lovers. I hold my head up high and grip his hand tightly. I give the unspoken male nod of acknowledgment to Gary on the way out. It was time to unwrap my gift.

CHAPTER 27

Our cab pulls up to a typical New-York-style neighborhood lined with brownstones. The multileveled brick homes appear alike with their fire escapes and ladders, but they are not comparable in size. The first floor to each building is a store, with the upper levels either being a continuation of the retailer, or someone's home. The street is quintessentially New York. It's like we stepped out on a classic New York City movie set. We step out of the cab on West 17th Street to make our way to a secluded bar called the Raines Law Room. It is here where he plans on gifting me my toy that fits so neatly in his inner jacket pocket.

Twilight diminishes under autumn's early darkness, blanketing the sky with ebony and twinkling stars. As we leisurely stroll to our destination, I analyze the businesses surrounding us.

Aimlessly walking without the Raines Law Room in sight, I ask, "Where is this place?"

The bar, Alexander explains, is named after a law passed to curb alcohol consumption. I'm amused by his knowledge of New York history.

He uses our walk to school to me. "New York City implemented a prohibition law increasing the drinking age from sixteen years old to eighteen years old. Only the patrons of the hotel were allowed to purchase and consume alcohol on Sundays. Back in those days, Sunday was the only time to relax and drink after a long work week. Men would check into hotels to drink freely and enjoy prostitutes."

The look of visceral satisfaction spread over my face. "So you're taking me to a whore house disguised as a bar?"

Suddenly, an oddly fitted black awning appears with the number forty-eight above it. It reminds me of the Tardis, from *Doctor Who*. Alexander pulls the heavy black entrance doors open, which reveal another flight of stairs leading down to something resembling a basement. A glowing porch lamp illuminates a copper sign with "Raines Law Room." There are simple instructions annotated on the wall to ring the doorbell.

The door cracks open, and we hear a female voice, "Yes?" coming from a fair-skinned beauty with black hair, wondrous jade eyes, and a welcoming smile.

She answers the door with typical hostess pleasantries. She glides her fingers down a list to verify Alexander's name has a reservation. After we are confirmed to enter, she leads us to our table.

The bar's clandestine location adds to its allure. One would think a secret passcode or an illuminati tattoo were needed to gain entrance. This secluded bar is off the beaten path but iconic enough to have a long wait list to get inside. It is the modern version of Jay Gatsby's house. This speakeasy is narrow and minimalistic in prohibition era decorum with oversized plush leather and velour seats. The open layout allows everyone to be visible, yet private enough for your table to converse without eavesdropping.

Alexander always takes me to reclusive elegant places, which is symbolic of his persona. He himself is tucked away, and only a few can get inside. My train of thought shifts upon entering the elongated room. The ambience emulates a seductive discretion with dimly lit candles and kerosene lanterns. The stylish vibe of Duke Ellington reverberate through the brick walls and intricate wood-paneled ceiling.

The area Alexander reserved is typically reserved for large parties, making it closed off with dark sheer drapes. Our setting consists of a cozy leather love seat placed up against the wall with a mahogany coffee table on which to place our food and drinks.

After easing ourselves into the stylish worn leather sofa, our waitress immediately greets us with a menu and ordering instructions. "Please request service by ringing the bell. We give our patrons the utmost privacy; therefore, we will not be constantly checking up on you. The waitstaff will only attend to you if you ring the bell requesting service." She motions to the location of the service drawstring, which is dangling close by the sofa and linked to a hanging bell outside the curtain.

Once the waitress walks away to tend to the tables with ringing bells, a wisenheimer grin emerges on my face. It dawns on me that we are out in the open, but hidden.

The drink selections on the menu are eclectic and mouthwatering with over forty choices. Mixology is an art form at the Raines Law Room. The drinks are not customary like typical menus. Each cocktail is freshly made with unique ingredients. I can't decide if I feel more like El Diablo or some Hanky Panky. I decide that Hanky Panky fits my mood.

Ratting off my order to Alexander, I excuse myself to freshen up. He seems ecstatic by my bathroom trip announcement, which catches me off guard.

Slyly, he asks, "Tell me what you think of the wallpaper." He additionally requests, "Let me know if you want to try anything."

A mystified expression blankets my face as I walk toward the bathroom. I try to quantify his words before pulling the door handle open. I enter the bathroom full of curiosity.

Staring hard at the walls like a crime scene, I mumble to myself, "What the hell?"

The beige-colored backdrop has thin black brushstrokes with vines replicating intertwining couples in a variety of sexual positions. It's the magnum opus of sexual hieroglyphics. Naturally, I pull out my cell phone and start taking pictures to show my friends. Sexual calligraphy should be documented and shared.

Upon my return to the table, I gleefully plop down next to Alexander. Reaching over to grab my Hanky Panky, I quietly savor it. Playing with the straw, while glancing around at my surroundings like a tourist, I deliberately avoid conversation.

His sultry eyes undress me when he asks, "What did you think?"

"I normally don't enjoy gin, but this drink is divine. What about you?"

Knowing I am being a pain in the ass, he clarifies, "What did you think of the loo?"

Wide-eyed with innocence, I tease, "The antique sink fixtures accompanied by the numerous mirrors were very fetching. Why do you ask?"

His ability to refrain is commendable. He admires me with a bright look of how to crack me, while I hold my tongue.

Innocently propping my head up on my right hand, I enthusiastically ask, "Are you wanting to know what I thought about the promiscuous wallpaper? It reminds me of the opening sequence of a James Bond movie, you know, like the opening montage of dancing naked silhouettes."

I imagine us in the bathroom picking out positions to try. Before placing my drink down on the table, I study him. "What position would you like off the Kama Sutra wall?"

"We can look later." For dramatic effect, he pauses. "My intentions are not exhibited on the bathroom wall."

He places his finished glass of Spanish wine next to mine. Reaching into his coat pocket, he pulls out a small white box embossed in gold with a single word, "Crave," then gently lays it in front of me. My nerves are fixated on the small object. Our night last night will be commemorated with jewelry and perverted wallpaper.

Alexander's excitement is layered with sweetness. "This is my gift to you. With your permission, I would like to show you how to use it."

Lifting the lid off the box, I discover an ash-colored suede pouch also branded with the word "Crave." I wriggle the pouch between two fingers to pull out the contents. A necklace resembling a cylinder-shaped pendant with a rounded tip slides out. A beautiful rose-gold-plated nail hypnotically dangles back and forth between my fingers.

"Thank you. It's a gorgeous necklace." Wrinkling my brows in confusion, I ask, "What exactly do you need to show me?"

I examine the smooth metal closely with certainty and wonderment. "Does it come with mystical powers? I mean, what does it do? Is this a bullshit detector sounding like a theremin when someone lies?"

"The mystical powers of the Vesper are from its multiple uses. You can wear it around your neck for jewelry or let it empower you."

Stumped by his words, I challenge, "Empower me?"

Even though the curtains are sheer enough to see through, the dark color is sufficient camouflage. Alexander reaches over to slide the necklace around his hand, then intertwines his fingers around the chain, to suspend the pendant up in the air.

"This isn't just a gold necklace. This is a vibrator disguised as jewelry. All you have to do is click on this tiny white button to turn it on, and then adjust the intensity setting for speed and vibrations."

I cast an eye over my gift to find the button. My fingers buoyantly roll the pendant around in the palm of his hand. Tapping the tiny button with eagerness, the nail vibrates to each setting. Distracted by unlocking the mysterious powers of the Vesper, Alexander moves closer, almost on top of me. He lightly brushes soft kisses with his lips along my neck, before suckling my ear lobe.

"These curtains are a false sense of privacy. We can be seen by anyone looking in our direction."

He breathes his intentions into my ear. "I want to watch you orgasm right here."

I comply to his request by relaxing my stance and leaning backward, allowing him to unlock its mystical magic. My eyes are transfixed on his focused stormy blue gaze. Delicately, his feather-like fingertips trace along my neckline, between my breasts, until reaching the bottom hem of my dress. His hand slides between my legs to ease them open with long, tickling, playful strokes. My head drops back, when my heartbeat flutters faster from anticipation. His fingers creating forward circular patterns along my inner thighs render me weak. His teasing fingertips explore the opening of my panties, already damp arousal.

I gasp loudly when his fingers press up into my sex. Wet and stimulated in response, I greedily force his open mouth into mine without a need for air. The rhythmic throbbing of his wine-drenched tongue steadily melts us into each other. Thirsty for more with each delicious exhale, my legs instinctively open wider. Feeling the rapid cadence of his pulsing fingers, I fantasize that he's fucking me. My body is on fire with drenched panties. The softness of his stroking fingers pause long enough to introduce the pendant. With a click, a vibration quakes between my legs. He works the Vesper around my sweet spot. I forcefully bite my lip to stop moaning. The humming between my legs is almost climatic.

The bustling chatter and clanking bar glasses drowns out my erratic breathing. The cold metal of the pulsating Vesper heats my sexual core. The intensity increases when he presses the second setting. Swallowing my excitement to maintain discretion, the pulsing tickles my senses. Alexander sucks the moans out of my mouth to muzzle the temperate buzzing sound between my legs. Ignoring all the eyes and voices around us, a trembling sensation takes control of my body.

Alexander clicks the Vesper to the maximum speed setting. He skillfully maneuvers his hand to fondle the wand between my inner thighs. The Vesper massages inside my curves to the point of eruption.

I pant, "This feels so good."

My body gyrates along with his rhythm. I tousle his hair with a tight grip, forcing his body against mine. Teasingly deliberate in bringing me to the edge of sensation, he then pulls away. Alexander flickers the slick metal back and forth within my sex until I spasm uncontrollably. His hand holds steady, while I erupt, shaking from release. The orgasmic throbbing between my legs subsides when my contracting muscles relax. I peacefully sink back into the sofa satisfied.

Alexander eases his weight off me by moving to his side of the sofa. The Vesper's compact power renders me speechless. His handsome face looks back at me with a sense of fulfillment.

Pridefully, he asks, "What did you think of your gift?"

He's still clutching the Vesper in his palm with parts of the chain swinging freely. I reach for his hand to place it against my wildly thumping heart. My lips feel dry, and my mouth is parched from gasping for air. I welcome the wetness of his kiss, drinking in this surreal moment before my brain shuts down. We are motionless, silent in a room full of commotion.

"Your gift is perfect."

With a drowsy smile, I ask, "Which one of us is going to wash this in the wallpaper porn bathroom?"

CHAPTER 28

The pitch-black autumn night is adorned with stars. The chill in the air sends shivers all over my body. I seek out Alexander's body heat by wrapping his arm around me and snuggle against him. Uncharacteristically silent after leaving the Raines Law Room, he's holding his thoughts for ransom. It will cost more than a penny to buy whatever weighs heavily on his mind.

I deliberately squeeze his hand. Alerting him to my presence, I ask, "Are you in the mood for dessert? How about a slice of humble pie?"

He appears agitated. "What makes you think something is wrong?"

"You've barely spoken a word since we left the bar. Your demeanor is like a doctor who is about to give a patient bad news."

The dead air feels like a storm cloud of emotions forming between us. He is carefully choosing his words. Breaking up the stillness, he philosophically asks, "Did you know men have a hard time processing fear and love at the same time?"

Feeling punch-drunk, I respond, "No, I didn't. Why in the world are you asking me this?"

He states the obvious with a tinge of coldness, "You are leaving tomorrow."

"Does my leaving bring you fear or rejection?"

He swiftly responds, "Both."

Perplexed, I press him to be clearer. "How am I rejecting you?"

I can see the hurt in his eyes. In a low, despondent voice full of dread, he states, "Tomorrow morning, you will be gone. You have no idea when you'll return. Not knowing makes me feel rejected."

Sounding like a caricature of Yoda, I philosophize, "Fear and love will always coexist together. Love puts everything into context. Your fears can alter reality by making it worse than it seems."

I abruptly add, "But I'm standing next to you, right here…now. Your fears are unfounded. I will return."

Nervous tension begins mounting between us. Our fears slowly seep out to project our insecurities onto each other. Alexander's therapy sessions were all about keeping an open mind. My mind has been open since arriving in New York City. Ironically, his foreshadowing of rejection is making him recoil by shutting me out.

Fighting to prevent our last night from becoming a total loss, I bring up Harley. He needs perspective in demystifying any sort of doom and gloom associated with goodbyes.

"The day before Harley left for college, I wanted to have a nervous breakdown. If I had let my fear of being alone consume me, it would have ruined our last day together. It turned out to be a fantastic gift…a cheesy love fest."

My face is forward to prevent an emotional response. But my eyes instinctively shift sideways to catch a glance of him. I become sentimental. "I cried when she drove off in the morning, but not because she left. We were both entering new chapters in our lives. We were both going down undiscovered paths on our own. I felt happy for her."

"But more importantly, our 'goodbye' isn't forever. It's more like a 'see you later' due to distance." I wrap both of my arms around his in comfort. "You are still this undiscovered entity in my life. I want to explore what's next."

Alexander is forthcoming. "How will we be discovering anything with an ocean between us?"

Frustrated, I snap, "We can go around in circles deconstructing my trip to Paris. Or we can discuss why you suddenly have this stick up your ass."

In a dignified British tone, he maintains, "It does appear redundant."

He seems to shut down as we continue our walk in silence. Pandora's box has been opened. The delicate newness of our feelings teeters on uncertainties.

Trying to lighten the mood, I flirtatiously quip, "Are there any other rooms in your house that you'd like to explore?"

He remains lost in thought and doesn't acknowledge my comment. The quietness unleashes insecurities I had just locked away. The city sounds fill the space between us. A mask of disappointment disguises his handsome face, and his stormy eyes torment me by being lost in introspective placidity. The cool breeze accentuates the stillness of our connection.

"What are we doing?" he finally asks.

"We are walking…in uncomfortable silence. You are sulking, and now, I'm pissed," I quickly respond.

Alexander begins psychologically evaluating our situation. He's restless, until he breaks down his thoughts.

"We're not being sensible. You want to explore life, and I don't. Be a true adventurer without worrying about maintaining a relationship with me. I don't even know if I'm ready for a relationship, especially a long-distance one."

Hearing him use the word "sensible" enrages me. His sessions with me were far from sensible, but more irrational, which made them fantastic.

Fiercely defending myself for wanting to be anything but ordinary, I blurt out, "Your assumptions are based on fear. How in the hell can you predict anything?"

I abruptly stop walking. Redirecting my rigid stance to his gaze, I admonish, "Don't ever tell me what I want or need. I'm a grown-ass woman capable of making decisions."

Boiling blood cascading through my veins diminishes the chill I once felt. Not giving a fuck about perception, I become confrontational. "This isn't about me. It's about your own insecurities. Your fears of rejection. You've been in this time loop of meaningless sexual encounters. You're so detached from human connection. I'm not like you. Brief exploits would make me feel cheap, not gratified."

My frustration is emphasized with flailing hands and a raised voice. "I want full-blown, 'Holy shit! I can't believe he chose me!' type love. And I want him to feel that way about me.

"I thought you were this guy, but apparently, you're not. You're a hypocrite. You teach others how to self-love through experiences, but you can't seem to take your own advice."

I loudly state, "Love yourself enough to love someone else."

Alexander is reduced to a little boy shamefully looking downward. His hands snugly placed inside his jacket pockets are hidden from my grasp. Trying to reconcile the situation, I rub his shoulders like a touchstone; he doesn't deny or argue my points.

His shoulders slouch with an unwillingness to meet my eyes. His voice sounds shallow and wounded. "Meeting you has been serendipitous."

Taking a deep breath, he looks at me dead in the eye. "I am not ready for a relationship, but you are. I'm not sure when I'll be ready. You shouldn't wait around for me. I can't give you the happiness you want…or deserve."

Tense with inflamed emotions, I snap, "Are you on your period? You just went from giving me a porn fantasy to singing the blues. Why are you telling me this now?"

"I live with regret every day. I don't want you to feel this way. If we tried the long-distance route, you might regret it, because I will. Relationships are hard. My own personal fears mixed in with you being on another continent doesn't help."

I shake my head in disbelief before asking, "What regrets are you living with?"

"I will regret not taking a chance with you. But I would really regret selfishly keeping you in New York City. Even if you stayed, there's no guarantee that we would work out. Paris will always be in the back of your mind."

Visibly shaken and hurt, he admits, "Paris will definitely be a good experience for you. Being with me… might not be as wonderful."

Anger rivaling Mount Vesuvius explodes through my mouth. "Let me get this straight. We need to part ways because of your fragile male ego? You are too chickenshit to even give this a chance? We're both old enough to know what we want in life, whether it's having jalapeños as a pizza topping or knowing what you want out of a relationship. Love and affection are choices." I pause before spotlighting, "You are choosing to let it go."

My fight-or-flight instincts kick in. I suddenly have the urge to run. His fears of a relationship project onto me with a heavy heart. I'm afraid his next words will be, "I'm sorry," or worse, "I can't give you what you want."

My perfect day comes crashing to a halt. The painful truth of what is happening makes me despondent. I stop and take a few steps backward. Without a conscious thought, I go no further with him.

I turn away in the opposite direction, stopping long enough to share my wariness and cynicism. "You are absolutely right. We're not being sensible. What is the meaning of this? I need to go. I don't want to say anything I might regret." I walk to the curb and raise my arm to hail down a cab.

Piercingly cold-hearted and straight-faced, I tell him, "I won't be leaving you tomorrow. I'm leaving you right now."

Alexander is shocked by my sudden white flag of defeat. When the cab pulls up curbside, I grip the handle and open the door. Something holds me there. My thoughts are suspended with my body, heavy like stone. I should have just jumped inside the car and recused myself from the situation. Unable to contain my emotions any longer, swelling surges from my heart to my eyes. I can't breathe. Tears overwhelming flow beyond my control.

In my haste to flee, his shadowing presence behind me goes unnoticed. He reaches for my arm to prevent me from getting inside the cab. Intuitively pulling me in tightly, shielding me from sadness, he wraps his arms tightly around me.

I bury my face in his neck. I already miss his smell. Our "almost relationship" is about to end. Regardless if it is true love, infatuation, or just filling a void, I feel an intense onset of grief.

In a consoling voice, Alexander speaks without imposition. "Emme, this is not how our night was supposed to end."

"Are you kidding? You just unloaded your emotional shit on me; how *was* this night supposed to end? A handshake, a hug, and a 'Cheerio?'" I look at him in disbelief.

Gripping me with sympathetic eyes, he explains, "My mind just works in actualities. I'm not ready for a relationship. I'm not willing to try, and you are leaving. It would never work out."

My head and heart feel heavy with my muscles stiff with disgust. I loudly snap, "How could you know?"

Alexander unintentionally adds fuel to the fire. "This conversation was not intended to upset you. If you want to experience true freedom, then don't tie yourself to me."

"This wasn't supposed to upset me? How am I supposed to feel? You just openly used a vibrator on me in a bar!" I pulled out the dangling necklace from underneath my collar. "You pretty much just jerked me out in the open, and now 'ta-ta'. Or as the Brits would say, 'Fuck off!'"

I stare at him with knife like precision. "My heart is not in my vagina. My heart isn't looking to explore new attractions like some sexual amusement park."

I hold his hand up to my chest, forcing his palm open against my skin to feel my rapidly thumping pulse.

"My heart is right here…and it's breaking."

I calmly take a step back to loosen his grip. He urgently responds by reaching out to pull me back into his arms. Defiant for even allowing myself to be vulnerable to him, I speak with severity. "For someone exposing me to new things, you should take your own advice about being open-minded. You're emotionally closed off. You're probably the type of guy always looking for the next best thing."

I jerk my arm away and snap, "Thanks for wasting my fucking time. Time that could've been spent doing something else."

"This concludes our sessions, Dr. Jameson."

Alexander freezes in his tracks. No movement or words, he holds the look of a confused lost child. His sparkling blue eyes convey hopelessness. Knowing there will be no resolution, I climb inside the cab and slam the door shut. Peering at him through the window, overcome with emotions, this is the last time I will see him.

There is no dramatic chase, no pleading with me to stay, or words of affirmation. The cab driver whisks me off as Alexander watches, helplessly dazed.

Hugging my arms across my chest to self-sooth, I brace myself for the sickness that accompanies heartache. My mind tricks me into replaying our conversation. All the things I should have said, but didn't. The angst in my heart turns into physical pain. A dry sour taste fills my mouth, turning my stomach upside down. Looking out the window, the shards of light bouncing off the concrete horizon subdue my mind into a trance. Angry with myself for falling hard and fast for someone I just met, I mutter, "Damn you, Judy Blume, for not teaching me about being dickmatized."

CHAPTER 29

Standing on the penthouse balcony, I absorb the city's vitality. I inhale a deep breath for introspection, then exhale zero regrets. My insides feel like a dumpster on fire. When I peer into the horizon, the world is thriving and carrying on, but I feel empty. Hurt by what transpired, my decision to leave New York City stands firm. The reasons for my return have changed.

My mind plays out different scenarios. In my epic romance novel ending, I envisioned Alexander waiting for me in the lobby, pleading with me to let him see me one last time, and then professing his desire to be with me. None of those things transpired.

I clutch the dangling Vesper around my neck like a crucifix, then unclasp the chain. The pendant slides off to spiral downward, piling into a golden ball resting in the palm of my hand. My thoughts muse how Alexander is comparable to the Vesper, a very attractive sex toy used to empower women.

My phone startles my thoughts. Harley's voice is a welcoming beacon of positivity.

"I am just checking in. Are you ready for Paris?"

My voice shook, I say, "I'm ready to get the hell out of here."

"Everything okay? You sound upset."

Too exhausted to mask my feelings, I confess, "The doctor from the auction…his name is Alexander. We clicked, and everything seemed fantastic. But he just ended things tonight. I was blindsided, so yes, Paris is looking pretty great."

"I'm so sorry, mama. Raw emotion makes things feel bleak and unsolvable. Maybe you both will work it out." She adds, "Even if you didn't, you lived life this week. Life didn't live you."

Snickering at her hippie logic. "What the hell does that mean?"

"It means you put your heels on. You got out of the house and embraced your inner siren. No matter how this week began or ended, the time in between was freaking incredible. Admit it, you had the time of your life."

I counter, "Isn't it the end that has the longest lasting effect?"

Harley's directness is forceful. "You can be a Debbie Downer and think about how today ended, or you can chalk it up as having the best week ever, and Paris is the 'cherry on top' of the proverbial second chance in life."

Sounding frustrated, she adds, "After Dad left, you were stuck in this weird suburban routine for a year. I worried about you."

My face crumpled up like a wad of paper. "How so? What did I do that was weird?"

"You quit being you."

Harley recollected one instance. "You had this peculiar obsession with adultery. For example, you were glued to Sirius XM at 1045 AM just to hear 'Ryan's Roses.' Hearing Ryan Seacrest bust out cheaters by offering them roses was your 'special time.' You would hush everyone, and then hold your breath, in anticipation of whom this person would send those free flowers to. And when it wasn't that person's significant other, you reacted as if you knew them. You invested yourself in other people's adultery. It was self-torment, like some sick version of *Groundhog Day*. Living through adultery again and again."

My heart sank hearing her describe my lunacy. "Holy hell. I'm ridiculous. You're right; I did have some sick fetish about busting cheaters."

I grumbled, "Hearing someone's adultery story unfold on the radio made me feel less alone. It's like sharing a tragedy with strangers, like group therapy. It didn't just happen to me, but to a lot of people."

Slightly shamefaced, I apologize. "It was a side effect of my nervous breakdown. I'm sorry I scared you."

"Why are you sorry? Grief is like confetti on New Year's Eve. Once it's released, it's everywhere. You can't clean it up in one sitting. Even when time passes, you'll open up your purse and find old confetti shards. A reminder of that particular night."

She sings her praises, "That was then…look at you now. The metamorphosis is complete. You've shed the past to spread your morpho wings. You're a goddess strutting around with a hot guy in New York City, but more importantly, experiencing romance. Regardless of finding Mr. Right, you still have the balls to go to Paris, even if things did work out."

Unwavering in her prose, she adds one more truth. "Be inspired by everything that's happened. Write that bestseller. It's pining to get out of you."

Overcome with emotion and pride, I beam, "You are going to make a great psychiatrist. You are the best of everything to me. I love you infinitely."

"I love you more." Harley's words linger in the air, "Go to Paris. Be wild. If he reaches out to you, please talk to him. Don't swat him away with your flirtatious insolence."

I scoff, "Me? Insolent? Never."

Ending the call with Harley gave me mixed feelings. The pang of excitement for Paris returned, but then there was hope for a resolution with Alexander.

******

I restlessly lay in bed tossing and turning. Rolling over, I reach for my cell phone on the nightstand to check the time. It's 12:05 a.m. Seeing a missed call from Alexander at 11:17 p.m. makes me sit up alert. My nervous heart beats rapidly calculating my options. Etiquette deems calling at this hour to be rude. I don't care. I'll gauge the repercussions by his response.

He picks up on the first ring, and surprisingly sounds wide-awake. "Can't sleep?"

"I'm sorry…I know it's late. I've been watching the city lights create a club scene rave effect on my bedroom ceiling. Why are you still up?"

Hushed in tone, he responds, "I couldn't sleep. I'm out on my balcony…just thinking."

"Are you thinking about how awesome our night ended?"

"Emme, I wasn't prepared for you. I haven't allowed myself to feel anything for anyone since Victoria died. This entire experience was unexpected but welcomed."

My stomach sinks, and my heart races when I hear him say, "Life keeps nudging you to take a leap of faith. Everything about this week has been 'new'; don't stop growing on my account. Go on the adventure you were meant to go on. This might include having experiences with other men…without guilt."

"What if you are my adventure?"

His softhearted tone pacifies me. "We had our adventure, and now you'll discover something new. This trip to Paris is about self-exploration, alone, not with me. Starting a relationship with me will only distract you."

He sounds skittish and weak. "This is what we talked about in the museum. Sex can serve a purpose without love or commitment."

"Was that the purpose I served you?"

His response was immediate, "No. Not at all."

Flicking my feet back and forth to find the coolness of the sheets—sweaty under the blankets from nerves and frustration—I argue, "There is nothing casual about us. There is a strong connection, explosive chemistry, and yes, feelings."

Knowing I have nothing to lose, I ask, "Don't you feel the same way?"

My breath is weighted down with dread. Waiting in silence for seconds felt like infinity.

He remains diplomatic. "I don't want to have this conversation over the phone. I know you leave for Paris tomorrow. Do you have time to meet for coffee in the morning?"

Remembering Harley's advice, I agree, "Yes, we can meet downstairs. There is a restaurant called, The Garden."

Content with our détente, we ended the call. I lay awake wondering how wonderful or wrong this could go.

******

Alexander and I are meeting at 8:00 a.m. My flight leaves at noon, which doesn't give us a lot of time. I must factor in traffic to the airport, and then terminal security check-in. Impatience sprinkled with nerves with a twist of heartache prompts me to arrive twenty minutes early.

Seated at a corner table gives me a full view of The Garden's layout. The ceiling-high African Acacia trees diffuse the bright sting of the sun with thick sprawled-out branches. The waking yawn of the New York City skyline pierces an aura of brilliance through the window. My sleepless eyes focus on stirring my cappuccino. Breaking up the intricate foam design feels satisfying.

Alexander stalks up to me unannounced. He asks, "May I join you?"

My mind's eye brings back our first encounter. It proves to be incomparable to this moment. My butter-flies flutter out of love, and not from infatuation. I quietly admire him with appreciation. His night of sleep deprivation gave him new wrinkles around his eyes. I memorize everything about his face. Not knowing if I'll see him again makes me savor this moment.

Trying to put up a stiff upper lip by forcing fake po-liteness, I ask, "How are you?"

Straining to smile, he replies, "I didn't get much sleep last night. How about you?"

"I spent my night wide-awake and staring at the ceil-ing. Then, I had an epiphany. I'm the color yellow in a bag of Starburst. Lemon is the least-favorable flavor com-pared to the reds. Yellow serves a purpose, by filling up space, and breaking up monotony."

Deflecting the questioning back to Alexander, I ask, "What kept you up?"

"Funny. I've always favored the lemon Starburst. It's sweet-and-sour taste isn't predictable. It's the brightest one in the bag," he smugly responds. A sneaking grin detracts from his sad eyes. "Last night, I was thinking about us, then you. I wondered what your plans were *after* Paris?"

Hearing him emphasize the word "after" sucker-punches my chest. Nervous energy makes my hands fidget. I inadvertently begin tapping the rim of my cappuccino cup. "I can't spend all day sightseeing. I'm bringing my laptop to write and be the cliché Bohemian.

"Depending on how long I'm in Paris and my creative energy, a finished novel would be great. I'll settle for a written first draft." I shrug my shoulders. "And if there isn't enough mojo for a novel, I'll submit magazine articles for publication. Maybe writing about being single from a divorced middle-aged perspective might be a fun blog, especially if I date online."

Smiling self-consciously, I continue. "The flood gates of inspiration are flowing rampant as we speak."

"Are you sticking with your original idea for a novel, a divorcée seeing a sex therapist? Or is there a new idea?" he asked.

Stoking the fires of blatant sarcasm, I say, "That storyline is too real for me to avoid. I figured the layout of the story, but I'm stuck. I can't seem to write a happy ending."

His eyes blaze blue trying to maintain levity. "If you need help developing the sex therapist character, I'm available to help. Maybe I can help you come up with a plausible ending."

A smirk crawled across my face. "No, thanks. You can just buy the book like everyone else."

Roused by curiosity, he sits up. "I'm proud of you. If your wit is any indication of your writing style, then it will be phenomenal."

"What about you? What will you be doing when I'm in Paris?"

Suddenly perked up, he happily shares his good news. "I found out my research on sexual deviancy will be published in the *Journal of Clinical Psychology*." He reclines backward and folds his arms, pridefully beaming. "If this works out, a guest professor spot is opening up in winter at Harvard. I've always wanted to lecture."

He adds, "It looks like we're both publishing something about sex."

Smiling at his good fortune, I confess, "With everything going on in your life, it seems like running off to Paris with me would be nonsensical. You have so many reasons to stay, but only one reason to go. I'm proud of you, and equally jealous of all the female students vying for your attention."

He smolders with an arched eyebrow. "You shouldn't be jealous of anyone. They might be jealous of you."

Finding his statement ridiculous, I chuckle. "They will never know about me. You will be the same smug sex pot single bachelor. Nothing will change."

We are both pretending to be happy for the sake of leaving on better terms. Waves of anxiety possess me to change course. "I'm sorry. I can't do this. I can't bullshit you for the sake of being pleasant."

Flopping backward into my seat, I crack my neck from side to side before speaking. "This isn't how we're supposed to end."

He patronizes me, "How were we 'supposed to' end?"

"You're letting me go…without a fight." I bite back, "I can't wrap my head around any ending with you. We were just getting started."

Gesturing his shoulders back and crawling his hands forward along the tabletop, he frees up his own subdued anxiety. "This is why I don't want a relationship. There are expectations I can't meet. This shiny newness will dull. There will be clarity. At this moment, you'll regret not leaving and exploring life. You have a newfound confidence that's sexy as hell. It's okay to self-love, before falling in love."

I look at him long and hard before speaking, "Words of wisdom from a guy who openly jerks me off only to end things. I feel tricked. We were becoming more than something casual. Well, that's what you led me to believe."

Frustrated, tongue-tied, and twisting in my seat, I say, "You suck."

"I suck?" Unleashing a boisterous laughter turning heads in our direction, he asks, "Is that your analysis of me?"

I wouldn't let him shake me. "Yes, it is. It's time I found a new therapist too."

"Why the change of heart?"

I fell hard for him. Telling him would just complicate things even more. I can't quantify why I feel this way. We barely know each other, but he's infected me. There is no logic, just two people perfect for each other.

"I don't want to spend time with Dr. Jameson, but Alexander, the deep introspective sex pistol with a silly side. I don't want the prim and proper psychologist with the ginormous stick up his ass."

His smile subsides. "Someone's best intentions are truly for selfish reasons."

I counter, "I am being selfish, but so are you. You gave so much of yourself to me, and now you're taking it away," I reprehended.

The weight of the past slumps his stature deep into his seat. "Victoria's physical and emotional needs were not being met by me. She was in Paris, and I was in New York City. The outcome might have been different if we were together. Being far apart complicates any relationship. It's not a nurturing environment."

I cynically reply, "Thank you for prescribing me *A Last Tango in Paris* type of vacation to heal my soul."

I want to lash out at him, but his sentiment is derived from deep pain. "If you quit being a slave to your past demons, you could freely explore falling in love again. I never want you to forget the love you lost. Realize the possibilities of loving someone again; if not now, then when?"

Hearing myself saying the word "love" blushed my cheeks cayenne red and sent shockwaves throughout my body. The early stages of romantic bliss are blinded by great sex and attention. The red flags were there. There is no expiration date on his grieving for Victoria.

"Your lack of closure equates to living a half-life. Figure your shit out. You are choosing the casual company of multiple partners..." I taper off to mumble, "rather than just being with me."

"I don't know when I'll be ready. We can still be in each other's lives…as friends." He says what I was dreading to hear: friends.

Heeding Basil's relationship advice from lunch, my blunt words cut. "Friendship is a consolation prize. I don't need you injecting yourself into my life to be relevant."

Pressing his lips down, sadness creeps over him. "Isn't friendship the basis for any relationship? If we aren't going to be physically together, what's wrong with being friends?"

My thoughtless words sting out of frustration. "I don't want to be friends or anything else after today. Thank you…for everything, even taking the time to say goodbye."

"I see." Caught off guard, there is something cryptic in his eyes. "Maybe you're right. It's best to end this journey. I would disappoint your expectations after today."

Calmly cloaking signs of my emotional devastation, I utter, "I appreciate the effort in concocting that bullshit answer with a straight face."

"I'm not trying to hurt you. You are one of my favorite people. I don't want you to cut me out of your life. That's your choice, but I understand why."

My face softly changed into the perfect pink shade of humiliation. I immediately use my flight as an excuse to run away. "I've enjoyed rediscovering myself through you. Take care of yourself, if not your heart."

According to Basil, the one who ends the relationship holds power. Yet, I feel powerless. Everything is a balancing act. Shift the weight one way or another, and everything falls. I found the perfect guy. There's nothing else to do, but let him go.

Thick tension fills the space between us like amber. We both sit across from each other in silence and stillness. Swallowing the lump in my throat, I'm about to ugly cry like Tammy Faye Bakker.

We stand up simultaneously. This is it. Our moment to say goodbye. He holds my eyes for a split second, before I move toward him. Stopping inches from his lovely face, I breathe him in one last time.

He brushes a strand of hair behind my ear. Masked disappointment trickles out with sweetness, and he whispers, "I'm going to miss the way you make me laugh, Emerson Vaughn."

"And I'm going to miss everything else, Dr. Alexander Jameson." I finally allow my emotional dam to break.

Immediately reactive, he protectively wraps his arms around me and pulls me in, squeezing me breathless. Looking up from the safety of his embrace, I throw my arms around his neck, drawing him down hard into my mouth with urgency. Feverishly devouring every ounce of unrequited love, I allow myself to cry. My streaming tears mix into our kiss. The taste of wet saltiness mixes into each of our regrets. The way our mouths breathlessly move in unison, while we cling on to each other, we don't need to say, "I love you." We feel it.

CHAPTER 30

Situating myself in my business class seat on Air France, I enthusiastically accept a glass of champagne offered by the flight attendant. I need self-medication after everything that's transpired. Glancing down to check my phone, I see texts from Alexander. In an effort to avoid opening the freshly cut wounds, I decide not to read them, holding on to my dignity and moving forward.

The woman seated next to me introduces herself as Helen. Appearing friendly and relatable, she initiates an ice-breaking repartee of basic pleasantries. She has matured gracefully, so it is hard to pinpoint her age. I guesstimate she is in her sixties. Her rich Irish-jade eyes are enhanced by perfectly coiffed silver hair. All the wisdom lines around her eyes and the firm apples of her cheeks make for a stunning ivory complexion. She is soothing and maternal with her charming British accent. My mind keeps wandering while she speaks.

She interrupts my transatlantic sulking by carefully nudging me to engage, asking, "Are you okay?"

The champagne's bubbles lower my defenses by turning into truth serum. Taking advantage of her sympathetic ear, I welcome the airline therapy session with Helen. Skipping over the sexual encounters from the past week, I oblige her curiosity with emotional facts. Helen focuses on each word. She nods without judgment, never interrupts me, and allows my storytelling to remain fluid. Her years of insight are set deep in the color of her eyes.

Heartfelt and gentle, she advises, "I was married once. Sadly, the marriage revealed itself for what it was. Divorce hurts no matter the reasons. I thought dating would be easy." She holds up her hands in a waving motion to indicate the enormity of the world. "With all the fish in the sea, I would never be alone, right?"

She lets out a big sigh before adding, "I was wrong."

She pivots her body to face me. "My single years were filled with bad dates or dysfunctional relationships. It was one bad experience after another. I wondered if true love was real. After a while, you think there's something wrong with you. This belief makes you give up trying."

Her consoling demeanor is comparable to having milk and cookies with your mother. She continues her recollection, "In my desperate attempt to find true love, I forgot to love myself."

Her eyes twinkle, "Being totally alone is empowering. Your level of happiness shouldn't be based on text messages, phone calls, or whether you're dining out alone. If you can't be confident by yourself, then who wants to be with you?"

Joyfully sipping her champagne, Helen savors the sweet bubbles, before advising me, "The greatest love stories are created out of patience. The love you deserve is not something you can rush. Love just doesn't hit you. It is a choice. You choose to love something. It has to grow and develop over time."

Her words highlight her face with a buttery golden glow. She recalls, "I found true love late in life. Unfortunately, we didn't acknowledge our feelings at the moment, so we ended it. It was during this time our feelings came to light."

Holding up her index finger to bookmark her teachable moment, she points out, "People turn their backs on love every day, but there are those who are willing to chase after it. They are making a choice to love you. Time apart gives you a sense of worth as well as perspective on your relationship. Are you worth the effort? Were you a priority or an option to him?"

Her words ring true. "In the end, you will learn what you feel isn't necessarily what you deserved or imagined."

Helen's sentiment makes me evaluate my feelings for Alexander. I wonder if my libido mistook passion for emotional connection. He clearly wasn't chasing after me. I question, "But isn't it sexist to expect a man to chase you?"

"A valuable woman never chases a man. She knows she is 'the catch.' Never think less of yourself for wanting more."

A smirk shoots across Helen's lips like lightning. She politely covers her mouth before becoming giddy with chuckles, before apologizing. She promises she isn't laughing at me.

Helen shares her life's mantra from her idol. She catches me off guard by quoting Dolly Parton: "Find out who you are. And do it on purpose." Her enthusiasm in those words make them profound.

"What is Dolly saying?" I ask.

Like a philosophy professor analyzing literary prose, she expounds, "I think Dolly is telling us that we should be focusing on being the best version of ourselves. The person who should love you the most…is you. If you can't love yourself, how can anyone else love you? Be the person you were meant to be. Even if this means being alone."

Helen grabs my hand with a smile, affectionately squeezing it to comfort me. I don't know how to thank her, not only for her advice, but for listening to me. When I boarded this flight to Paris, I felt as desirable as an orange-flavored Ring Pop. After this conversation, I feel inspired to be strong and beautiful like the priceless Sancy diamond.

After hours of friendly idle chatter and champagne, I feel drowsy. Turning away from Helen, I put on my headphones to block out everything. Staring out the window, I fixate on the clouds, drifting so seamlessly without being lost in a tempest. As I peer out the window, the sky looks enviable. I wonder how many people down below are turning their backs on love. New York was a mind-blowing extravaganza of the senses, but Paris will be an adventure.

My seven-hour flight begins its descent to Paris Charles de Gaulle Airport. My nerves are all over the place. Excitement, fear, and wonder swirl in the pit of my stomach. I've finally made it to Paris. The adventure I always dreamed of would now begin.

******

It's been five days since I left New York City. The first day is the hardest. There isn't enough bread or wine in Paris to detoxify my heartache. Not speaking to

Alexander makes me anxious. He became a part of me in such a short amount of time.

I'm finally seeing and doing everything I've ever wanted, but I have love on the brain. Walking around makes me reflect on the movie *Eternal Sunshine of the Spotless Mind.* I wish I could extinguish painful memories forever, but without them, I wouldn't be here. Shaking the pity party from my head, I leisurely stroll to the Flame of Liberty, the unofficial memorial to Princess Diana. The copper gilded flame is set upon gray-and-black marble, with flowers and photographs of Princess Diana adorning the ground. I examine all the gracious mementos with fascination.

Crossing the bridge of Pont de l'Alma, the sun's brightness simmers down. The cool breeze coming off the water combined with gray threatening skies rob the sun's radiance. The day is turning bleak. I make my way over to a crowd of tourists at the overpass of the tunnel. Everyone seems to be gawking at French graffiti marking where Princess Diana tragically died. Bypassing the inscribed messages of love and respect, something catches my eye: the majestic Eiffel Tower perched on the horizon, a spectacle beyond the greenish hue of the Seine. My pace quickens toward that direction.

Ominous rain clouds invade my picture-perfect postcard day. Frantically, I look around for possible places to duck into for shelter. The sudden ringing of my cell phone startles me.

My favorite Southern twang sings through the phone, "Hello, sweetheart, how's the path to enlightenment going?"

"It warps my mind seeing all the things from magazines and travel shows. Being enlightened is more about me being detached from everything, not overstimulated."

At the end of the day, I am surrounded by love. I shake off any sense of romance, by revealing my excursion. "I was hoping to contribute to the Love Lock Bridge, but that ceases to exist. Maybe I'll visit Jim Morrison's grave today."

I quip, "I'll have to ask him where realms of bliss and sweet delight exist."

"Maybe you weren't meant to lock up your heart and throw away the key," Ashley says.

Laughing before throwing in sassy Texas diction, she says, "Bliss was the light we were born with, so you've always had it." Poking fun at me, she snaps, "You just had to hawk your ass on your feet and move forward."

Changing the topic, Ashley asks, "You sounded nervous on the phone upon your arrival to in Paris. Now that a few days have passed, is traveling alone what you expected?"

I reply, "Walking around is a constant reminder of why Paris is the City of Love. Romance is embodied in the architecture, every bite of delicious cuisine, and hand-holding couples. Yet, I'm okay with being alone."

I confess, "I set aside a few hours a day to feel like a poser, sitting in cafés writing on my laptop. There's an undeniable creative energy here compelling me to write. I love it. I needed this more than anything."

The sky is about to dump buckets everywhere. I express my need to get off the phone to find shelter.

She helpfully asks, "Where are you?"

After sharing my location, Ashley recommends, "Google Maps says you're close to the Pont de Bir-Hakeim. The tunnel under the bridge will keep you dry; the Eiffel Tower will be in full spectacle view. Perhaps, that's where you'll find the realm of bliss and sweet delight. Maybe…what you're looking for is there waiting for you."

Puzzled by her fortune cookie logic, I ask, "Are you implying there's a boulangerie there? I must admit, bliss is a warm baguette slathered in butter." My stomach growls just thinking of a warm loaf of bread on a rainy day.

After ending the call with Ashley, I scurry to the Pont de Bir-Hakeim. It turns out to be the perfect safe haven. Just as big chubby raindrops splash on the ground, I find my way under the central arch of the bridge. Admiring the surrounding Parisian architecture, self-satisfaction creeps on my lips with a congratulatory smile. I'm finally doing something selfish and frivolous. I lean up against the wall feeling liberated and drink in the grand view of the Eiffel Tower. The rainy romantic ambience of Paris reminds me of great sex. Tugging on my Vesper hidden underneath my sweater, I procure the metal between my fingers. Playfully, I twirl it to self-soothe. Knowing that I'm wearing a vibrator as jewelry unleashes a fit of giggles echoing through the tunnel.

I'm startled hearing quickening footsteps reverberating along the cobble streets behind me. The scratching walking pattern abruptly stops. There is an unknowing presence inches from my back. Dread mixed with adrenaline gives me the nerve to be confrontational. Right before I can whip around, I freeze. I hear a distinctive, cocky British male voice. My heart and body are catatonic. I'm suspended in disbelief, mindlessly staring at the Eiffel Tower. My mind is racing with questions. I nervously twiddle the Vesper between my fingers like a rosary counting prayers. Closing my eyes, the lyrics to "La Vie En Rose" play in my head: "Everyday words turn into a love song."

"Do you mind if I wait here with you? It's pretty crowded over there." I hear the gregarious grin in his voice.

My throat constricts taking in his words.

He continues, "Or are you waiting for someone?"

A Cheshire-cat-sized grin flashes across my burgundy-painted lips. Recounting this previous exchange on the first night we met, butterflies flutter upward throughout my body, kick-starting my weak heartbeat. I maintain a forward-facing position and play along.

Forcing myself to push down thoughts of jumping up and down and clapping my hands like an idiot, I play it cool. "Yes, I've been waiting for someone."

He moves in closer. His breath on my neck tickles my body. Unlocking my inner teen girl exuberance, my senses are blissfully aroused. Boyishly charming with masculine confidence, he toys with me, "I see. Are you waiting for your boyfriend? Husband? Girlfriend?"

"No husband. I should consider a girlfriend. I'm surrounded by strong women. They haven't fucked me over yet."

Trying not to choke up, I add, "No boyfriend. I thought I met someone who checked those boxes. Sadly, he wasn't interested, and that was a kick in the nuts. Instead of sulking, I took my sex therapist's advice; he recommended that I sow my wild oats."

"Your sex therapist sounds very intuitive and smart."

Knowing he can't see my wicked sneering expression, I respond, "No. He sucked. I couldn't continue therapy with him. I chose to do my own sexual healing, alone, and in Paris. Love, food, and wine is a billboard for sex."

Shamelessly coy, I append, "Unfortunately, after a few days of aimlessly wandering these streets, I still haven't met the right guy to bring out my inner porn star."

He cracks, "Maybe you'll find this guy sooner than you think."

"You're right. I should download French Tinder and swipe on the local hotties. Maybe they can teach me something new. I can have a liaison with my tongue. Isn't this the birthplace of French kissing?"

I hear his smile through his voice. "Is your inner porn star auditioning younger men or just men in your decade?"

I turn around to finally look at him. Alexander's eyes ignite my heart like the aurora borealis. He doesn't have to say anything. The look of absolution envelopes his face. Helen was right. It was only a matter of time before the outcome revealed itself. My first instinct is to touch him, pulling him with a big passionate French kiss to say hello. I deliberately hold still.

"I thought you had work, a book to be published, teaching at Harvard…"

Waving his hands like an umpire to strike out any miscommunication, he says, "You're right. I have a lot of reasons to stay, but I had one reason to come here. All of that can wait. It will be there when I return. I need to attend to more important matters…us. I didn't want to miss my opportunity to be with you."

Joy spreads over my face, before asking with utmost curiosity, "How did you find me?"

"I flew out here on a whim last night. I only thought about what to say to you, then once I got here, I had no idea where you were staying or where you'd be. Naturally, I called Ashley for guidance."

He reiterates his conversation with Ashley. "She basically threatened to stick her foot up my uptight British ass if I didn't end this bullshit."

My laughter bellows throughout the tunnel. "The female power of persuasion. Texas Barbie threatened you with her shit-kicking boots?"

"Ashley said I would find bliss in this location. She was sheepishly referring to you, and I was hoping for warm bread with butter."

The blue in his gaze penetrates me into feeling hopeful, yet nervous. Closing the space between us, he reaches out toward the Vesper and begins rubbing the jewelry's shape with his thumb.

He wonders out loud, "Were you planning on empowering yourself publicly while enjoying the view?"

Devilishly grinning, he adds, "Need any help?"

Feeling stripped down to raw emotion, I didn't mince words. "Why are you here?"

Alexander isn't prepared to explain his intentions. His voice reduces to a shy whisper, "These past few days caught me off guard. I reevaluated my stance on relationships, when we stopped talking. There was something missing from my life: you."

He tapers off before regaining his composure. "There is an exhilarating absurdity when we are together."

"I'm a mess." He pauses long enough to inject a note of caution, "There are no guarantees when it comes to love."

He surprisingly adds, "The day after you left. I was consumed with regret."

I quickly respond with a quote from Clint Eastwood: "'If you want a guarantee, buy a toaster.'"[4]

Suddenly stupefied by what he just said, I stammer, "Love. Is this love?"

He beholds me in a trance as if his life depends on it. "We've known each other for such a short amount of time. It's somewhat mental, but I'm crazy about you."

The blistering rain beats down against the pavement, creating a static watery echo throughout the tunnel. The sound is mesmerizing, soothing me, while he keeps his response a secret. There is no impatience for the mere seconds that have transpired, just a stomach full of knots and nerves. The answer might not be what I expect, but it's what I need to hear.

He delicately traces my jawline with his fingertips. Moving his fingers to outline my lips, my insides tickle with anticipation. Tilting my head back, welcoming me to his lips, I surrender. Prompting my mouth slightly open, I breathe out anticipation. Our lips press against each other with a slow tease of soft kisses. Our tongues groove deeper, making me feel it all the way down to my inner thighs. The minty wet taste of his peppermint tongue, combined with the woodsy spice of his neck, leaves me intoxicated.

---

[4] Brainy Quote, "Clint Eastwood,"
https://www.brainyquote.com/quotes/clint_eastwood_103537

He deliberately breaks away, leaving me disoriented. Looking into my eyes for attention, he uncomfortably searches for the right thing to say. "I'm constantly helping couples connect with their partners, but I was afraid to connect with you. Turning my back on falling in love would've been easy. But not as easy as falling in love with you."

He shyly admits, "Yes. I love you."

The word "love" rings through my ears, elevating my heartbeat through my fingertips. The magnanimous number of butterflies fluttering in my stomach feels more like a roost heading north to migrate. He didn't turn his back on love, but chased it all the way to Paris.

He takes a long hard look at me before professing, "I love your smart mouth, the way you challenge me with humor. It's like I discovered laughter again. You're beautiful in every way. Being with you makes me feel… happy. It's been a while since I've felt this way."

Surprisingly unguarded, he calculates, "Even if you don't feel the same way, I wanted to see you one last time, just to tell you."

This is the epitome of grand romantic gestures. My adrenaline-induced heart is overcome with an unusual combination of hysteria calmed by balls-out bliss. Unloading so much emotion forces his eyes down, bracing for my response.

Lifting his chin up to face me, I study him. "A therapist admitting he's crazy. I feel the irony burning between my legs like a lidless scorching cup of coffee."

He laughs. "There is a fine line between love and madness. Both make you act out in unusual ways."

My hands cradle his sincere unguarded face, leaning in to crash his mouth onto mine. Delicately sweet sugary kisses, melt us into each other. My heart swells until I suffocate.

Resurfacing for air, I gasp, "I love you too."

My eyes crease from beaming. I am overwhelmed with undiscovered emotions. "I can't believe you're here…in Paris…with me."

His hand brush loose wisps of hair from tickling against my cheeks. We hold each other tightly, accepting the love we are offering each other.

Hearing the rain subside, the sun lights up every ounce of darkness cast down. Alexander weaves his hand into mine. "Would you like me to show you Paris?"

Guiding me away from our hiding spot, he abruptly stops, then looks around. Grinning at me sideways, he offers a second option, "Or would you like to take advantage of our location?"

"What's advantageous about being in a tunnel?"

Reiterating my fantasy, he says, "Using this secluded area inappropriately…"

Dauntlessly leering, I ask, "How inappropriate?"

He whispers in my ear, "Very inappropriate."

Walking me backward up against the wall, he slides his hands behind my lower back, edging downward to trace my curves. Restraining my hands behind me, he finds that sweet spot on my neck. An arousing warmth between my legs overtakes me.

Our foray into unusual therapy began in a penthouse in New York City and ended under a bridge with a spectacular view of the Eiffel Tower in Paris. In this time and space, there is nothing in the world that I want more than him. The seductive pull of Paris is incomparable to the love I feel now.

Breathlessly smiling to accept his invitation, I exhale, "Paris can wait."

314